WORTH THE RISK

ETERNITY SERIES
BOOK ONE

JENNIFER J WILLIAMS

Cover design: KB Barrett Designs

Cover Photographer: Lindee Robinson

Cover Models: Josh and Julia

Editing by Brenda Bastien

For anyone who has ever had a three-way.
Get your mind out of the gutter.
It's a Cincinnati chili dish, you heathens.
But also: I love your dirty mind.

Play List

Listen to the Playlist on Spotify
I Knew You Were Trouble - Taylor Swift
Paparazzi - Lady Gaga
Players - T-Wayne, Altruist
Starships - Nicki Minaj
Only Girl (In The World) - Rihanna
DJ Got Us Fallin' In Love - Usher, Pitfall
As It Was - Harry Styles
Cruel Summer - Taylor Swift
Calm Down - Rama, Selena Gomez
Golden Hour - JVKE
I Ain't Worried - OneRepublic
Last Night - Morgan Waller
Until I Found You - Stephen Sanchez, Em Behold

Chapter 1

Hannah

❧ ⛰ ❧

I groan as I lift up my pillow, slamming it against my face, begging the bed to quit shaking from the loud music next door. I swear, whoever lives there must hate everyone. They have absolutely no respect for quiet hours. I peer out from under the pillow to grab at the nightstand, finding my watch. Fuck. Fuck! It's three in the morning! Who plays music this loud at three a.m.?

I have to be up at six. I'm starting my new job as the social media coordinator for the Denver Wolves, an NHL team. I'm a little surprised I got this job, to be honest. I don't know a damn thing about hockey. I grew up in southern Georgia. Not exactly a hockey haven, ya know? I can school anyone on college football, but hockey isn't in my wheelhouse just yet.

I just turned twenty-eight, and I spent the last four years as the social media coordinator for the University of Southern Georgia's football team, so I definitely know how to work my way around all things social media. It also helps that my Uncle Bennett is one of the coaches here, and he recommended me for the job. He knew I wanted out of Georgia. Not only was there some drama with an ex-boyfriend, but my relationship with my parents wasn't the best. Moving to Colorado is a dream come true.

I'm staying in my Aunt Caroline's incredibly nice apartment. My aunt is only ten years older than me, but she's had a successful career in real estate. The Colorado real estate market has been booming, and because of that, she was able to take six months off to fulfill a lifelong dream to travel. She is taking a sabbatical and traveling across Europe, so she's allowing me to stay here until I find my own place. The cost of living here is bonkers. Coming from Georgia, I was not prepared for this. A one-bedroom apartment going for twenty-five hundred a month? You've got to be kidding me. My job pays fairly well, but not *that* well.

I was honestly surprised when Aunt Caroline offered her apartment to me. We've never been close. I've always had a better relationship with my Uncle Bennett, but chalked it up to us having the commonality of loving sports. Caroline is ... odd. No matter the situation, she remains stiff and poised. My mother routinely compared the two of us whenever she wanted me to change something about myself. *Be more like your aunt, Hannah Ann.* But, as I've never been good at living like a borderline robot, I could never take on the Caroline Davenport outlook.

It's the beginning of August, but the players won't report for training until mid-September. This gives me a few weeks to memorize the roster, learn the ins and outs of the team, and get my footing. I'm starting tomorrow — well, actually, today — when my uncle will get me sorted with Human Resources.

A loud crash next door jars me as I'm finally drifting off, and I shout out in frustration. That's it. I'm pissed. I throw the covers off and stomp out of the bedroom, swiftly walking to the apartment door, throwing it open, and walking to pound on the offending neighbor's door as hard as I can, non-stop.

"Jesus, stop already," I hear a male voice mutter from the other side of the door, and then a few giggles from what sounds like more than one woman. *Good Lord. What am I walking into?*

"Open the god damn door!" I shout.

The door swings open, and I'm stunned speechless.

The most beautiful man I've ever seen is standing there, shirtless, holding a glass of amber liquid. Behind him are three women, all in various stages of undress. The man has tattoos down both arms, across his chest, and onto his washboard abs. He's built like a brick wall, well over six feet tall, and his bronzed skin shines with perspiration. I don't realize I'm staring until he waves a hand in front of my face.

"Eyes up here, darlin'," he drawls with a smirk.

My eyes narrow as they whip up to his, and I growl. I literally growl. This gorgeous man is now enemy number one.

"Oh, you're a spunky little pixie, huh," he says with a wink as his eyes take a lengthy perusal down my body. "You always say hello to the neighbors in lingerie?"

Holy shit. I glance down at my body and realize I'm wearing next to nothing. A small camisole and a pair of booty shorts. I was so angry at being woken up, I didn't even think about my state of undress.

"Do you have any idea what time it is?" I say menacingly.

"Umm, it's about three, ain't it, Luke?" one of the girls says as she walks behind him and slides her hands across his stomach.

"Do none of you work?" I shout incredulously. The girl has the audacity to shrug at me.

The gorgeous man, Luke, stares at me.

"Don't you know who I am?" he asks.

"An annoying and disrespectful neighbor? Yes, I'm aware of that," I retort.

"I'm not ..." he starts, and I hold up a hand to stop him.

"Yes. Yes, you are. It's three a.m. I have to get up in three hours. Your shenanigans have kept me up all night. For the love of all that is holy, settle the fuck down," I snarl, my hands on my hips.

"Jesus, woman, just chill. We'll be quieter. Unless you want to come in and party with us?"

I snort.

3

"And get whatever venereal diseases y'all are passing around? No thanks," I say as I spin around and saunter back to my open door.

"See ya around, pixie," he calls after me as I slam my door shut. I lean against the door, and I can hear them talking.

"Luke, come back inside," I hear one of the women whine. She straight up whines. Do men actually find that attractive? No wonder I'm not in a relationship. I couldn't whine for attention if my life depended on it. Not only do I think it is remarkably unattractive to whine, but I was raised in a debutante world. *A lady must be poised and well-spoken at all times.* Ugh. I even say that crap in my momma's voice.

"Nah. Think it's time for you ladies to leave. Gotta be a good neighbor and shit," the guy says. I hear the women sputtering and all talking at once, trying to convince him otherwise. "Ladies, I've made myself clear. You need to leave."

I can still hear some muttering and shuffling around.

"Fuck! Get the fuck out of my apartment!" I jolt against the door as he yells at the women, who all seem to quickly get the memo and leave. His door slams moments later.

"Stupid bitchy neighbor. She's probably jealous. I bet he turned her down. She's fat anyway," one of them says. I stare down at my thighs. Yeah, they're thick. I've never met a donut I didn't enjoy. But at best, I'm a size ten. My weight fluctuates. I've been as high as a sixteen, but only as small as a size eight. I'm happy where I am. Confident. I rock these curves.

"Totes. We'll find him again this weekend. He'll invite us up again. You know how he is," another answers.

I hear the ding of the elevator, and moments later, it's quiet. Ahh, blissful silence.

I head back to the bedroom and slide under the sheets.

I finally fall asleep again around four, and visions of the shirtless tatted up hottie from next door dance behind my eyelids.

I hit snooze six times. I simply cannot successfully operate on this little sleep. As I check out the dark circles under my eyes, I sigh and grab my trusty bottle of concealer. Gonna need a thick layer today. I need to be out the door by seven-thirty, so this makeup look is going to be simple and quick.

I dress in a pair of ankle-length slim-fitting trousers, a white tank top, and a deep blue blazer. My long wavy blonde hair is loose and flows over one shoulder. Uncle Bennett says the dress code is casual, but I want to make a good impression on my first day. Grabbing my favorite pair of heels, I head out to the kitchen to grab some breakfast. Not only am I horrible without sleep, but I'm also definitely not a morning person. It's a pop tart kind of morning.

I grab my purse and laptop bag in one hand, and as I'm closing the door, hottie's door opens. His deep brown eyes are remarkably bright as he quickly looks me up and down. How the hell is he this awake?

"Hey, pixie," he says with a smile. I glower at him. Oh, he's a morning person. The worst kind of person.

"Don't call me that," I mutter. He's adjusting his shirt as he locks his door, and is sporting his hat backwards and wearing running shoes.

"Why? You're pint size and scrappy. Perfect for a pixie," he tells me. "And since I don't know your name, Pixie it is."

I sigh. I know he's trying to goad me into telling him my name, and I'm refusing to fall under his spell. I stare at the elevator door, willing it to open. I'm half tempted to take the stairs just because the thought of being stuck in the elevator with him is too much for me to handle.

The elevator dings, signaling its arrival, and I march onto it, secretly hoping he doesn't get on. Of course, he does. He smells divine. I stand ramrod straight, facing the closing elevator doors. He leans against the wall, studying me.

"You need to get fucked," he says casually.

My head whips toward him, and he smiles wickedly.

"Excuse me?" I snarl.

"You're wound too tightly. You need to get fucked. Loosen you up a bit, Pix. Couple of orgasms would do you good," he says.

"You really shouldn't comment on a woman's sex life. It's uncouth," I say snottily.

"You mean your lack of sex life. Anyone can tell you're not getting any, Pix."

"You know nothing about me," I stammer. He's hitting a little too close to home. It's been ... way too long since I've had sex. Let's not even talk about how I've never had an orgasm by a man, since apparently, the clit is a long-lost treasure men just can't seem to find.

Hottie sneaks up behind me before speaking. "Someone needs to yank that pole out of your ass, Pixie. But I bet you're not into ass play. You'd definitely relax with that kind of orgasm, though."

I'm gobsmacked. This entire conversation is unlike anything I've ever had with a man. Southern men, especially the men my parents approve of, do not proposition women in elevators, and they certainly don't talk about anal sex within a few hours of meeting. But, I mean, he's not wrong. It's been well over a year since I've had sex. And good sex? Multiple orgasm kind of sex? Well, that's never happened. I've only been with a couple of guys, and they've always played the 'I come first and hopefully you do too' game. So, guess what? I never did.

The elevator slows at the fourth floor, opening for a group of people to get on. Hottie moves over to stand directly behind me, and I catch a whiff of his scent. I exhale slowly as his scent overwhelms me. Manly, woodsy, and sheer testosterone infiltrate my senses. I feel him step closer to me as his chest hits my shoulders. His head bends down so his mouth is next to my ear.

"You wanna get fucked, Pixie?" he whispers against my ear. My eyes close reflexively as my body sways with hunger. Jesus. I've never had this kind of reaction to a man. Every nerve ending is firing as my skin prickles with goosebumps. Even if I wanted to, I can't answer him. My tongue seems to have stopped working. But even if I could speak, I wouldn't. It'll be a cold day in hell before this man gets me to admit anything about my sex life. As I'm trying to come up with a retort, Hottie stops me dead in my tracks. "Not gonna be me, though. You couldn't handle me with how tight you're wound. You ever decide to stop this bitch act and show me the *real* Pixie, you know where I'm at. I could loosen you up."

My head snaps up as the elevator arrives at the lobby. Hottie slides past me, and strides out into the lobby without a backward glance. As the doors close, I can't move. My feet are rooted to the ground. Uptight bitch? That's basically what he called me in no uncertain terms. Is that what he thinks of me? He doesn't even know me.

But it's not the first time I've been called uptight. Or frigid. Or just a bitch. I've always let the nasty comments roll off my back, but for some reason it's hitting differently with this guy. It's somehow worse.

I try to hold in the tears that threaten to cascade in rivulets down my cheeks, but to no avail. I ride the elevator back up to my aunt's apartment to regain my composure before heading back downstairs. I had hoped to live here for at least a few months before finding a more permanent residence, but I immediately fire off a text to my aunt to ask for realtor recommendations. Honestly, I had a little bit of a panic attack on my way back up to Aunt Caroline's apartment. Being called frigid, uptight, or a bitch brings up memories. Bad memories from Georgia. Southern women are supposed to appear regal, refined, and cultured. But men expect them to be sirens in the bedroom. I never got that memo, and more than one man called me out on it after high school.

Once I've finally gained my composure and walked out of the building, I falter when I see my new neighbor standing right outside. Probably shouldn't call him hottie, since he's clearly an asshole. Was he waiting for me? No fucking way. Shit. I have no idea if my makeup is running, or if there are mascara marks on my face. Great. Just another thing he can bring up the next time he corners me. I square my shoulders and stiffly walk past him. Totally proving the whole frigid bitch thing right now, but I can't make myself do anything else.

I walk the three blocks to the arena. I'm so glad my Aunt Caroline suggested I stay at her apartment for the time being. Being able to walk to work is a definite plus. I have a car, but the drivers here are absolutely crazy. All traffic laws seem to be suggestions, and it's incredibly disconcerting. Atlanta at rush hour pales in comparison to the chaos in Denver at any time of day. I'm sure when it snows it'll be complete mayhem.

I find the entrance Uncle Bennett told me to use, and head inside.

"May I help you?" the security guard asks courteously.

"Yes, hello. My name is Hannah Beauregard. I'm starting work here today. My uncle Bennett Davenport is supposed to meet me here, I think," I stammer nervously. For as good as I am on social media, my in-person people skills suck.

"Ahh, yes. Welcome, Ms. Beauregard. Coach Davenport told me you'd be coming in today. I'll call him and let him know you're here," he says warmly, as he picks up the phone. "Hey Coach, your niece is here."

I look around the small employee entrance and see a few framed photos. Some are of hockey, and some are of basketball. The arena is shared by the Wolves and the NBA basketball team, the Colorado Altitude. I start to walk over to take a closer look at a hockey team pic, when a door opens.

"Hey kiddo," my uncle says, opening his arms to give me a hug.

"Hi Uncle Bennett," I say quietly.

"You settling in at Caroline's place okay?" he asks, and I nod. I'm not telling him about my run-in with the neighbor. He'd probably want to come over, and that would be all kinds of embarrassing.

"Yep, settling in just fine."

"Okay. Let me give you a really quick tour and then get you to HR so you can fill out all the employment forms. I have a conference call in about an hour, so I can't give you any more time than that. We can meet later today, or tomorrow, for a more in depth tour, okay?" he says, gesturing for me to walk through the doorway and into the tunnels beneath the arena.

My uncle talks a million miles a minute, and I'm barely focusing. I know next to nothing about hockey, but I can smell it. I can smell the ice. And it's intoxicating. I can almost feel the blades gliding across the ice. I've never been ice skating either, but I'm almost giddy thinking about attempting it now. Hell, I've never even been to a hockey game. This is all brand new.

As we walk through the hallways, he points out a variety of different rooms. I'm slightly taken aback by the barren nature of the facility. This doesn't seem like a world-class institution that pays athletes millions of dollars to skate around and beat each other up. Okay, I know that's a novice opinion, and an over simplification. I must have a disgruntled look on my face, because my uncle chuckles.

"Confused?" he asks.

"Uh, yeah, actually," I admit with a sheepish smile. "The college had a better setup than this. Are you sure this is the NHL?"

"This is just where they play, Han. This isn't where they practice. The majority of the time they're at a different facility. That place has all the bells and whistles you expected," he explains.

"Okay, well, where is that? And where will I be working?" I ask. I was under the assumption I'd be at the arena all the time.

"The practice facility is about a mile from here. It's a huge complex with other sports fields. Baseball fields, lacrosse, you name it. And in regards to where you'll be working, you go where the team goes. If they're practicing, you are with them. If they're getting ready at the arena, you're there too. You know you'll travel with them on occasion, right?"

My jaw drops open. Obviously, I didn't know that.

"What? Seriously?" I am not the best traveler. In fact, I'm petrified of flying. The only reason I was able to complete my job at Georgia State was because they only traveled half the games, and many were driving distance. In four years as their social media manager, I only flew six times. And of those six, I had four panic attacks. The other two times one of my co-workers basically knocked me out with a Xanax.

"Hannah, are you still afraid of flying?" my uncle asks. I don't even have to answer him. I can feel the blood draining from my face. "Shit. I thought you would have gotten over this by now. Well, you're gonna need to figure something out. Forty-one away games, Han. You have to be at a chunk of them."

I nod slowly as a wave of nausea overtakes me. I guess it never occurred to me that hockey is a much more involved sport, and the schedule is intense. Of course there would be traveling.

"Listen. I have a therapist. Let me call her and see if she can fit you in this month, and get you some kind of anxiety medication or something. You gotta get over this, Hannah. You can't work this kind of job anywhere in this field without being able to fly," my uncle says.

"I know. I know! I just ... I guess I didn't think I'd have to go everywhere with the team," I say softly.

"We'll figure this out. Let's finish this tour and then I'll take you up to HR. You can get your paperwork filled out while I go to my meeting. We can grab lunch before heading over to the practice facility to show you the ropes over there."

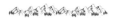

*A*fter what felt like an hour of paperwork and guidelines being discussed in Human Resources, Uncle Bennett grabs us some lunch from a food truck, and we head to the practice facility. He tells me it's just referred to as the Sports Facility Zone. The massive building houses a practice rink, administrative offices, a couple of gift shops, a food court, indoor golf, and even an entertainment complex. Baseball and lacrosse fields outside seem to go on for miles.

Uncle Bennett leads me in a side door near a private parking lot for Wolves players and employees. We enter into a spacious lobby with multiple security guards standing before an elevator.

"Gentlemen, this is my niece Hannah Beauregard. She is the new social media coordinator, so she'll be coming and going throughout the day," my uncle introduces me. The men all smile warmly at me, or at least attempt to smile. They all look mean and miserable, which I guess is a good thing for security. I smile back at them and drop my head to look at the floor. I'm overwhelmed.

My uncle shows me how to use my brand-spanking-new ID to access the elevator, and we zoom up a couple of floors to the administration wing. I'm introduced to a handful of people, all of whose names I've already forgotten, and then Uncle Bennett deposits me into my new office.

"This is yours. I need to go check on something, so stay here for a minute." He jogs off down the hallway, and I turn to take in my new office.

Barren walls and an empty desk greet me, but the massive window behind the desk has the most exquisite view of the Rocky Mountains I've ever seen. It takes my breath away. I gasp with glee.

"Beautiful, isn't it?" a voice says from behind me, and I jolt. Turning, I find a striking man leaning against the doorframe. "Sorry to scare you. Just wanted to come meet Coach's niece. I'm Gabe."

He extends his hand to shake mine, and I slide my hand into his. He shakes it, but doesn't let go.

"Coach didn't tell us how beautiful you were," he comments. I snort and roll my eyes.

"That's how you're gonna play this?" I ask him with a cocked eyebrow. I didn't expect his first sentence to be a line. He grins widely.

"Yep. What's your name, beautiful?" he asks, still holding my hand.

"Her name is off limits, Dawson. My niece is off limits. Spread the word to the team. I better not hear about any of you hitting on her," my uncle says from behind Gabe.

Gabe is still holding my hand with his eyes on mine. His thumb skirts over mine in a light stroke.

"You might need to let go of my hand," I whisper. He shakes his head slightly.

"Not sure I can do that, beautiful. Not sure I can," he responds with a flirty wink, and I can't help but giggle.

"Enough! Dawson, get the fuck out of here. Leave my niece alone," my uncle yells. Gabe finally lets go of my hand, but doesn't leave my office. He takes an exaggerated look at the nameplate on the door before turning back to me.

"Til next time, Ms. Beauregard. I'll be seeing you again real soon," he says with a sultry promising tone.

"The fuck you will," my uncle snarls. "You just got yourself twenty extra minutes of drills today, Casanova."

I have no idea what that means, but Gabe does. He winces slightly, but then gives me another big smile.

"Worth it," he says, then taps the doorframe before sauntering away.

My uncle looks over at me.

"Stay away from him."

"Uhh, okay?"

"Seriously, Hannah. Stay away from him. He's trouble. Well, actually he's not trouble, as he seems to stay out of the limelight, but still stay away from him. Just stay away from all of them. Especially Santo. He's the worst," my uncle mutters.

"I don't really intend on hooking up with the entire hockey team, Uncle Bennett," I respond wryly.

"Jesus. I didn't need that thought in my head, Hannah banana. To me, you're still six years old."

"Yeah, well, I'm not. I'm twenty-eight, and I've had sex, so quit acting like I'm an innocent flower these dirty little hockey players are going to corrupt. I've been corrupted. It's done," I tell him. He squeezes his eyes shut. "And seriously, you're not even that much older than me. I bet you've sowed your wild oats enough for the both of us."

"I'm a dude. It's different."

"Oh, is it?" I ask, popping a hand on my hip and staring at him. "How positively antiquated, Uncle Bennett. Shall I have all gentlemen callers speak with you first for your blessing?"

"You're not gonna make this easy on me, are you?" he says with a tilt to his lips that tells me he's not actually angry.

"Probably not."

"Fan-fucking-tastic."

Chapter 2

*L*uca

*S*tanding outside my building, I begin my stretching routine before my run. I've positioned myself so I can see the pixie walk out. No clue where she came from, or how she got into the apartment next to mine. Caroline Davenport was living there, and her brother is one of the coaches on my team. So I'm guessing the pixie knows Caroline somehow. They might be related, as I could hear a southern twang in Pixie's voice when she was yelling at me last night, and I vaguely remember Coach Davenport talking about family somewhere in the south.

Fifteen minutes after I left the elevator, the pixie still hasn't come outside. Yeah, I get my fair share of pussy. But I don't go out of my way to be cruel to women. Something about this girl has me off my game. I'm feeling a bit worried, and as I'm about to head back into the building to make sure she's okay, she strides out. She sees me and her steps falter, but I see her square her shoulders as she swiftly walks past me. I don't miss the reddening of her eyes though. Fuck. Maybe calling her a bitch was a little rough, even for me.

She's a damn vision. Beautiful blonde curls I want to feel in the palm of my hand. Eyes that aren't quite green, yet not hazel, and rimmed in thick lashes. Tiny, yes. I'm six foot four, so basically all women are tiny. I don't think she's more than a couple inches over five feet, though. But curves for days. Curves I want to get to know intimately. Best ass I've seen in a long time. Watching her walk back to her apartment last night? Spank bank material. Got myself off right after, thinking about her.

Not like anything will happen with her anyway. I mean, she caught me with three women. No coming back from that. I don't even know what I was doing. I didn't even kiss any of them, let alone anything more physical. In fact, I don't even remember the last time I had sex. I know things need to change, because I'm in a downward spiral. That's for damn sure. Thank fuck none of that was broadcast on social media. My agent, and the team, would have had my head for that.

As I begin my run in the opposite direction from where the pixie walked, I turn my hat around and tuck it as far down on my forehead as I can. I hate being recognized in public. And it happens more often than I'd like. I'm one of the most recognized defensemen in the NHL, and with my track record off the ice, it can get really bad. I'm photographed all the fucking time. It's ridiculous. I probably should just run on a treadmill in my building's gym, but it's August in Colorado. Gotta take advantage of warm weather when I can.

I've been in the NHL for ten years. They've all been here in Denver, but my agent has warned me this year that I better shape up. My contract is up at the end of this upcoming season, and the owners have been not too discreetly muttering about a trade. My off ice antics are draining them. I get it, they're draining me too. But I can't seem to stop making bad decisions. Like last night. Why the fuck did I invite *three* women back to my apartment? I don't even like bringing any women home to my space, choosing instead to go to their places. My apartment is a haven for me. Three women, though? What the fuck was I thinking? It's like I'm just trying to see how far I can go before I completely fuck myself.

I don't know what the fuck I'm doing. I'm from here. It was a dream come true to get drafted by Denver and get to stay here. I played college here, so to stay and play for the team I idolized growing up? Absolute perfection. So I really can't explain why I'm so hellbent on messing it up.

As I'm finishing up my six-mile run, my AirPods buzz with a call. I don't even have to look at my phone. I know it's my agent. He calls me at the same damn time every fucking morning.

"I'm still alive, Max," I sigh.

"Well, with you I have to check daily, asshole," he mutters. I chuckle. Max and I have been friends since high school. He's one of the few people I trust completely. While his hockey career ended due to an injury, he parlayed that into a successful job as a sports agent. He doesn't get around as much as I do, but he gets his fair share of pussy.

"You'll be happy to know I kicked out the women that I went home with last night," I tell him.

"Women? As in, plural? More than one?" he asks.

"Uh, yeah. Three, actually."

"Jesus, man. You really are a whore."

"Thanks."

"Well, what do you want me to say? Not gonna congratulate you on a harem, bro. You're gonna need to start getting tested every other day. Who the fuck knows what these puck bunnies have," he counters.

"Yeah, that's what my neighbor told me last night when she came over yelling at us to keep it down."

"Which one? The older lady? Or was it Caroline who yelled at you?"

"Oh, shit. No, some other chick. Maybe a relative. Sounded southern? I don't know. Cute little pixie with an amazing ass," I say, envisioning her walking away from me. My cock twitches.

"Don't do it."

"What?"

"Don't do the neighbor. Seriously, man, don't. I don't know what her relation is to Caroline, but if she's possibly family, you cannot fuck this up. Coach Davenport will have your head."

"I know that. I'm not gonna do anything with her. She's too uptight anyway. Can't risk running into her all the time," I tell him. I already don't have a good relationship with Caroline or Coach Davenport. I don't need to add insult to injury. Besides, Caroline is weird. I never quite know if she'll go full stalker on me, or try to get me kicked out of the building.

"Good. Alright, I'm sending over a couple of events I'd like you to attend this month. All great publicity. And the director of marketing at the children's hospital called again, asking when you'd like to come back in," Max tells me.

"Will it be off the record again?" I ask.

"Yeah, they know you want this to be under the radar," he answers. Good. I hate when athletes only show up for anything if it's going to help their image. My image is in the shitter, but I'm not gonna try to capitalize off sick kids.

"I got a conference call to get on, so I'll let you go. No orgies tonight, okay, Luca? No public fights, no chaos. I have plans tomorrow and I don't want to spend the whole day putting out your fucking fires," Max says.

"No promises."

"Lovely."

I snicker as I end the call. I make the mistake of removing my hat to wipe my forehead, and I immediately hear a screech.

"Oh my God! Luke Santo!"

A tall thin woman is suddenly in front of me, grabbing my arm and jumping up and down giddily.

"I'm such a big fan of yours!" she says breathily as she pushes her tits into my body. Normally I would slide my arm around her and give her a big smile, but I'm not in the mood.

"Hey, thanks. Glad to have you as a fan," I say as I gently step away from her and pull my arm from her grasp. She doesn't get the memo and steps into me again.

"I'd love to ask you some questions about hockey, Luke. You wanna grab some breakfast?" she asks huskily as her eyes dart toward my building. What the fuck? This chick knows where I live? This means she's either a crazed fan, or she's with the news or a paparazzo.

"Did you really just sit and wait here for me?" I ask her bluntly. Her eyes widen as she stammers a response.

"Well, umm, not exactly, but..."

"Which station are you with?" I ask. Bet this is an intern fresh out of college, trying to get her big break for one of the local channels.

She opens her mouth to speak, and I can see the denial coming. I subtly shake my head, and she giggles, before straightening and pushing her shoulders back. "I'm with NBC here. If you could just let me ask you a couple of questions —"

"Yeah, no. You need to leave. I'm calling security."

I swivel and march into the lobby of my building. The security guard is already approaching me with his phone out.

"See that woman? She's not allowed in. She just cornered me, and knew this was my building. Said she's with NBC," I tell him.

"On it, Mr. Santo."

As he walks outside to see if he can talk to her, I watch as she quickly crosses the street and talks to a man holding a telephoto lens camera. Fucking great. I was just set up. Is she really with NBC, or is she really working for a gossip site that makes up stories to go with photographs? Wouldn't be the first time I experienced that, and it probably won't be the last.

Shooting off a quick text to Max, I sigh as I board the elevator going up to my fifteenth floor apartment. My apartment isn't massive. I have some teammates that live in palatial apartments, or even larger homes on the outskirts of Denver. But I like living close to the arena and near all the nightlife. Well, I used to. Now it's all become grating. Thirty-year-olds should not be out at bars trolling for chicks. I've begun asking to see their ID's because some don't look legal, and I'll be damned if I get arrested for statutory rape.

I keep my three bedroom apartment tidy. My mom and my nonna helped me pick out all the furniture and decorate it. I come from a huge Italian family. I have six siblings: three brothers and three sisters. I'm the third youngest. My oldest two brothers, Alex and Dominic, were both married with a slew of kids. Dom is divorced, and Alex's wife passed away in a car accident a while ago. He was deployed at the time and didn't find out about her death until a week later. Neither have remarried, and both claim they'll never have another relationship.

The twins, Leonardo and Gianna, who go by Leo and Gia, are a couple of years older than me. Leo is in the Army, and Gia works with my family. Gia is the only happily married one. Leo is a tech wiz, and set up our hotel website. When he's here, he enjoys helping out wherever he can, but especially likes to help with the grounds crew. Hell, most of my family works for the same hotel that has been in my family for ages here in our hometown. Everlasting Inn and Spa.

My sisters Isabella and Ariana are both single. My mother cries often about her poor little unmarried daughters. My sisters are not amused. Isabella owns a bakery in town, and supplies all the fresh pastries and desserts for the hotel. Arianna runs the hotel spa and hot springs.

When I think back to my childhood, I have more memories at the hotel than I do from our actual home. Everyone in our family, even distant cousins, has helped out there in one way or another. Folding towels when a stomach flu took out half the housekeeping staff. Emptying dishwashers after an unexpectedly busy Fourth of July buffet dinner. Answering phones for the concierge ... which Arianna and I were *not* asked to do again once our mom realized we were speaking only in pig Latin and answered every question with a question. While it wasn't expected that we all would end up working there, it was implied.

Honestly, had I not found my passion for hockey, I'd undoubtedly be puttering around there in some aspect. As soon as my parents saw how much I loved hockey, however, they knew I was destined for different things. I know I'm fucking lucky. Not only do I love hockey, but I play it well enough to survive in the NHL. Only about one in every one thousand boys who start playing hockey as kids make it into the NHL. The fact that I've been here, successfully, for ten years? I know I'm lucky. Even luckier that I get to do it for the Denver Wolves, the team I grew up rooting for, and I'm an hour away from my hometown.

Eternity Springs is a small town west of Denver, full of personality, touristy spots, well-known hot springs, and my entire family. It's not just my immediate family. The Santo clan rolls deep in Eternity. In fact, if at least one of my family members hasn't been featured on the town gossip site, *The Eagle Has Landed*, then I know something major must have happened. Us Santo kids tend to be featured pretty often. We're all pretty dramatic like that.

After a quick shower, I settle down on my couch to watch a movie. I should be watching tapes. I know there are rookies gunning for my spot. But at this moment, I'm just so fucking drained. Ten years may not seem like a lot in normal careers, but hockey is ridiculously physical. Maybe a hockey career is like dog years, or Hollywood marriages. Ten years in hockey is like thirty in a normal job. And frankly, I know my time is coming. Hell, it's probably already passed. But I don't have a fucking clue what I want to do with the rest of my life, and that scares the shit outta me. So I put on a mindless action movie and drown out the voices in my head screaming at me to be a better man. Because at this moment, I don't have the ability to be better for anyone.

*N*ot surprisingly, the woman who approached me in front of my building did set me up. Pictures appear online within a few hours and show me in a horrible light. It blows my mind how a paparazzo can take an innocent situation and paint it in a completely different manner. The photos make it look like the woman and I are having an intimate conversation. There's even a shot of me looking back at my building, as if I'm suggesting she come inside. The woman went on record saying that I rocked her world, and then forced her to leave because I had another woman coming over. She legit just made up a fucking story.

I text Max the link and ask if we can sue. He texts back that he'll contact the site and ask for a retraction and correction. The woman was "unnamed" in the article, so it would be difficult to sue her. And, he tells me, it's a he said-she said situation, which never pans out well for the celebrity. He also added that, since I'm the "celebrity" here, I'll be guilty until proven not guilty, and even then, most won't believe the truth. The public no longer thinks I'm a good guy. They just assume that I'm the devil. I fucking hate this.

I'm thirty fucking years old. Yeah, I've had a bunch of transgressions on my record. I'm not perfect. I've done stupid shit, and thanks to social media, I get butchered for everything. But people just straight up lying about me? That makes me want to quit hockey and become a hermit. Move up into the mountains and never come back. Just get groceries delivered, and never see another human being again. I don't even think I could move home to Eternity Springs, because the paparazzi would just follow me, and I can't bring that on my family.

I take a long pull of my beer as I contemplate what I want to watch while I eat dinner. The lobby just called, saying my Chinese food delivery was on its way up. I'm in no mood for public interaction, and Max advised me to lay low for a few days anyway. I hear the soft knock letting me know the delivery has been left at the door, and I grab my food at the same time the elevator is opening. Pixie steps out and our eyes meet. My mouth salivates as I see her. Fuck she's gorgeous. She has on sky-high fuck me red heels and her trousers accentuate that amazing ass. I'd comment on that, but one look at her face has me stopping in my tracks. Pure hatred pours off of her as she glares at me.

I don't say a word as she walks to her door and unlocks it. I take one last look at her ass before sliding my gaze up to her face and see that she's watching me. Her glare has changed slightly, and I now see heat. Lust. Confusion. She hesitates for one second, and I open my mouth, ready to invite her in for dinner. But she shakes her head before I can speak and slams the door.

Fuck.

I stand there for a couple minutes, flustered at my reaction to her. I don't even know her fucking name. She obviously hates me. Hell, I hate myself, so I don't blame her. But, damn. I hate how my body is reacting to this woman. That'll only make me hate myself more, because I'm thinking about getting off to the image of someone who may, or may not, be related to one of my coaches.

The elevator dings again, jarring me from my thoughts. My other neighbor is a seventy-three-year-old widow named Edith. Edith and I do not get along. She thinks, assuredly so, that I'm a man-whore with no morals. I haven't given her any indication of being other-wise. Pretty good thing she didn't see the three women leaving early this morning, or Edith would probably try to get me kicked out of the building.

My mind is not operating at one hundred percent, or I would have thought to enter my apartment quickly as soon as I saw Edith in the elevator. Instead, since all the blood has inconveniently rushed straight to my cock at the sight of Pixie's ass, I stand in my door and stare at Edith.

"Young man! Have you no shame?" Edith yells out, clutching at her pearl necklace. Yep, she literally wears pearls, and she clutches them often. I furrow my brow in confusion. What the hell is the old bat spouting off about?

She points at my crotch.

Oh, fuck.

Yeah, that's noticeable.

I'm wearing grey sweatpants. It's pretty damn obvious that I'm aroused. Jesus. Now she's really going to try and get me kicked out of the building.

"You are an atrocity! Shame, shame!" Edith shouts, and before I can respond, Pixie's door opens.

"Is everything okay?" she asks, only looking at Edith. Great. She hasn't noticed my erection.

"Oh, hello. You must be Hannah. Caroline told me about you," Edith says warmly. Pixie's name is Hannah. Holy fuck, that suits her. She's a Hannah. I smile slightly as I finally know her name. "Stay away from that heathen, Hannah. He's a monster, standing here all aroused just waiting for people to walk past!"

Pixie's eyes automatically lower and then bounce right back up to my face, horrified. Blush covers her cheeks...and not the cheeks that I'd like to make blush. Fuck. These thoughts aren't gonna help my erection calm the fuck down.

"Mrs. Willowby, I apologize for this. Really, I do. I was just grabbing my delivery. I'm going inside now. Gonna go drown myself," I mumble as I walk back into my apartment and close the door. I lean against the door and listen.

"Hannah, Caroline told me to keep an eye out for you. You stay away from that boy, you hear me? He's trouble. Always has women coming in and out at weird hours, makes tons of noise. No respect for the other tenants. Just a disrespectful hooligan."

I roll my eyes in frustration. Women don't come in and out at all hours. Exaggerate much, Edith? Unless you count my mom or sisters, it's a rarity for me to bring women back here. Excluding last night.

"I'll keep that in mind, Mrs. Willowby."

I take a look out the peephole and see Edith has gone into her apartment, but Hannah still stands in the hallway. She looks over at my door, and I hold my breath. Her eyes reach the peephole as if she knows I'm watching her. She turns slowly toward her door and hesitates, her head again turning towards my door. Her hands slide up the sides of her legs and onto her ass as she struts into her apartment. Right before she closes the door, she lightly taps her right ass cheek. I groan loudly, and I hear her light giggle as she closes her door.

What the actual fuck was that?

Chapter 3

*H*annah

have absolutely no idea what came over me. I just knew he'd enjoy the show. I'd caught hottie staring at my ass again. While his 'frigid bitch' comment threw me off this morning, I did catch his eyes lingering on my backside. And frankly, I felt a little tease was needed after he'd been a complete jackass to me that morning.

I have a big ass. It is what it is. I've tried to lose it, tried dieting and stretching, cardio and weight lifting. I'm just predisposed to having a large ass. Thank God big asses are 'in' right now because nothing is taking this off of me.

After having Gabe flirt with me today, and then seeing hottie and the straight lust flowing off of him in waves, I was feeling sassy as I sauntered back into the apartment. I was half tempted to knock on his door and ask him to help me get rid of the whole 'frigid bitch' tattoo that's apparently stamped on my forehead.

I'm not comfortable with men. I never have been. It's ironic that I've chosen a career field where I'm surrounded by men. While I may not know hockey yet, I love sports. I love the sportsmanship, the traditions, and even the weird rituals all athletes seem to have. I love the fan base, the excitement of the crowd, and even the agony of defeat. It's all such a complete whirlwind that gobbles me up every day.

But interacting with men in my job? I'm absolutely horrendous at it. I stumble over myself, stammer, and always seem to say the wrong thing. It's why I've only had a couple relationships in my life. And why I have almost no sexual experience whatsoever. I've had three sexual partners in my life. Two were in serious relationships, and from what I can gauge, they were both what would be termed 'vanilla.' I've seen some porn. I know what *could* happen. But in those relationships, it was missionary, or me on top. That's it. My third sexual partner was a horrifying one-night stand that involved me doing the walk of shame with one shoe and a broken phone. My mother brings up that travesty almost every Thanksgiving: the time Hannah embarrassed the family. It's really no wonder I moved across the country.

I learned very quickly at the University of Southern Georgia that I needed just to do my job, and keep any interactions with the players completely off-the-table. Focusing on my job, and the task at hand, helped me to steer clear of any opportunities to put my own foot in my mouth. It's also why I couldn't send any player/peer recommendations to the Wolves organization, because no one at USG really knew me. I kept to myself as much as possible.

As I'm contemplating going back into the hallway and knocking on hottie's door, my phone rings. I grimace, knowing it's going to be a family member. I don't have a good relationship with any of my family back in Georgia. They had high expectations for me to find a rich husband and settle down into southern socialite life. When I actually wanted a career — gasp — they were horrified. I became the black sheep of the family simply because I had career aspirations. Well, in all honesty, I was the black sheep before that. I asked too many questions as a child, skinned too many knees, and didn't do exactly as my parents told me. Shame, shame.

I sigh as I look at the screen. Yep, it's my mother. I refuse to call her 'mom.' That would insinuate a close and connected relationship where she actually attempted to raise me.

"Hello, mother," I say dryly.

"Hannah Ann."

My mother always refers to me with my middle name. It's a southern thing. Once I was eighteen, and legally an adult, I told people to stop calling me Hannah Ann. It infuriates her, which makes me even happier.

"What can I do for you, mother?" I ask.

"Your cousin Annabelle has accepted a proposal of marriage from Dalton Whithers. His daddy is a senator. You've met Dalton, yes?" my mother asks. I roll my eyes.

"Yes, mother, you've introduced me to him multiple times."

"Oh. So then you know what a great catch he is, and how excited Annabelle's parents are for this match," she says.

"Yep."

"That's yes ma'am, Hannah Ann."

I loudly sigh.

"Is Annabelle excited to share Dalton?" I ask.

"I beg your pardon?"

"Dalton isn't monogamous, mother. In fact, Dalton doesn't even stay on one side of the field. He plays both sides," I tell her. Dalton enjoys some MM side action. My mother is as conservative as they come, so I'm sure this will be unacceptable to her.

"Well," she stammers, "he's an attorney, and needs to let off steam. That's understandable."

My mouth drops open.

"So you're saying it's completely acceptable for Dalton to step out on my cousin because his job is stressful?" I am completely shocked. No way can my mother think this is okay.

"It's the way of life, Hannah Ann. It doesn't matter what men do outside of their marriage, as long as they come home to their wives."

"You have *got* to be kidding me, mother. You can't seriously act like this is okay!"

"Annabelle will be marrying well, and she'll be set for life. I'm sure she's aware of Dalton's extracurricular activities. In fact, Dalton's older brother Wesley is single. I could set up an introduction," my mother says, and I can hear the victorious smile in her voice. Absolutely not.

"Umm, I'm pretty sure Wesley is single because he doesn't just play both sides of the field, mother. He strictly plays one side. And it's not the side I reside on," I tell her. Wesley is not exactly in the closet, but not fully out either. When you come from a large society family in the south, lots of things are expected from you. I'm betting he's single because his family won't accept his lifestyle.

"He still needs a wife. That would be perfect for you! He could continue living however he wants, and you could do whatever it is that you do with the sports," my mother comments.

She calls it 'the sports.' You'd think a southern woman would at least understand football, but my mother is completely clueless about all sports.

"Yeah, I'll pass. I'm not going to marry a homosexual man just because our two families expect, or demand, it," I tell her.

"Hannah Ann, we've allowed this to go on too long. You need to come back home and take your rightful place in the family. You have expectations to fulfill, and it's time you delivered. It's bad enough you left poor Jefferson here, fending for himself, with all the ridiculous rumors about your breakup," my mother chastises.

"I'm twenty-eight years old, mother. It's time *you* realize I'm an adult and no longer under your thumb. I'm never coming back to Georgia. Get that through your thick skull. And the rumors about Jefferson? I can only assume that most, if not all, are true. Don't call me again with one of these little tirades, mother. It's quite unbecoming," I tell her and then end the call, throwing the phone on the bed. I can feel a massive headache coming on. No one knows how to aggravate me more than my mother. I specifically chose to use the word "unbecoming" because my mother used it to describe every behavior she didn't like of mine growing up. *It's unbecoming to frown. Don't pick at your fingernails, Hannah Ann. It's unbecoming. You will not raise your voice to your date, Hannah Ann. It's unbecoming to show disrespect.*

The phone immediately rings again, and I power it down. I have no desire to hear anything she has to say. She's getting worse with the controlling power trips as I get older. If I don't do exactly what she wants, or what she expects, it's like the world is ending. Absolutely ridiculous.

I have an older sister and a younger brother. My sister, Chastity, married a rich businessman in Atlanta, and immediately popped out two cherubic little nightmares in the form of my niece and nephew. Oh, they play the parts. They're both incredibly photogenic, and they perform perfectly at high society functions. In private, however, their horns come out. Since Chastity would rather spend her time 'lunching with the ladies' and bathing in whiskey, her disasters wreak havoc on the people hired to care for them.

My brother, Martin Jr, has managed to turn a normal four-year collegiate program into six years. He's changed his major four times, somehow still manages to live in his fraternity house, and has had multiple close calls with fatherhood. He's supposed to take over the family business, which he has no desire to do. He goes by MJ, because he hates the name Martin, and to attempt to separate himself from the family name.

My father runs a multi-state construction company supplying windows and doors to home and commercial builders. It's not exactly exciting, but it's lucrative. Selling windows is the furthest thing from MJ's mind. I can commiserate with him, as the thought of working with my father makes me nauseous.

I hate that my mother brought up Jefferson, my ex-boyfriend. He was a multi-year mistake on my part. It should have been concerning to me that my parents introduced me to him, being the prominent son of a couple from their country club. At first, Jefferson and I hit it off. It took quite a while for me to realize he wasn't a nice guy. He slowly and methodically broke my resolve and confidence, one small infraction at a time. *You could stand to lose a few pounds,*

Hannah. Did you look at that man, sweetheart? My friends are your friends now. You shouldn't be with your single friends now that you have me. Did you use profanity in front of my mother? Did you raise your voice at me? It's your fault I slapped you, Hannah. You knew you wanted my dick like that.

I'm a fairly resilient woman. While my home life was never picture-perfect on the inside, I remained steadfast in my hope for happiness. Once I realized that Jefferson was a vile person, I began taking steps to escape the stranglehold of southern Georgia. I stayed with him much longer than I should have, and allowed people like my parents to reason with me on Jefferson's actions. "He didn't really mean he'd sexually assault you, darling. He was just angry. Jefferson is a good man, from a good family. You don't want to give that up." All it took was him hitting me once, and I regretted ever letting my parents into my head.

Heading into the bathroom, I decide to run a bath. Caroline has an Alexa in every room so I'm able to play some music and relax in the tub. I light a few candles and dump in an unhealthy amount of rose scented Epsom salts and bubble bath, then add in one of my favorite bath bombs. I'm too keyed up to relax any other way. I hate when my mother calls me. It's never for a good reason.

I let out a blissful exhale as I slowly sink into the scalding water. I have Alexa playing some light jazz music, and I can feel my muscles begin to relax. Closing my eyes, I run through the craziness of the day in my mind. And I keep coming back to the hottie next door.

Subconsciously my hand drifts between my legs as I picture him answering the door this morning with only pants on. Then I remember just moments ago, seeing him VERY aroused. Hottie is rocking quite the nice little package. Well, definitely not little. Above average package? Girthy package? Hell, I don't know what to call it. It appeared larger than any I've ever been acquainted with, but that's not saying much.

My fingers are now circling my clit faster and faster as I remember him standing behind me in the elevator. His hot breath on my neck. My other hand joins the party, sliding into my channel. I let out a loud moan as I feel my orgasm building. I imagine it's Hottie's hands touching me, his fingers hammering in and out of me at a brisk pace as he whispers dirty thoughts into my ear. I cry out as I come, shuddering through the pleasure.

A crash sounds next to me and I hear a muffled "Fuck!"

I still my body as I listen, and I hear a groan. Oh my fucking god. The bathroom backs up to Hottie's apartment. Did he hear me? Does he know what I did? Before I can convince myself otherwise, I hear him very clearly speaking to me.

"Was that as good for you as it was for me, Pix?" he says.

My mouth drops open in disbelief. How fucking thin are these walls? Jesus, this is a nice apartment complex. Did they just decide insulation wasn't necessary?

"Did you really just listen to me?" I yell out.

"Kinda hard to miss, Hannah. You aren't quiet."

I have no response. I'm sure my face is incredibly red. Shame is burning my cheeks.

"Were you thinking of me?" Hottie calls out. When I don't respond, he says, "That's what I thought. Just so you know, I was thinking of you, too. And I can do much better in person than whatever you just fantasized about."

Considering the harem of women he partied with last night, I have no doubt about that.

Chapter 4

*L*uca

✦✦✦✦✦✦✦✦

*J*esus.

That was unexpected.

I was just gonna soak in my tub for a few minutes. Ran a little too hard this morning and my legs were sore. When I heard her filling up her tub, I stayed in mine. It was incredibly erotic, knowing we were that close together, naked in our tubs, with only a couple pieces of drywall between us.

Then she started moaning, and I lost my fucking mind.

I knew what she was doing. I was hard as a rock, thinking about her touching herself. Knowing she was thinking about me. Well, *hoping* she was thinking about me. I could tell when she was about to come because her moans began to crescendo. I couldn't *not* go along for the ride.

Grabbing my dick, I only had to stroke a couple of times thinking about her. As I came, I threw my head back in bliss, only to knock over my phone, a bottle of beer, and a glass container of Epsom salts I keep next to my tub. Fortunately, nothing shattered. I'd have been more pissed about losing the Epsom salts than the beer. Epsom salts are great for muscle strains and when I've overused my legs.

Dead silence next door meant she knew I was listening. So I

figured I'd test the waters. Every time she refused to answer, I knew I was correct. Which only made me want her more.

As she drained her tub, I made a mental note to track down the name of the construction company who built this building and send them a fruit basket or something. Because clearly they fucked up the insulation between our tubs, and I'm *very* happy about that.

Gingerly getting out of my tub, I put on some boxer briefs and then grab my foam roller. The foam roller is one of the only things I have to have with me at all times. It is instrumental in helping relieve muscle soreness and tension. I spend a few minutes loosening up my calves, then focus on my quads. It has become a ritual for me to do this before bed every night, no matter where I am. And hockey players are incredibly superstitious with our rituals.

My phone vibrates with a text message, and I automatically assume it's a sibling. Most likely one of my sisters. My brother, Dom, isn't really the texting type, and my other two brothers are typically really busy with their military careers. Leo is currently deployed overseas on a mission so secretive he wouldn't even tell us where he was headed. Other than knowing the time zone, he's given no details about his location. We don't even know when he'll return. While my parents are proud to say their son is an Army Ranger, I know they're unbelievably stressed about all the unknowns. Our mom prays often that Leo will decide to end his enlistment soon.

Picking up my phone, I see it's my sister Isabella.

Isabella: Are you ever coming home again, or have we lost you forever?

Me: Dramatic much, sis? I was home two weeks ago.

Isabella: I hardly saw you.

Me: I was there for a month. Not my fault you chose a career that has you in bed before dinner.

36

Isabella: You certainly don't complain when you get fresh donuts.

Me: I'd enjoy the donuts just as much at lunchtime.

Isabella: Anyway, when are you coming home again?

Me: I don't know. Training is ramping up again.

Isabella: Which is why you need to come home NOW. With Leo and Alex both gone, and Dom being his typical growly self, we need some more manpower around here. Dad hurt his hip again.

Me: Fuck. That's like the fourth time this year.

Isabella: I know. You know Mom and Arianna just coddle him.

Me: Has he been to a doctor?

Isabella: Nope. He claims after seeing that stupid wedding movie that Windex does actually help with pain.

Me: My Big Fat Greek Wedding?

Isabella: Yeah.

Me: We're Italian.

Isabella: I'm aware. You try telling him that.

Me: So I need to come help out, and then tell our father that Windex doesn't actually cure pain?

Isabella: Yep. Hit a Costco on your way for those pickles I like. Love you, byeeeee!

> Me: I am not buying you another five gallon tub of pickles.

> Me: Who needs that much?

> Me: Did you finish the last one? Shit, Belle, I just bought those three months ago. No human should go through that many pickles.

> Me: This is why you're still single.

> Isabella: Oh yeah? What's YOUR excuse?

I chuckle as I turn off the screen and toss my phone onto my bed. Taking a quick look around my room, I notice how stark it is. My mom and sisters decorated, so there *are* things on the walls. Weird knickknacks on furniture. But it's not me. The modern edges and minimalist furniture doesn't scream *Luca Santo, ice hockey god*. Okay, that was awful. Regardless, it's not me. How could I make this space more comfortable for me?

Sighing, I turn my phone back on to look at my schedule. I have three days with no practice where I can head home and see what help is needed. I think I'll call a realtor while I'm home. It would be nice to have a property there so I didn't have to stay at the hotel. Or worse, with my parents. The month I was home scarred me in more ways than one. While it's wonderful to see that my parents still clearly love and crave each other, I shouldn't have to literally *see* them. Hell, maybe that's why my dad keeps messing up his hip. I shudder and shake my head to clear the visual of how I saw them in the kitchen. Gross.

It's only nine o'clock, but I'm beat. The party last night wasn't a good call. I don't even know what I was thinking. Pisses me off to know if I hadn't brought those three girls home, I might have had a chance with Hannah. Who am I kidding, I'll never have a chance with her. She's above my pay grade.

*T*he following morning, I'm up and at the practice arena early. We aren't technically in training camp yet, but we can still use the facility for work outs and ice time. Sports Facility Zone has lots of children's leagues for hockey. So, we have set times for Wolves players when we can access the ice.

The ice is my happy place. It's where there's no drama. No paparazzi. No meddling mother, no dramatic sisters, or crazy brothers. No worries about the future. Just me, the puck and my stick. The ice is where I can breathe. I take a few laps around the perimeter, just settling in to the moment and relaxing.

"Santo!"

I look over my shoulder and see a couple of coaches off by the wall. I skate over with a smile.

"Looking above average out there, Santzy," Coach Woodward calls as I approach. Above average. Nice. And once someone calls you something in hockey, it sticks. I've been called Santzy since I was five. And above average? That's hitting below the belt.

"Looking forward to being back out there, coach," I answer.

"Listen, we have a new social media manager and we're setting up times for all the players to meet her. Get with your agent and set up a time, okay?" Coach Davenport says, his eyes studying me. Davenport and I have never gotten along. He's just a general prick. He's only five years older than me, but his career was more glorified than mine is. He's got a ring. Now he's coaching, and he thinks he's better than me. Pisses me off.

"Sure thing, coach. Is she hot?" I ask. Coach Davenport glares at me. Stupid easy making him mad.

"Off limits, asshole."

"Yeah, yeah."

We're told often that any employee in the Wolves organization is off limits. There isn't technically a no-fraternization policy, but we're highly encouraged to steer clear of anyone working here. Don't shit where you eat, Coach Woodward tells us often.

"You and Daws gonna be kosher this season, or more of the same bullshit antics as last year?" Coach Erikson, the skills coach, asks me. I shrug.

"He's the one with the issues, not me," I say cockily.

"You antagonize him and you know it, Santo," Coach Davenport retorts.

"Eh. It's too easy to piss him off. Fun to watch him blow his top," I say with a smile. "Remember that time when he threw the chair and broke the urinal?"

The coaches all laugh except for Coach Davenport.

"If I recall, it was because *you* suggested you had slept with his sister the night before..." he trails off pointedly. Oh, fuck. I had forgotten that. I've never met Dawson's sister. But damn, that really pissed him off. Woodward's smile drops from his face as his gaze narrows on me. I'm not completely sure, but I think I hear him growl.

"Tone it down, alright, Santzy? Sick of reading about you in gossip rags, and seeing bad videos on ESPN. Act like the professional we *pay* you to be. We don't want to have to review your contract," Woodward says, as he turns toward the coaches, effectively ending the conversation, and shutting me out.

Holy fuck. Did he basically just threaten to cut me if I mess up? Or just not give me another contract? My contract is up for an extension at the end of this season. I had hoped to get a couple more years in before retiring. I know I'm getting up there in age. These young guns right out of the minors and college are so much faster than me.

I skate over to the bench and grab my phone, texting Max about what the coach said. Maybe I'm getting too in my head about this. Hopefully, Max can calm my nerves.

Heading to the locker room, I pass Dawson and a couple of the other guys. They all greet me except for Dawson. Jesus, this dude is such a douche.

My phone dings with a response from Max.

> Max: I'm not surprised. Word on the street is they're waiting for you to fuck up so they can drop you.

Well, that certainly doesn't help my anxiety.

> Me: What the fuck??

> Max: They're sick of negative publicity. Your antics last season overshadowed their playoff run.

The news reported some ridiculous shit last year that wasn't true. Evidently, I got into a fist fight with someone in Aspen, while simultaneously having a rambunctious party in my apartment that the cops had to break up. Oh, and I have a love child with a prior teammate's ex-wife, I secretly belong to an underground sex club, and I make women sign an NDA before I let them see my dick. No NDA for sex. Just for *seeing* my dick. Who comes up with this shit?

> Me: I didn't even do any of the shit that was reported.

> Max: I know that, but there's so much you HAVE done in the past that they don't believe us when we say you didn't do stuff now.

> Me: Is there anything I can do? I don't want my career to be over yet.

> Max: Keep your head down and don't fuck up.

Lovely.

Chapter 5

Hannah

It's been two weeks since I started my new job with the Denver Wolves. I'm starting to feel like I have my wits about me with the job, living here, and making friends. Well, that last bit has been more difficult than I'd hoped. Frankly, I've never made a lot of friends. The family I come from, and their place in society, made it hard to discern who wanted to be my friend for *me*, and who wanted it for my family. It became easier to not let anyone in.

I was raised to be seen and not heard. Politeness, cooperation, and subservience. The men rule the show, and the women are there to look pretty. The first time I raised my voice to Jefferson, he looked at me like I was crazy. The last time I did it, I got slapped. I knew I wasn't made to live that kind of life. My sister didn't mind it. She wanted the money, the prestige, and the perks. I just wanted to be my own person, and have people accept me for me.

I'll never forget how I felt once I crossed over the Tennessee border on the interstate. Like a weight was lifted. I was leaving Hannah Ann Beauregard behind. The girl who couldn't stand up for herself. The girl who embarrassed her family by choosing a career with sports. A girl who refused to be beaten down, both physically and emotionally, by a man hand-picked by her parents.

I cried when I saw the "Welcome to Colorful Colorado" sign.

So while I'm exhausted, I've never been happier. I'm living my life for me now, and that is such an exquisite thing.

I could do with some friends, though.

My one and only friend is my crazy neighbor Edith. Aunt Caroline assured me that Edith has good intentions, but she's bat-shit crazy and sassy as all get-out. Edith invited me over for dinner last week and I learned all about every single neighbor in the apartment building. Considering there are twenty floors, and multiple units per floor, it took a while to list them all. She spent an inordinate amount of time discussing Hottie, though.

While I remember the harem from the first night referring to him as Luke, Edith calls him Luca. Luca suits him. He's got that tall, dark, and handsome vibe, and I could definitely see him wining and dining someone while speaking Italian at sunset in Rome. Okay, maybe I could see that person being *me*. Ugh. So hot, yet such a jackass.

I've only seen him a handful of times since he heard me in the bath, and every time he gives me this knowing smile with a wicked gleam in his eyes. He's calling me by my first name, but he says it in such a way that screams uninhibited sex and pleasure. "Hannah." He breathes it huskily, and I can feel the word skip across my skin like a tender caress. I have a visceral reaction every single time he does it, and he fucking knows it.

We've talked a few times, and I've found him quite engaging. Even when I've barely answered him, he's consistently continued as if I was participating fully. His cheerful disposition is wearing on me. Yesterday he talked to me all about his love of *bagels*, for crying out loud.

It's obvious Luca loves to antagonize me, and unfortunately, I play right into his hands every damn time. I've never met a man so infuriating. He teases me mercilessly. A couple of times I've managed to get in jabs. There's been a lack of noise at his apartment, suggesting he hasn't been partying as much. Even Edith commented on it.

When Luca isn't calling me Hannah, he's referring to me as Pixie. I'm not exactly short, he's just incredibly tall. I bet he could manhandle me, and put me just where he wants me. Ugh. I have to stop thinking about him and sex. I've never been the type to jump into bed with a man, and that certainly won't start now.

✦ ✦ ✦ ✦ ✦

*D*uring my second week of work, I've begun meeting with players. I probably could have met with players earlier, but my uncle is definitely treating me with kid gloves. Lots and lots of HR courses. Tons of reading and research. Did I really need to watch the 1996 NHL finals? Really, Uncle Bennett? Doubtful. I get it: my knowledge is in football, not hockey. But I figured I'd learn as I go. Keeping me away from the players is absurd. Can't do my job unless I work with them. Not only do I need to get to know them, but they're basically teaching me about their positions on the team.

I've spent quite a few hours at home doing hardcore Hockey 101 research at night. Gabe Dawson basically abducted me and took me on the ice for the first time, and I only fell a few times. Well, more than a few times. But it was fun. Made me realize hockey is *much* harder than I thought it would be. I can barely skate a straight line, yet they're running around with a stick, and keeping track of a tiny puck that whizzes by at upwards of eighty miles per hour.

By the end of the third week, I'm exhausted. I have an entire box of notes and files from my sessions so far to look through all weekend before I meet with the remaining players. I'm compiling spreadsheets with all kinds of information to help me put together a social media strategy for the upcoming year. While many of the players have their own social media accounts, I'll be covering all of the team accounts, for now, and correlating some media release information.

I was also told this week I'll be taking on two interns, both in their senior year of college. While it could be nice to have someone else to do the grunt work, I'm not looking forward to training two more people. And after looking both of them up on social media, and finding out they're barely twenty-one, and not even majoring in anything sports related, I can only assume they're in this for the boys, and not for the job, or experience. Another co-worker tells me they're related to the owner's family, which frustrates me even more. Either they'll assume they can get away with murder because of their family, or they may run to the owners and complain about everything. I hope I'm wrong on both accounts.

Heading into the elevator, I slump against the wall as the doors close. One of the files I'm holding slips through my hands, and onto the floor, at the same time a hand slashes through to open the doors again.

"Could have held the doors for me, Pixie," Luca drawls with a wink. I sigh. I'm too tired to put up with his shenanigans. I bend down to retrieve the file and stuff it back into the box.

"No. You could have waited. Let me have a few moments of peace before your Friday night activities undoubtedly keep me awake." I have no idea where this snark is coming from. I've never been a woman who talks back, but it's oddly refreshing and exhilarating. Jefferson would have *never* allowed this.

"Nothing planned tonight, Pix. Unless you want me to keep you awake? I've got things we could do to keep you up all night, *bella*," he says huskily. Dammit. Him calling me *bella*? Shivers. Legit shivers.

"I doubt you could handle me," I say breathily.

"You might be right. But it would be fun to try," he responds.

"Nah. Lord only knows what diseases you have. Bet you've been ridden more than the A line to the airport," I say with a shudder. Luca throws his head back and barks out a laugh.

"Means I know what I'm doing ..." he says, but stops when the elevator jolts severely and the lights go out.

"Fuck!" I scream, dropping the files again, as I'm launched across the elevator. Luca grabs my arm and pulls me toward him as the elevator drops for a moment before stopping.

"What the fuck was that?" I whisper against his chest. I'm trembling. I'm not the best in dark and enclosed areas.

"Not sure, *bella*," Luca whispers back. I'm gripping his shirt on his sides, and I know he can tell I'm incredibly frightened. I'm slightly claustrophobic, especially in the dark. I'd be okay if the lights were on... I think. His left hand begins to slowly stroke my back.

"I can't breathe ..." I whimper.

"I've got you, Hannah. Just breathe in through your nose and out through your mouth, okay? Slowly."

I count to ten, slowly inhaling. This is going to be okay. I'm okay. There is nothing to worry about.

"This is security, is anyone in there?" a voice asks over the intercom.

"Yes, there are two of us in here," Luca answers.

"The fire department is on the way."

The elevator moves slightly and I cry out.

"Oh my God! I can't die like this, I can't! I have too much to do, too many things I haven't experienced. I can't die right now ..." I sob.

"You got a bucket list, Pix?" Luca asks quietly, continuing to stroke my back as I cry into his chest.

"Yes. Doesn't everyone?"

He makes a noncommittal hum before asking, "What's on yours?"

I think for a moment.

"Dancing in the rain. Climbing one of those beautiful mountains. Sky diving. Having the best first kiss, like in a romance book. Sunrise while on a horse. Someone cooking me dinner, and us eating it by candlelight. Eating sushi. Going to Europe. Oh! I want to see the Eiffel Tower so badly! Getting a puppy, buying a house, getting married. Oh, and having an orgasm by someone other than me!" I gasp, shocked that I blurted that out.

"That's a hell of a list, Pixie," Luca comments. "That last one ..."

"You didn't hear that," I mumble.

"Oh, but I did."

"Dammit."

"Yeah. Never had an orgasm by a man?" he asks. I sigh, and nod against his chest. "Jesus, woman. How could a man not focus on you? I'd make you come so many fucking times you wouldn't be able to walk afterward."

I inhale sharply as my pussy clenches in wanton need. Could he? Could he actually make me come? I figured I was broken.

"Yeah, *bella*. I know I could make you come. Bet I could make you come with just my fingers. Then my tongue. Then on my cock. Bet you come spectacularly," he whispers as his head dips down and he kisses the side of my neck reverently. I whimper and clutch his waist. "Bet I could make you come just by talking to you. Kissing your tits. Holding that sweet ass as you rock against me. Fuck, could I make you come."

Luca touches his tongue to my neck and slides it up to my ear, sucking the lobe into his mouth before nibbling on it. I let out a low moan as my hands circle around his waist and grab his lower back. His shirt has skirted up slightly so I'm able to touch his skin. Ripples of tension flow along his spine as my fingers trace and touch.

"You gonna come to my place tonight, *bella*? You gonna let me make you feel good? Say yes, Pix, please say yes," he breathes against my neck as he slowly raises his head and rests his forehead against mine. "I'll make you feel so good. Make you forget the rest of the world. Just you and me."

His lips are feathering across mine with each word, so close to a full kiss but so far away. As I'm about to push up on my tiptoes to close the distance, the elevator door opens with a flourish.

I push Luca away from me and step as far away as I can as light fills the elevator cab.

"You two okay?" the fireman asks.

"Yep!" I chirp, grabbing my bags. and the files, and pushing past him. We're on the fourth floor. Great. Gonna hoof it up the stairs.

"Hey, you're Luke …" I hear as I run through the door to the stairs and start hauling up the flights. I'm out of breath within two floors.

This Georgia girl is not used to mile high altitude. I sound like I'm hyperventilating when I get to the tenth floor.

I hear a door opening somewhere under me, which propels me faster.

"Pixie, wait up!" Luca calls from below. I don't wait. I'm incredibly embarrassed by what just happened in the elevator. Not only did he witness me almost having a panic attack, which would be the second time he's been near me when that happened, but I also almost kissed him. And I'm not sure if that would have been a mistake or not.

I can hear Luca approaching quickly as I reach our floor, but I manage to unlock the apartment door and get inside before he enters from the stairwell. I'm panting as I throw my bags down and grab a bottle of water from the fridge, keeping one ear focused on the doorway.

Within a minute, there's a knock at the door.

"Hannah."

I debate on not answering and acting like I've disappeared.

"I know you're in there, Pix. Open the door."

Fuck. I can hear it in his voice. He just oozes sex appeal. If I open the door, I won't be able to stop myself from getting a taste.

"Hannah, please. Open the door … Hannah. Please."

God dammit! The way he says my name…

I throw open the door.

Luca is braced against the door with both hands gripping the doorframe. His eyes are black as midnight as he stares at me with intensity and lust. Promise of pleasure and bliss dance in his eyes. Our eyes are connected as he lets go of the doorframe and lunges toward me, kicking the door closed as he grabs me around the waist and picks me up. My back is against the wall as his lips crash onto mine in a kiss so passionate, so searing, that I feel all aspects of my surroundings wash away as my focus goes solely to Luca. His tongue slides into my mouth and he groans as one hand slides down to grip my ass.

"Jesus, woman, this ass," he mutters as he peppers kisses down my neck and onto my shoulder. "Been dreaming about this ass." His hand slides further in between my legs and he pushes his palm against my pussy. He bites my shoulder blade as I shamelessly rock against his hand.

"Luca," I moan.

"Fuck, baby. Say my name again," he groans against my neck.

"Luca."

He lifts his head to give me another scorching kiss that takes my breath away. I suck his tongue into my mouth and he moans. I've got both of my hands in his hair, gripping on for dear life as I bring myself closer to orgasm.

"So beautiful, *bella*. So fucking beautiful," he murmurs as he leans away from me slightly, watching me. "Wanna watch you come. Wanna see you break apart for me, Pix."

I can feel the orgasm building. I'm so close. Closest I've ever been with a man. And as I'm right there, just as I'm about to fall off the cliff ... the doorbell rings.

"Hannah? You home? I made some cookies for you!" Good ole cockblocking Edith, my friendly bat-shit crazy neighbor.

I stiffen as my eyes meet Luca's. I'm suddenly overcome with humiliation.

"Put me down," I whisper as my eyes drop from his and I slide my legs down from his waist. He's still holding me up so we are eye level. He's a foot taller than me, and he's not letting me down.

"No."

"Luca, put me down."

"Not until you say we continue this later."

"That's not a good idea and you know it," I whisper. Edith knocks loudly on the door and rings the doorbell again.

"*Bella*, we're continuing this," Luca says.

"No."

"Yes."

"No!"

"Hannah, I can hear you. What's going on? Are you okay?" Edith calls out. Fucking hell.

"I swear to God, baby, don't let that cockblocker in here," Luca hisses as he finally puts me down.

I glare at him as I throw open the door.

"Hi, Edith," I say to her as she looks behind me and gasps.

"I told you to stay away from that heathen!" she yells.

"Hello to you too, Mrs. Willowby."

"Oh don't you sass me, young man," Edith snaps, which makes Luca smile even wider.

"Seriously don't antagonize her," I tell him as he gives me an innocent smile. I bite my lip to keep from giggling, and his eyes lower to stare at my lips. He licks his, and Edith growls. Little ole Edith actually growls.

"Dearie, I told you. I warned you. You're gonna regret getting involved with this bottom-dweller. It won't end well for you," Edith warns as she shoves a plate of cookies into my hands and stomps back to her apartment door. "Damn women and their inability to stay away from bad boys."

As she slams her door after that last remark, I let out a laugh. Luca stalks toward me and begins to kiss me again. I'm about to wrap my arms around his neck and close the door when his cell phone rings. I giggle as the ringtone says, "Warning! Sister alert! Sister alert! Please use extreme caution!"

"It's my sister Arianna," he says as he answers the phone. "Hey sis ..." He trails off as I can hear someone shouting on the other line and speaking incredibly quickly. "Woah, slow down! What happened?"

I turn to place the plate of cookies on the kitchen counter to give Luca a bit of privacy. I'm not sure how to respond in this situation. I'm not close with either of my siblings. Luca seems connected to his sister, which is incredibly foreign to me.

"Okay, I'll be there in twenty minutes," he says as he ends the call. Luca turns to me. "I have to go. My sister was in a car accident. I have to get to the hospital."

"Oh, Luca, I'm so sorry. Was that her? Is she going to be okay?" I ask.

"Yeah, that was her. She's the youngest and she's pretty dramatic, so I really don't know if it's as bad as she's making it out to be. But she's shaken up, so I gotta go," he tells me as he walks toward the door.

"Okay. I hope she's okay," I tell him, and he stops walking. Turning quickly, he grabs me and picks me up again, kissing me breathless.

"This isn't over, Pixie," he mumbles against my lips. I sigh.

"Okay."

I feel him smile against my mouth.

"At least that's one thing off your bucket list, yeah?"

"Huh?" I ask, confused.

"The perfect first kiss."

My eyes widen as I remember what I told him in the elevator. Holy shit. Him kissing me against the wall *was* the perfect first kiss. Wow.

"I'll work on the rest of that list soon," he says huskily, as he puts my feet back on the ground and walks confidently out into the hallway. "Lock up, baby."

I stand still, in shock. The elevator dings and I'm still standing in the doorway.

"Pix."

I look up at Luca, who is grinning knowingly at me.

"Huh?"

"Lock up."

"Oh, uh-huh. Yeah."

I close the door as I hear him chuckle.

I'm reeling. Not only was that the best first kiss, it was the best kiss I've ever had. Hands down. Knew I shouldn't have opened the door.

Chapter 6

*L*uca

⸙⸙⸙⸙⸙⸙

*N*ever been more pissed at my little sister than I am right now. First Edith was cockblocking me, and then Arianna joined in. Fucking hell. That kiss ... I'll be adding that to the spank bank. Never had a kiss like that. And I've done quite a bit of kissing. Probably too much, amongst other things.

Arianna is the baby of the family, but she's also my best friend. She's only a handful of years younger than me, so we really grew up together. You'd have thought she and Isabella would be really close, but they aren't. Belle really marches to the beat of her own drum. And while Arianna does as well, we just vibed more than either of us did with Belle. We ran in the same circles growing up. Same friends, same experiences. We're similar in a lot of ways, except for dramatics. Arianna is full-blown melodramatic about everything. Well, I guess we are sort of the same there. I just beat the shit out of people on the ice when I decide to get dramatic.

I pull on a hoodie and hat as I stop my car at the valet at the hospital. Arianna was in an accident heading home from Eternity Springs, and she's been taken to a hospital in the western Denver suburbs near her apartment. Now is not the time to get recognized, and I'm suddenly thankful that I drive a relatively normal SUV instead of some of the outlandish cars some of the other players drive. Granted, it's an Infiniti QX80 with all the bells and whistles, so it's definitely not your average suburban mom vehicle.

As I slide out of the driver's seat and hand the key fob to the valet attendant, he whistles low as he looks at the interior. I had it custom detailed to match the exterior, and it's fucking beautiful. I give him a quick nod with my head down as I trudge inside. The security guard notices me, and I quietly ask him if he can help me. The ER is quite busy, and I know if I'm just standing in line waiting to speak to the people at the desk, I'm going to get recognized. I hate pulling the celebrity card, but sometimes I have to.

The security guard whisks me through the doors and leads me to Arianna's triage room. I silently walk in and see my sister with her arm dramatically thrown over her eyes and chuckle.

"You dying, sis?" I ask.

"Yes, you asshole. I'm dying," she mutters while flipping me the bird.

"Well, you look...alive, I guess. What happened?"

Arianna snorts and then winces as she attempts to push herself up into a sitting position.

"Some jerk swerved into my lane on the interstate, and I swerved to try and miss him. I smashed into the concrete divider. My car is trashed," she says miserably.

"Damn, Ari, that sucks. Did he hit you on the passenger side or the driver's side?" I ask.

"Passenger, thankfully. He was hauling ass, though. No clue what he thought he was doing. The doctor thinks I have bruised ribs from the seatbelt, a concussion, and possibly a broken wrist. I'm waiting to get x-rays."

Well, shit. Now I feel bad for assuming she was exaggerating. I grab the only chair in the triage room and pull it next to the bed.

"Take my mind off of this, please, Luca. Did I interrupt anything fun tonight?" she asks. I smile sheepishly and she laughs. "I knew it! What did you do?"

"Well, I would have done *more* if you hadn't managed to cock-block me, sis," I tell her.

"Okay don't give me that many details. Who was it? Another puck bunny, or someone actually worthwhile? Would be nice for you to actually date someone for a change," Arianna says.

"Nah. Our history is already too complicated. Doubt she'd be into me that way. I'm too fucked up for anyone to want to be with..." I stop when my sister throws her arm up and slaps her hand across my mouth.

"You are not fucked up! Why would you even say that, Luca? That's such bullshit," she says. I stick my tongue out and she shrieks, yanking her hand away and immediately wiping it off on the hospital sheets.

"You worried about cooties, sis?" I tease.

"With how much you get around, yes. I am worried about a few specific forms of cooties," she mutters.

"See, that's what I'm talking about. Everyone knows I get around. Lucky Luca, the one who gets all the play. No self-respecting woman would choose to be with me," I say with a sigh. Arianna cocks her head to the side and studies me.

"I'm teasing you, Luca. I know you don't get around *quite* as much as the media portrays. But it sounds like even you're getting sick of that narrative, and sick of all the games. Am I right? Because maybe, you finally want someone to choose you," she says. I take a moment before I nod. I think I do. I'm sick of being alone. I want a partner. Someone to come home to, someone who supports me at the end of every day. Someone that I get to support.

"Yeah, Ari. I do want that. But everyone knows my history, and they assume the worst. Even the girl tonight ... she caught me with multiple girls the first night we met. She lives next door to me. She's beautiful, and so fucking out of my league," I tell her.

"So what happened tonight that made you think differently? If you say I cockblocked you, something definitely happened," she says pointedly.

"We got stuck in the elevator together. There was ... chemistry. And the best fucking kiss of my life. And then you called."

"Oh. Shit. Sorry, bro."

I chuckle.

"Not your fault. She would have come to her senses at some point."

As Arianna is about to say something, a nurse comes in, ready to take her for her x-rays. I stay in the triage room, contemplating the events of the night. Pondering how maybe, in an alternate universe, Hannah and I could be together. I lean my head back and close my eyes, reminiscing about that kiss. How Hannah felt in my arms. Jesus, she felt so good. So right. That's never happened to me before. It would be so complicated, starting something with her. She's my *neighbor*. If she's related to Caroline, that could spell long-term issues. And does she even think about me, like I think about her?

I doze off in the chair as I relive the kiss, and I swear I smell Hannah in my dreams.

I end up staying with Arianna over the weekend to help her get settled at her apartment. She did end up breaking her wrist. Isabella's voice loops in my head about helping out more with the family, and clearly my baby sister needs my help right now. She's easier than my parents, though. Weeks ago, when I helped out for a few days, they had me running around doing all kinds of odd jobs. Waiting on Arianna is easier than maintenance at the hotel, that's for sure.

Arianna is nothing if not resourceful ... meaning she orders me around to do everything for her. I spoon fed her two meals before I realized she broke her non-dominant wrist, and she didn't even have the decency to appear guilty. I was thrilled when I managed to escape late Sunday night and head back to my apartment.

One thing Ari did help me with was a realtor. I've put in an offer on an amazing mountain home about twenty minutes west of Eternity Springs. Five bedrooms, six bathrooms, a fully finished basement with a theater room, and every aspect of a state-of-the-art home I could want. Not only did it hit every major expectation I wanted for a home, but the design screams *me*. Exposed beams, a two-story great room featuring both floor-to-ceiling windows and a massive fireplace, and the biggest shower I've ever seen. When I closed my eyes briefly in the kitchen, a picture of Hannah flew through my mind. Would she like this house? What does she want in her future? Hell, does she even want to stay in Colorado? Obviously, Hannah was never far from my thoughts.

The entire weekend I was acutely aware of not having any way of contacting Hannah. Mentally bitched myself out multiple times for not getting her number before I left Friday night. I thought about her nonstop.

It's almost midnight when I get home, and when I arrive at my floor, I contemplate knocking on her door. I stand outside the elevator and wait, when suddenly her door flies open. Hannah stands there in just a camisole and booty shorts, just like the first night I met her, and her eyes are wild.

"Hi," she says breathlessly.

"Hi," I respond as I stalk toward her and pick her up, our lips locked together immediately. She wraps her legs around my waist as I walk into her apartment and slam the door. The kiss turns wild and carnal quickly as my tongue caresses hers. Hannah drags her nails up my scalp and I groan into her mouth. "Where's your bedroom, *bella*?"

She points down a hallway and I quickly throw my keys and phone onto her counter before walking us to her bedroom. I'm not taking any chances of getting interrupted again. I need time with this woman.

"Luca," she whispers as I kiss her neck and lay her down across the bed. Her legs grip me tightly, and I trail my lips back up to take hers in a searing kiss. Fuck. I could kiss her endlessly. Her lips are pillow soft, and taste of strawberries and cream.

"Tell me what you want, baby," I say quietly as I raise my head so I can look into her eyes. "Tell me what you need."

She looks at me and I can see a raging war between lust and apprehension.

"I...I'm not the one night stand kind of girl," she says softly. I stroke her cheek and cup her face tenderly.

"I don't want you to be just one night, *bella*."

"Really?" she asks, her eyes wide with shock.

Even I'm a little surprised at how quickly I answer her. "Really. I'm cool with this going at your pace."

She leans up and places a soft kiss on my lips. "Can we just see where this goes? I'm not sure I'm ready for all..." she gestures down toward my cock, "...for all of that, Luca. I think I might need a little time to get ready for you. For that. For us."

I chuckle.

"Perfectly fine, baby. It's been a really long weekend. How about we just sleep for now?" I ask, and her eyes widen.

"Oh my God! I totally forgot. How's your sister?" she asks. My grin widens.

"She'll be fine. Broke her wrist, has a concussion, and some bruised ribs. So she wasn't being as overdramatic as I thought she was," I tell Hannah. "I stayed with her all weekend to help her get around. My mom and my other sister are going to help her this week while I'm working."

"I'm glad she's okay," Hannah says as I shift us up to the top of her bed. "How many siblings do you have?"

"Six."

Her eyes widen comically.

"Six?" she yells. "Holy shit! That must have been chaos growing up."

"Yeah, it was. But it was fun, too. I'm the third youngest, but we're all stacked into a little over ten years. I don't remember a lot of my oldest brother though. But we're pretty close now," I tell her. "Is it okay if I take off my jeans? I mean, if you're not comfortable with that, I can sleep with them on, but..."

"No, it's fine," she says, interrupting me. "I've seen you in less, if I remember correctly."

I give her a smile and a wink as I take off my shirt and jeans. I don't miss her eyes tracking down my body. Slipping under the comforter, I pull her to me. Little spoon to big spoon. I sigh in contented peace.

"Is it weird to say I missed you this weekend?" I say softly against her ear. Her breath hitches before she answers.

"I missed you too, Luca."

I fall asleep with my arms wrapped around Hannah, and it's the best sleep I've gotten in months.

Chapter 7

Hannah

As a small amount of light begins to filter under the curtains in the bedroom windows, I'm aware of being incredibly hot. Stiflingly hot. Unbearably hot.

It takes me a few moments to remember *why* I feel this hot. Luca is sprawled over me, sound asleep, with one hand wrapped up in my hair and the other hand cupping my breast. His impressive morning wood is jammed up between my ass cheeks and one leg is thrown over mine.

As he takes a long breath and sighs, his breath hits the back of my neck and I involuntarily shiver. Wetness pools between my legs as I reflexively shimmy my ass against him. He moans and pulls me closer to him, grinding his cock against me.

I whimper as his fingers pinch my nipple and his lips meet the back of my neck. His hand tightens in my hair as he pulls my head back. His lips dance across my shoulder and collarbone as he plucks my nipple into a diamond peak.

"Pixie," he growls against my neck. The hand that was rolling my nipple between his fingers slides down my abdomen and into my underwear, finding my clit. "Fuck, *bella*. You're soaked."

I moan incoherently as his thumb strokes circles around my clit.

My hand slides between our bodies to grip his shaft tightly, and it's his turn to moan.

"Damn, woman. This is the best fucking way to wake up," he says as he pushes two fingers inside of me. I'm so incredibly turned on, actively writhing against his hand as I slide my hand beneath his boxers to feel his cock. Tightly squeezing and stroking, Luca grunts against my neck. I can feel my orgasm building as he finds that elusive G-spot and pushes against it. "Come for me, baby. Come for your man, Hannah."

Oh shit. Calling himself my man? That does it. My orgasm overwhelms me as waves of pleasure crest from my tiptoes throughout every nerve ending of my body. I shudder blissfully as I feel Luca swell in my hand and roar out his own release.

Oh. My. God.

I just had my first orgasm by a man. I'm not broken. *I'm not broken!*

"No, baby, you're not broken. Just with the wrong men," Luca chuckles. Didn't realize I said that last part out loud.

My alarm on my phone blares, jolting me. I'm suddenly incredibly self-conscious and embarrassed about what just happened. I struggle to remove myself from Luca's embrace and won't look him in the eye. I grab my phone, silencing it, but stay sitting on the edge of the bed.

"Hannah."

"Hmm?" I respond, as I stand up and make a big display of organizing my jewelry tray next to the bed.

"Look at me, baby."

I sigh as I turn toward the bed and slowly bring my eyes to his. His expression is tender and soft.

"Don't regret this, Hannah. Don't get in your head," Luca says as he throws his legs over the side of the bed and pulls me to stand between his legs. Even with him sitting, our height difference makes us almost eye level.

"Okay," I whisper as he leans his forehead against mine.

"Another one done," he says, and I furrow my brow in confusion. "Your bucket list. I'm just slowly checking them off, one by one." He gives me a saucy grin before kissing me quickly. "I gotta get home so I can go to work. Can you give me your number? I'd like to be able to actually get in touch with you without midnight booty call type situations."

"Is that what that was?" I say, horrified. He barks out a laugh.

"No, Hannah. I swear, it wasn't. Give me your number so I don't have to knock on your door at all. I can text you first," he says cheekily as he puts on his jeans.

I walk into the kitchen to start some coffee. I have a long day ahead, meeting with four players and strategizing with the marketing team on player profiles.

Luca trails behind me, slipping on his shoes and grabbing his phone.

"What's your number, baby?" he asks, and I rattle off the numbers. I hear my phone go off in the bedroom. "Now you have mine, too."

"Okay," I say quietly.

Luca smiles at me and leans in, giving me a soft kiss as he strokes my cheek.

"Dinner tonight?" he asks softly. I nod as he kisses me again. "I'll text you later. Bye, baby."

As I lock the door behind him, I let out a deep exhale.

I sure hope the rest of the day pans out as well as my morning.

*M*y two morning meetings ran long and I was forced to eat lunch at my desk while catching up on emails. My two afternoon sessions are with the Russian goalie, Alexei Pavlov, and with the guy my uncle warned me about Luke Santo. To finish up the day, I'm meeting with my two interns. Kill me now.

Alexei is stoic and mostly answers me with one word responses.

It's like pulling teeth. He's going to be a hard nut to crack, and I fear doing any kind of player profile on him where I have to make him appear personable. Other players and some staff have warned me that he's very closed-off and private. I hate that people try to warn me about the players. This is why I didn't do any research. I wanted to meet them without any preconceived notions. But since I was warned Alexei is closed-off, it makes me frustrated more quickly, and then I get very awkward with my conversation. Any attempt at a joke was either completely ignored, or went over his head. Possibly a language barrier? I don't know. But the meeting was incredibly uncomfortable and felt like it dragged on for hours.

As I'm finishing up my notes, my uncle pops his head into my office.

"Hey, Han. How's it going?" he asks.

"Good. Just have one last player interview and then I've officially met the whole team," I tell him.

"Who is left?"

"Luke Santo."

"Oh."

"Don't sound so thrilled," I tease him.

"I just don't like the guy. He's a douche," Uncle Bennett mutters.

"I'll keep that in mind."

"Just watch yourself around him. He's a player and he'd have no qualms about taking you down, consequences be damned."

"Jesus, Uncle Bennett! How about a little respect for *me* here? I can handle myself," I tell him. He gives me a crooked smile.

"I know you can, pot pie," he teases me. I roll my eyes.

"You are seriously only like nine years older than me, Uncle Bennett. Don't treat me like a child," I tell him. His smile fades.

"I know that, Hannah. I just want you to be careful. You could have a real career here. I know you were really unhappy in Georgia, and getting away from your parents was a goal for you. I don't want you to fuck it up," he says.

My mother and my uncle never got along. My mother was fifteen when my Aunt Caroline was born, and then a few years later Uncle Bennett came along. My mother had already met my dad when Bennett was only a toddler. My grandparents moved from Atlanta to Denver, but my mom stayed in Georgia for my dad. Well, for his family. For his wealth, his connections, his status. I was born a few years later and became a pawn in my mother's goal to become a southern socialite.

"Don't worry about me, Uncle Bennett. I can handle myself. Let me do my job, okay?" I tell him somewhat stiffly, but give him a small smile to let him know I'm not upset. He nods in understanding.

"Okay. Let's have dinner this weekend to catch up before the season really gets going."

"Sounds good."

As my uncle leaves, I stand to stretch and face the windows of my office. Taking in the beautiful mountain view, I stretch my arms up high and bend my back as someone knocks on my door.

"Hi, I'm Luke Santo, I'm here for the meeting..."

I stiffen and forget how to breathe. I know that voice. Intimately. I had it in my ear only hours ago as I orgasmed by a man for the first time. My hand goes to my mouth as I swiftly turn around and take in Luca's stunned expression.

"Hannah?" he asks incredulously. I don't answer. I can't answer.

"Your name is Luke?" I finally ask, but he shakes his head.

"I go by Luke in hockey. I go by Luca in my personal life..." he trails off. "What the fuck, Hannah? Did you know it was me?" His eyes become angry and accusatory.

"No. No! I swear I didn't know! I didn't research anyone, I wanted to meet everyone first without any preconceived opinions." I can hear the emotion battling in my voice. My heart feels broken. I barely know Luca, but the connection felt real.

We stare at each other, neither one knowing how to move forward. His eyes search mine, looking for answers I can't give. Answers I don't know how to give. Answers I wish were different.

I feel my eyes fill with tears as I realize at the same time as Luca that any relationship we may have had is done. His head shakes emphatically as he walks toward me.

"No, *bella*, no. We can figure this out," he says, but he stops before he gets to me. Luca reaches around to grab the back of his neck in frustration. "I don't know how, but we have to figure this out. Fuck. We have to."

A tear slides down my cheek and I wipe it away furiously. I'm so pissed at the universe right now. This isn't fair.

"It's not fair," I whisper to myself. Luca looks up at me with pain in his eyes.

"Yeah. It's not fair."

We stand quietly for a few moments, both of us clearly in our own heads. I close my eyes as I remember last night and this morning. How perfect it felt. How for the first time in my life, I felt like I was with the right person. I mentally shake my head at that thought. How could I think that? I barely know the guy. I didn't even know his last name.

The quiet allows me to control my emotions as I focus on my breathing. In and out. This will be okay. I can handle this. In and out.

A knock on the door startles me back to the present.

"Hannah, I just wanted to touch base with you about the schedule...oh, hey, Santo. This your first meeting with Hannah?" Coach Woodward says as he struts into my office authoritatively. At this moment, I despise the head coach. Frankly, I haven't gotten a good feed on him from the moment I met him. He seems really sketchy and snakelike. And right now, I loathe him for interrupting whatever this is with Luca.

"Uh, yeah, coach. First time meeting Hannah," Luca says, his eyes meeting mine with uncertainty.

"I hope Santo hasn't been giving you any trouble, Hannah. I can tell your uncle if he is."

"Uncle?" Luca says quietly.

Woodward sneers at Luca. "Coach Davenport is Hannah's uncle. Surely you knew that?"

Luca's eyes meet mine briefly, and I see the pain I feel. Just another complication. My heart drops as he takes a step back toward the door. "Uh, no. I didn't. It was nice meeting you, Hannah. Let me know when you need me to do anything for the social stuff."

I nod, unable to find the ability to talk. I watch Luca's retreating back as he walks to the door, glancing my way one last time before exiting my office.

"Hope he didn't give you any trouble," the coach says as he walks behind my desk to stand beside me. "Santo is a loose cannon. I don't think he'll be with us after this year."

My back stiffens as I feel the innate need to jam my stiletto heel into his condescending forehead, and I count backward slowly from five to calm myself before I respond.

"Oh, I didn't get that impression at all. He was composed and very respectful. I think he'll be great for social media campaigns," I tell him pointedly. He looks taken aback by my vehemence, and even I'm a little surprised at how I defended Luca. Obviously, I don't know him well at all. Maybe I should have done research on the players before meeting them. Then I'd have known to steer clear of Luke/Luca.

Even I know that's a lie. I was screwed the moment I set eyes on him.

"You're new here, so I'll give you the benefit of the doubt. But trust me. That boy is going nowhere. Don't let him drag you down with him," the coach says as he sets a hand on my bare shoulder, his thumb briefly stroking the skin. I recoil, suddenly upset with myself for wearing a sleeveless dress to work today. And now I know my initial gut feeling on Coach Woodward was correct. He's a skeevy snake, and I need to steer clear of him at all costs.

After the coach leaves, I sit at my desk. Suddenly incredibly exhausted and emotional. I wish I had friends to talk to right now. Making friends has never been easy for me, and it's not like I can talk to Uncle Bennett about this. I'm tempted to call my aunt, but I don't even know what country she's in, let alone the time zone. Aunt Caroline and I have never been close, and I don't know how she'd handle me talking about her next door neighbor, his skeevy boss, and how out-of-sorts I'm feeling.

My phone buzzes with a text, and I know immediately who it's from. I hadn't even programmed his name in yet.

Unknown: I wish things were different.

Tears fill my eyes as I respond.

Me: Me too.

The bubbles appear and disappear countless times before disappearing altogether. I don't know what Luca intended to say, and yet I completely understand at the same time. There's nothing either of us can say to make this any better. We're screwed.

⚘⚘⚘⚘⚘

By the time I manage to leave the arena at well past dinnertime, I'm beyond exhausted. I'm so physically and mentally drained. The meeting with my interns was as bad as I thought it would be. Lindsay and Jessica looked down their noses at me, blatantly asked what the rules were for dating players, and asked for a tour of the locker room. When I explained that their job duties would be more administrative, and on the backside of social media, they asked if they would still get college credit if they didn't show up much.

Old Hannah would have been nice. Tried to appease the mean girls. Kept them happy to ensure I didn't ruffle any feathers this early on at my new job. But this Hannah, the one who wanted Luca way too badly, is just pissed off now.

"No, I'll make sure you don't get any credit at all, ladies," I snap.

"Woah, you don't have to be a bitch about it," Lindsay says standoffishly.

"Yeah," Jessica adds. "Uber bitchy."

"And?" I ask. They both stare at me in confusion. "You're going to have to do better than that, girls. I don't care if you think I'm a bitch. I'm your *boss*. This is a job. And if you don't do the job you're assigned, I'll make sure you don't get college credit. End of story. You're expected to be here for twenty hours a week. I will send you your schedules a week in advance. No, your schedules are not open for debate. You work around *my* schedule, and the *team's* schedule, so don't even suggest that I change something. Understood?"

"It's giving uber bitch vibes," Jessica mutters.

"That's boss bitch to you, sweetie. You're dismissed," I sneer. I watch as both girls stand and stalk out of my office before Lindsay slams the door. If I hadn't seen her age on her application, I'd have thought she was a teenager with that little tantrum.

I might be a bitch, or a frigid bitch as many have pointed out, but I'm the boss. And I control their schedules. Looks like Jessica and Lindsay are going to be on admin duty for the foreseeable future, and definitely at opposite times of the team.

They're just the type of women I'd expect to see with Luca. And now that I know he works here, I'll do my best to keep them away from him. I may not be able to have Luca, but I'll be damned if either of them get a piece of him.

Chapter 8

*L*uca

⁘⁘⁘⁘⁘⁘⁘⁘⁘⁘

*T*here have been times in my life where I've felt like the universe has it out for me. But none more than right now. Right fucking now, I'm furious.

She works for the team. The team that I play for. She's gonna travel with us. I'll see her everywhere. And I can't be with her. Can't talk to her. Touch her. *Feel* her. She can't be mine. I know this, but my heart is screaming at me to figure out a fucking way.

Our team doesn't have a no-fraternization policy, but it's definitely inferred. No relationships with players and team employees. That's not to say some players haven't had quick fucks here or there along the way, but there haven't been any relationships. And I don't want Hannah for a quick fuck. I want her to be mine in every way.

I was supposed to have a session with a trainer, but I just leave. I can't be here right now. I'm so fucking pissed. I left her apartment this morning riding a high. Already hit the market for ingredients to make her dinner. A candlelight dinner, to cross another item off her bucket list. Got her flowers, too. First fucking time in my life I've bought a woman flowers, other than my mom or sisters.

When I get into my car, I grip the steering wheel so tightly my knuckles turn white.

"Fuck!" I roar as I hit the wheel hard.

I wrack my brain, trying to come up with any way I can make this work. Keep my job, keep the owners happy, and keep Hannah. Keep my Pixie. I don't fucking know how to do this without screwing something up.

I pick up my phone, ready to call my sister and ask for advice. Arianna probably won't have anything good to offer, but she's a great sounding board for me. Somehow I end up clicking on Hannah's name and firing off a text with the first thing that comes to mind.

> Me: I wish things were different.

> Hannah: Me too.

I start and erase a response to her a dozen times before throwing my phone into the passenger seat in disgust. There's nothing I can say to make any of this better. We're screwed.

Maybe I could have figured out a way around this. But her uncle already doesn't like me. If they'd had the same last name I might have realized it quicker. Hell, who am I kidding? My dick took over almost every damn time I was in the same vicinity as Hannah.

As I drive out of the player parking lot at The Sports Facility Zone, I find myself on I-70 heading west of town. I don't know where I'm going, just that I can't go back to my apartment. Knowing she'll be right there … I just can't. I drive in a daze, my car seemingly taking me somewhere it knows I need to go. I end up at a hole-in-the-wall bar outside Golden. A friend owns the place. We haven't fully discussed what the bar is a front for, but it has to be something. Sebastian Garcia exudes confidence, danger, and lives on the edge of his seat at all times. While I wouldn't necessarily be surprised if he was into some less than legal business ventures, everything I've ever known about Sebastian has been on the straight-and-narrow.

As I swing into the parking lot, I see his motorcycle. He's in a MC, and he's invited me to a couple of their parties. They are wild. Definitely not my kind of scene.

Heading in to the bar, I see the bartender nodding at me. Todd has been bartending here as long as I've known Sebastian.

"He's in the back," he says to me as he continues to dry off beer mugs, jutting his head in the direction of the back offices.

"Thanks," I say as I walk toward the back. I hear Sebastian speaking quickly in Spanish as I approach. I'm not even remotely bilingual, so I have no idea what he's talking about. I do catch the word '*perra*,' which means 'bitch,' so I assume he's yelling about a woman. He ends the call and throws his phone onto his desk in disgust.

"Fucking women!" he snarls out as runs his hands through his hair in frustration. Finally noticing me, he gives me a half smile. "Haven't seen you in a while, Luca. What's going on?"

Clearly I only come up here when I'm either in trouble, or avoiding something. I walk into his office and settle into a chair opposite his desk.

"Fucking women," I respond wryly. He chuckles. "What's your woman problem, Sebastian?"

He shrugs.

"Got a girl claiming to be pregnant by one of my members. Now she's refusing to go get an ultrasound, or get tested to confirm the paternity. She's also refusing to leave the clubhouse, locking herself in one of the rooms. It's a mess," he confesses.

"Damn. Might be worse than my woman drama," I comment. Sebastian looks up at me.

"You have woman drama? You, the king of the puck bunny kingdom?" he muses. I give him a half smile.

"Am I really considered to be the king of the puck bunny kingdom?"

Sebastian shrugs. "I don't know. The media certainly thinks so."

"It's all bullshit though. You know that, right? Like this fucking reporter shows up at my apartment and corners me outside. Claims she's a fan, then suggests we go up to my apartment. I refuse, and tell my doorman to make sure she stays outside. The next day, there's an article from her claiming she slept with me, and pictures that are staged so perfectly it looks like we're having this intimate conversation. The bitch completely set me up."

"Jesus Christ," Sebastian swears. "What are you gonna do?"

"I put my agent on it. He'll send a cease and desist to the news station and tell them to issue a retraction. But the damage is done. The article was front page. The retraction won't get the same treatment."

"It sounds like you're over the lifestyle."

"Yeah. And this girl ..."

"Oh, do tell. This I gotta hear."

I hesitate, trying to formulate how I need to explain what the fuck just happened.

"New neighbor moved in, we've had some moments, and when we decided to give it a go with things, we find out she works for the Wolves. Oh, and she's the niece of one of my coaches," I tell him.

"Holy fuck."

"Yeah. That's accurate."

"What are you gonna do?" he asks.

"Nothing."

"What?!?"

"Nothing I can do. We both need to keep our jobs. I already think the head coach is out to get me. He's made some comments to my face ... I don't think I can rock the boat at all. He's gunning for any reason to aggravate me. I think he's hoping for bad publicity so he can trade me," I tell Sebastian quietly. He leans back in his chair and studies me.

"Doesn't sound like the Luca I know. Since when have you backed down from a challenge?" he asks.

"Not the same as something dumb like chugging a bottle of tequila, or asking three women out at the same time, man," I say roughly, rolling my eyes. He laughs.

"No, but you've also never let anyone tell you what to do, or how to act other than your mom. You want this girl?" he asks, and I nod. "Then figure out a way to get her."

"I don't know, man," I sigh. "Could be more trouble than it's worth."

"Speaking of trouble," Sebastian says as he clears his throat, "how's your sister doing?"

I raise an eyebrow, studying him. "Which sister?"

"Isabella."

"How do you know my sister, Seb?"

He clears his throat again, scratching at his arm. "Run into her a few times here and there. I've used her bakery for a couple of events here, as well as club events."

"I didn't know that."

"Well, now you do."

"Are you interested in my sister, Seb?" I ask. He looks at me nervously, and I have to admit that it's difficult to keep a straight face. This larger-than-life MC president is nervous to talk to me about my sister. Some guys might stand taller and act all big, but I'm not like that. Sebastian might be able to take me down if he wanted to, but Isabella is no slouch. She'd eat him alive.

"Nah. I mean, I don't think your sister has any interest in me. She's bitten my head off more than once," he admits.

"Really? For what?"

A slight pink dampens Sebastian's neck as he chuckles. "I may have insinuated she couldn't carry a couple dozen cupcakes into the bar."

"And why did you do that?"

"I was trying to be fucking gallant, Luca. I wanted to impress her, obviously. And she just lit into me," Sebastian shouts. I throw my head back in laughter.

"If you want to get with my sister, Seb, you have to figure out the way to her heart."

"What is it?"

"I'm not fucking telling you that. You gotta figure it out," I tease. While I'm not completely sure what Belle would want or expect from a man, I do know she doesn't want a man to come in and take care of her. She's a proud and confident woman. If Seb is the man for her, he'll figure it out.

Dominic and Leo are going to destroy him once they get wind of his interest, though. No man will ever be good enough for Belle in their eyes. My oldest brother, Alex, won't care. He's as nonchalant about our sisters having relationships as I am.

"Listen, Luca, if I *were* to pursue your sister, are you really okay with that? I don't want to rock the boat here." I resist the urge to smile, but damn I can't wait to watch this all go down.

"It's cool, man. Go for it. She's gonna put you through the wringer. You know that, right?"

Sebastian chuckles. "I wouldn't expect any less."

Studying him, I'm overcome with jealousy. There's nothing holding him back from going to Isabella right now and telling her he's interested. No workplace drama. No aggravating boss, or nosey neighbors. He could take Belle out tonight, in public, and enjoy being with her. For the first time in my life, I'm fucking jealous of a man who wants a relationship.

I know I need to forget about Hannah. There are too many complications there. I have to forget about her.

Easier said than done.

As I'm leaving Sebastian's bar, Arianna calls me.

"You get things worked out with your girl?" she asks cheerfully when I answer the phone.

"Sure. Turns out she works for the team, and she's the niece of one of the coaches, which also makes her my next door neighbor's niece as well, so yeah. Totally worked out," I respond sarcastically.

"No way!" Ari shouts. "You're joking."

"Wish I was."

Arianna remains quiet, a feat in itself, as I explain everything that occurred since I left her apartment.

Chapter 9

*H*annah

✦═══✦═══✦═══✦

I make it back to the apartment building in a daze. I'm not too proud to admit that I sneak into the apartment building and trudge up the fifteen flights of stairs, all because I'm petrified of running into Luca.

I pause as I reach our floor and struggle to contain my panting breaths as I strain to hear if anyone is in the hallway by our doors. I cautiously open the door and step out, only to stop dead in my tracks when I see a woman standing between our doors.

I'm hit with a wave of jealousy immediately, until she turns to face me. Her eyes match Luca's, and she has the same nose. Her right wrist is wrapped in a cast.

"You must be Arianna," I blurt out, and her eyes widen.

"You're the neighbor," she responds.

"Hannah."

"Hi, Hannah. Luca didn't tell me your name. Just told me I accidentally cockblocked him," she says with a smile. I laugh quietly. "Do you know where he is?"

"Umm, no, I'm sorry. I don't," I tell her, looking down at my feet. She cocks her head to one side as she studies me.

"Something happened. What did he do?" she asks.

"Nothing intentionally," I tell her. "It's just not going to work out."

I walk to my aunt's door and unlock it.

"Hold up. I need more information. He was completely smitten with you!" she says. "I've never seen him so taken with someone. He talked about you all weekend."

I sigh as I open the door.

"I work for the Wolves. I'll be traveling with the team. We can't ... we can't be together."

"Oh, yeah. He may have mentioned that. Are you as bummed as he is?"

"Yep."

I step into my aunt's apartment and am turning to say goodbye when she hustles in right behind me. Huh. Okay, come in, I guess.

"Wait. There's not an actual rule, though, right? I mean, it's the twenty-first century. There's no way it's an actual rule you can't date a player," she says as she throws her purse down on the counter and meanders over to the couch to sit down. I stare at her incredulously, and she gives me a wide smile. "We're friends now, Hannah. This is how I make friends."

I laugh nervously. I don't have many friends, and I'm unsure if this is normal.

"Do you have any wine? This feels like a wine conversation."

"Uhh, actually, I do. My aunt sent me a bottle of wine from Italy," I tell Arianna as I walk to my fridge and pull it out.

"She sent you wine from Italy?" Arianna screeches.

"No," I giggle, "she sent me wine from the liquor store down the street. But she said it was made in Italy, and the grapes came from a vineyard she toured."

"Sweet. Let's pop that sucker open and tell each other all our deepest and darkest secrets!" Arianna says with glee. She grabs the bottle from my hand and stares at the label. "This is a vineyard in California, not Italy. She must have just ordered the wrong one. But wine is wine, and I never let alcohol go to waste."

I learn about Arianna's job at a hotel, and her opinions on the lack of dateable men in her town. She tells me how her parents are still so in love forty years after they got married, and how she won't settle for anything less than what she has witnessed her entire life. She does say her dad can be crabby, as well as one of her older brothers.

I'm not sure when we began singing to an eighties playlist on her phone, but it happened. I also don't remember switching from wine to liquor. All I know is Arianna Santo made me feel completely comfortable, and it was such a relief to feel like I finally had my first friend in Colorado. Well, besides Luca, if I could call him a friend.

It probably helped that Arianna continued to hand me shots. Since I was never allowed to have more than one glass of wine under the watchful eyes of my parents, or Jefferson, I had no idea drinking could be so fun. I've never giggled this much in my life.

And that is how I got completely drunk with Luca's little sister.

$\mathcal{R}$ing.
            Ring.
Ring, ring.
Jesus, what is that?
Ring. Riiiiiiiing.

"Dammit, shut that up!" Arianna mutters, her face plastered into the back of the couch cushions.

"What is it? I don't know what it is!" I moan. It's pitch black in the apartment. I don't know what time it is.

Ring.

Thump, thump, thump.

"PIXIE!"

I jump up, then immediately grab my head as the room spins. Arianna and I polished off the bottle of wine and then tackled an entire bottle of rum. I don't think I've ever had this much alcohol.

"Is that my brother? He calls you Pixie. Oh my God, that's so fucking adorable. You are like a little pixie," Arianna muses as she rolls over and stretches.

I start to laugh, finding the entire situation suddenly hysterical. I continue giggling as I weave my way over to the door, throwing it open to find a very angry Luca standing on the other side.

"What the fuck, Hannah? I've been calling, texting, and knocking for the last twenty minutes!"

"Jesus, calm your tits, Luca," Arianna calls from the couch. Luca's eyes widen and I giggle.

"Is that my sister? What the fuck?" he says as he pushes past me and strides into the apartment.

"Helllooooooooo big brother!" Arianna yells and waves maniacally at him. He looks at her, a bemused smile stretching across his face.

"Are you ladies drunk?" he asks.

"Little bit," Arianna answers. He turns to me with his eyebrow cocked.

"She made me be her friend," I blurt out, then laugh at the absurdity of it all.

"That's right! I made her be my friend. We're best friends now," Arianna screams. I clutch my head and moan.

"Not so loud, woman," I mutter. "What time is it?"

"Around ten," Luca answers.

"In the morning???" I whisper, horrified. He chuckles.

"No, *bella*. At night," he responds.

"God you guys are disgusting. Pixie ... *bella* ... bet he calls you baby, too. I need a fucking man," Arianna mutters. Visions of the evening come back to me.

"Did we ... did we put on Journey and karaoke to it?" I ask her, and she nods emphatically.

"You've got the *best* voice, Hannah, it was ah-*maz*-ing," she says. Jesus.

I'm suddenly aware that I'm swaying, and nausea overtakes me.

"Oh God …" I say, covering my mouth as I sprint for the bathroom. I barely make it before emptying all the rum. "I'm never drinking with you again, Arianna …"

She cackles from the other room. "Famous last words, bestie. I'll convince you again."

I stiffen when I feel a hand on my back as my hair is pulled away from my face. Luca shushes me as he rubs my back while I vomit.

"Go away," I mutter.

"No, baby."

"Yes! Go away. I don't need your perfect ass in here while I'm throwing up. Why do you have to be so perfect?" I moan, laying my head on the toilet seat. He chuckles quietly.

"Not perfect, *bella*. Not perfect at all. You make me wanna try to be perfect though," he says softly. God. He makes me want to cry. Stupid damn job and stupid damn team.

"Stupidfuckinghockey," I mumble. "Don'twannadothisitsnotfair."

"I know, baby. Gonna take Arianna back to my apartment and then I'll be back to help you into bed, okay?" Luca says, and I nod against the toilet. I swear I feel his lips ghost over my forehead, but I'm three sheets to the wind and possibly hallucinating.

I hear Arianna mumbling incoherently as Luca tries to get her up. Lifting my head, I peer out into the living room to see him unceremoniously throw her over his shoulder. He gives me a wink as he walks toward the door. Once I hear the door close, I exhale in relief. Even trashed I recognize how insanely hot he is, and how much I want him. How much I feel like I need him. God, this is so fucked up.

I try to pull myself up to the sink, but I don't have the strength. I begin to crawl down the hallway to the main bedroom so I can get to my toothbrush. My mouth feels like I've been sucking on cotton, and tastes like I lived inside a distillery for a few months. I can't sleep unless my mouth feels fresh.

I make it to my bathroom and pull myself up to grab my toothbrush. Laying my head on the counter, I begin to brush as I hear the apartment door open again.

"What the fuck?" I hear Luca say and I incoherently call out to him with the toothbrush in my mouth.

"Jesus, woman, what are you doing?" he chuckles.

"Teeth."

"I can see that. Did you put toothpaste on there?" he asks.

Well, fuck.

I take the toothbrush out and try to look at it. Why are there two toothbrushes? I attempt to close one eye to see clearer. When my eyes focus, I clearly see my toothbrush with no toothpaste. I harumph with frustration as I sway next to the sink. Luca grabs onto my waist as he chuckles.

"Let me help, *bella*," he says quietly as he grabs the toothpaste and puts a pea-sized dab on the toothbrush. "Open."

I dutifully open my mouth as he brushes my teeth. I suddenly find my hand drifting up his chest to touch his face. He's way too pretty. His nose is slightly crooked, and I bet it's a hockey-related injury. He gives me a small, crooked smile as he continues to brush my teeth. I don't care what he says, he's fucking perfect. This is bullshit.

"Spit."

I turn, taking the toothbrush out of his hand so I can spit and clean the toothbrush. His hands find my waist and circle around to hold me against him. Luca drops his head so his forehead rests against the top of my head. We both sigh.

"Luca," I whisper.

He doesn't respond. He doesn't need to. I know he's thinking the same thoughts as me. I know we can't be together. There's no way. But he feels so right.

"Let's get you to bed, Hannah," he says softly against my hair. I feel his lips press against my temple and I shiver, whimpering.

"Luca, I need you ..." I trail off. He exhales against my neck.

"I know, baby. I need you, too. But, the job, my job ... I don't know how to do this," he says.

I nod as tears fill my eyes.

Luca moves and puts one arm behind my knees to lift me, carrying me to my bed. As I slip under the covers, he steps away from the bed. My eyes are closed and I assume he slipped out.

"It's not fair," I mumble out loud.

"I know."

My eyes squint open as I look up to see Luca leaning against the wall, watching me with a closed-off expression on his face. I can't read him.

"Why are you still here?" I ask him bluntly. He shrugs.

"Can't seem to move my feet to leave."

"Oh. Okay."

"Just go to sleep, baby. Wanna watch you for a minute, yeah?"

I nod as I close my eyes, feeling a weird sense of comfort that he's here, even though I know he shouldn't be.

As I'm beginning to drift off, I feel his lips touch my forehead softly as his scent wafts over my body in a comforting embrace.

"I think I could fall in love with you so easily, Pix," he whispers. Or maybe I dreamed that part. God, what an amazing dream that would be.

Chapter 10

*L*uca

⁓⁓⁓

*S*he smiled in her sleep when I told her I could fall in love with her. Problem is, I think I already have. Maybe? I don't know. I've never felt this way before. It's so different from how I've felt from any other woman. I can't seem to leave the room. I know I need to go check on my sister, but I can't leave Hannah. Never met someone who seemed to complete me like she does.

When Hannah lets out a very unladylike snore and rolls over, I decide I need to leave. I lean down to give her one last kiss across her forehead and breathe her in. Jesus, she smells so fucking good. Vanilla and something else, I'm not sure of what. If I'm gonna survive the whole season with her near me, when I'm not allowed to touch her, I can't decide if I should bottle that scent up to keep with me or plug my nose any time she's close by. Her scent could be the death of me.

I leave her a note that I have her keys so I could lock the door, and head back into my apartment to check on Arianna. She's dead asleep, snoring like a freight train in my guest bedroom. Essentially it's her bedroom. She's stayed here so many times after drinking too much at bars near here and barged in here for a bed.

I grab a bottle of water and quietly go out to my balcony. It's a beautiful night heading into autumn. A crispness to the air tells me my days of running outside are limited. Lots of people here still run in the winter, but I choose to stick to a treadmill. One slip on a patch of black ice, and my career is over.

Pulling out my phone, I text my dad.

> Me: You up?

> Dad: I'm not going to Netflix and chill with you, Luca.

> Me: Nice.

> Dad: Is this how you interact with all of your partners? It's a wonder you get as much ass as you do.

> Me: It's after ten, Dad. I just wanted to be sure you were awake. Can I call you about something?

My phone immediately rings.

"Hey, Dad."

"Son. If you're calling to tell me about an illegitimate child, we need to figure out a plan to tell your mother so she doesn't have a stroke."

"You really are on a roll tonight," I respond sarcastically. "Love knowing how highly my family thinks of me."

"We are teasing you, Luca. I know you aren't that way. We all know that. You've had some periods where you definitely went through women like it was an Olympic competition, but that's not who you are. In all honesty, you were tamer than Alex in high school."

"Why does everyone bring it up, then?" I ask quietly.

Dad sighs. "Habit, I think. But you're right. We shouldn't. I'll talk to the girls, and remind them to treat you respectfully. They do it in jest, Luca. They'd annihilate anyone else who said it."

I know that. My sisters would cut a bitch without question.

86

"So what's on your mind?" he asks.

"When you met Mom, did you know she was the one?" I blurt out.

"I did. I think I knew immediately. I felt a pull to her that I'd never felt before. Like I was attached to an invisible rope, slowly getting pulled into her orbit." I can hear the smile in his voice. My father is a quiet man, always introspective and watchful. Except around my mom. His love and adoration for her is evident to everyone. "Did you meet someone, son?"

I hesitate briefly. "I did. It's exactly like you said, Dad. Everything is different with her."

"Are you in love with her?"

"It's … complicated. She works for the team."

"Ah. What would happen if you pursued her?" he asks.

"I don't know. I've never heard of any specific rule for employees dating players. I think it might just be frowned upon. But it gets a little more complicated because her uncle is one of my coaches."

My dad swears under his breath before chuckling. "Of course."

"What's that mean?"

"It means that I'm not surprised you've found your one in such a complicated manner. But, son, is she worth it?"

I think of Hannah, asleep and smiling as I tell her I could fall for her, and answer, "Yeah, Dad. I think she's worth it."

He sighs. "I really messed up when I tried to get involved with Gianna's relationship with Travis, and your mother made me swear I wouldn't do the same with any of you. I trust you, son. If you think she's worth it, figure out a way to make it work."

I head back inside and go to my room, slipping into bed after brushing my teeth. My eyes squeeze shut as I remember the look on Hannah's face when I brushed her teeth for her. I've never done that before. Never taken care of a woman like that who wasn't related to me. Never wanted to. But I *want* to take care of her. The look of adoration and reverence on her face, albeit her drunk face, was something I'll never forget.

Has anyone ever taken care of her before?

I fall asleep with Hannah's face on my mind, and I dream about a life with her.

*L*oud music penetrates my sleep. I groan, rolling over to grab my phone. Shit. It's nine o'clock in the morning. I'm about to miss morning skate. Fuck. Coach is gonna be pissed. I see I've missed fourteen calls from various people in the Wolves organization. Nothing from the one person I want to talk to, though.

After relieving myself, I head into the kitchen. Arianna is dancing and singing well off-key as she scrambles eggs.

"Sis," I say as I walk around her. She screams as she whips around to face me.

"OH MY GOD!" she screeches. "I thought you were gone!"

"Yeah, obviously I'm not," I drawl, amused.

"Aren't you supposed to be at the Sports Facility Zone?" she asks.

"Yep. They're pissed. Haven't even checked my messages. There's like ten voicemails and a bunch of texts. I overslept," I tell her as I pull out a protein shake from the fridge.

"Well, at least now we get to chat about Hannah," she says with a wicked glint in her eye. I sigh.

"Nothing to talk about."

"The fuck there isn't!"

"Jesus, Ari, calm down."

"Nope. Not gonna happen. Gotta help you figure this out," she says as she attempts to flip the eggs with her non-casted arm.

"Jesus, you suck at that," I comment.

"I know," she mutters. "The domestication gene obviously missed me."

I grab the spatula from her and push her out of the way. Arianna sits at the counter, studying me. As she opens her mouth, I hold up the spatula.

"There's nothing to figure out. We can't be together. End of discussion," I tell her as I finish the eggs.

"I don't accept that answer," she says vehemently. I begin to speak and she throws her hand up to stop me. "Let me finish. I've *never* seen you like this, Luca. And now that I've met her, she's fucking *perfect* for you. I get that the circumstances are fucked up, but there has to be a way! You can't just give up on her, on the possibility of a relationship with her."

"Ari, I love that you're invested like this. But it's not so simple. I'm pretty sure the coach has it out for me. This could get me kicked off the team. He's started making comments *to my face* about my contract, my behavior, and other shit," I tell her.

"But is there an actual rule that says you two can't be together?" she asks. I shrug.

"Listen, I don't know. I really don't. I always thought it was kinda inferred that you don't date employees. I know a few players have fucked around with some girls, but no one has ever *dated* a co-worker. And it's even more of a gray area because of Hannah's job. She has to travel with us a lot, sis," I tell her.

"Damn."

"Yeah."

Arianna is quiet as I plate up the eggs. Fortunately, she made enough for both of us. I take both plates to the table and we eat quietly for a few minutes.

"If I ask you a hard question, will you promise to be honest with me?" Arianna asks.

"I'll try."

"It's just ..." she trails off.

"What?"

Ari sighs. "I've watched you play hockey my entire life. The joy that always emanated from you from the moment you stepped on the ice until well after you stepped off. That's gone, Luca. It almost seems like it's work now. Are you still enjoying it? Is this job, and this team, worth possibly losing what might be life-changing for you with Hannah?"

I didn't expect that deep question from my little sister, that's for damn sure. "It's all I know, Ari. I don't know who I am without hockey."

"Hockey is just what you're good at, Luca. It's not your identity. Honestly, I always thought you'd quit after a couple years and be a coach."

I stare at her. "Seriously?"

"Yeah. You're great with kids of all ages. Look at how you took Matt's step-daughter under your wing," Arianna says with a shrug. Our cousin Matt recently married a single mom. Her oldest daughter, Molly, is an exceptional hockey player. To say she enjoys playing in a co-ed league is a massive understatement. I've never seen anyone, male or female, enjoy taking people out quite as much as Molly does.

I let those thoughts resonate quietly while finishing the eggs.

"How are you gonna handle being around her so much?" she asks quietly.

"I don't fucking know."

"Do you think you could date her and not tell anyone?" she asks hopefully.

"Maybe. I don't know. The thing is, I don't *want* to hide it. I want to be with her. I want to do the damn thing and have everyone know she's taken. That I'm taken. I don't want it to be a secret thing," I admit.

"I'm sorry, bro. I hate this," Arianna says. I nod. I hate it too. "Can I ask you one thing?"

I chuckle. It's never 'one' thing with Arianna.

"Yeah, what?"

"Can I still be friends with her? Cuz she's kinda amazing and I feel like she's my person," Arianna says with a hesitant smile. I bark out a laugh.

"Yeah, sis. You can still be friends with her," I tell her. It'll kill me to see her with Hannah, but I can't take away a friendship from my sister. Arianna has had some really shitty relationships and has had a few back-stabbing bitches in her past. I know Hannah will be a great friend for her. And I feel like Hannah needs Arianna in her life.

⁕⁕⁕⁕⁕⁕⁕⁕⁕⁕

I've managed to steer clear of Hannah for a week. I've only seen her a couple times, and fortunately our paths haven't crossed at the arena, or the Sports Facility Zone. Until today in my apartment building. This is one incredibly uncomfortable elevator ride, and all I can think of was being stuck in the elevator with her. I'm sure she's thinking the same thing. I can hear her breathing accelerating, but I'm trying to remain as silent and stoic as possible. It's better if she doesn't know how much she's affecting me.

As Hannah runs out of the elevator, I loiter in the lobby for a few minutes. I'm on my way to the Sports Facility Zone for a veteran meeting, so I assume she's going there too. I don't want to follow her there and then have to walk behind her into the building. That ass ... I can't not stare at her ass if she's in front of me.

After waiting about ten minutes, I head to the garage and get in my car. I hope she's long gone and already in the Sports Facility Zone parking lot so I can relax. But suddenly, she stands in front of my car with a worried expression on her face.

I jump out of my SUV immediately.

"What happened? Are you okay?" I blurt out, walking quickly to her and reflexively grabbing her face between my hands.

"Umm, I think someone slashed my tires," she whispers. My heart drops. Holy shit, someone slashed her tires?

"Show me," I tell her, as I lock my car and grab her hand, pulling her in the direction where I know her car is. Yeah, I know. A little bit stalkerish, but I needed to know where she might be so I avoided the area. All tenants have assigned parking spots. I never paid attention to where Caroline parked, but now I know. I know everything when it relates to Hannah.

Hannah's hand is shaking in mine as we approach her car. She has a small sedan that would probably be fine in Georgia, but it's not meant for Colorado winters. I make a mental note to price out SUV's for her, then realize how fucking ridiculous that sounds. We aren't together. I can't buy her a car. Can I? Wait. No. No, I can't buy her a car. Fuck.

"Okay, baby, we need to call the police. And the building security. They have cameras in the garage. They probably caught something, okay?" I say to her. I catch how she winces when I call her baby. "Shit, I'm sorry. I can't say that anymore. I'm sorry, Hannah."

"I know," she whispers brokenly. "Can you call my uncle, too?"

I wince, having forgotten about her relationship to my coach.

"I can call him. Why don't you go back into the lobby and ask security to come out here? I'll call Coach while you're gone," I tell her. As she walks away ... and yes, I watched her ass ... I pull up Coach Davenport's number. I take a deep breath as the phone rings, almost willing it to go to voicemail.

"Santo."

Fuck.

"Coach Davenport, um, I have a weird situation here," I begin, and he cuts me off.

"What. Did. You. Do."

Jesus. They just *assume* I've done something wrong.

"I didn't do anything. Um, you know I live in the same complex as your sister, right?" I say.

"Uhh, yeah ..."

"Well, I live in the apartment next to her ..." I trail off, trying to formulate my words correctly.

"Shit. Hannah."

"Yeah, so Hannah ..."

"What happened? Is she okay?"

"Yeah, she's fine, but ..."

"Did you do something to her?

"Jesus, *no*! Why would you automatically think that?"

"Because it's *you*, Santo, and you've always been trouble."

"Fuck, man, I didn't do anything to her."

"Well, are you gonna tell me what the fuck happened?

"Stop interrupting me and I'll get to it!" At this point, I'm literally yelling at him. I'm so fucking pissed. My fist is clenched, my fingernails digging into my palm, as I pace in front of Hannah's car. This asshole has some nerve being all judgmental when I'm helping his niece right now.

"Fine."

"I was on my way to the Sports Facility Zone and she appeared in front of my car in the building garage. She told me all four of her tires were slashed," I blurt out.

Silence.

"Uhh, coach?" I ask.

I hear a loud exhale.

"I'm on my way."

"I don't think she wants you here, she just wanted you to know because she'd be late for work ... coach? Are you there?" I pull my phone away from my ear to see he's already ended the call. Great.

Hannah is walking toward me with one of the security guards.

"Did you call my uncle?"

"Yeah, he said he's on his way."

Her eyes widen dramatically.

"I didn't mean he needed to come here!" she shouts.

"I know, and I tried to tell him that, but he hung up on me," I explain. She rubs her forehead and temples as her eyes close in frustration.

The security guard circles the car and takes a few pictures.

"Ms. Beauregard, we have to call the police and have them involved. You'll need to file a report," the guard explains. Hannah sighs and I hear a tremble in her throat. Before I can think twice, I reach over and grab her tightly, resting my head on hers.

"This sucks," she whimpers. I nod my head in agreement.

"Do you think this was random? It had to have been another

tenant, right?" I ask the guard. He gives me a subtle shake of his head.

"The thing is, we've been training a new guy, and we think he's been letting some people have access to the building when they shouldn't, so ... well, there's no real guess on who might have done it," the guard says sheepishly as he scratches his neck. I glare at him.

"I want his name," I growl. Hannah tenses in my arms and pulls away from me. I look down at her. "The owners of this building tout it being one of the safest in downtown Denver. If they're gonna hire people who don't take the job seriously, they need to be held accountable."

I hear footsteps running down the lobby hallway and release Hannah from my arms right as her uncle barrels into the garage. He stops dead in his tracks when he looks at me. His eyes narrow as he approaches Hannah and takes her in his arms, his eyes still on me.

Fuck.

"What are you still doing here, Santo?" he mutters, malice evident in his tone.

"Just wanted to make sure she was okay, Coach," I mumble.

"You okay, pot pie?" he says quietly to Hannah. Pot pie? He calls her pot pie? Jesus he can't be more than six or eight years older than her. They're more like cousins.

"I'm okay. I'm so glad Luca was still here when I saw the car," she says, looking over at me and giving me a cautious smile. Coach is still staring me down.

"You call him Luca?" Coach says to Hannah.

"Well, yeah, that's how he introduced himself to me," she stammers.

"I only use Luke in hockey, Coach. To everyone else, I'm Luca," I tell him honestly. Seriously, if he's mad about the name she uses for me, there's no fucking chance we can ever be together.

Coach glares at me some more.

"Well, now that you're here, I'll be on my way," I say, as I turn and begin walking back to my car.

"Luca, wait!"

I turn around and see Hannah running over to me.

"Thank you," she whispers, looking up at me with so much sweetness in her eyes that I can't help but place my hand on her cheek and smile at her tenderly.

"I'll do anything for you, *bella*. You know that, right?" I say quietly, and she nods. "Take care of yourself, Pix."

As she turns and walks back to her car, I see Coach Davenport with fury emanating off of him in waves.

Shit. He knows.

This isn't going to end well for me.

Chapter 11

Hannah

⸻✦⸻

I'm not surprised when my uncle interrogates me for the rest of the morning. After doing the police report, Uncle Bennett drove me to the Sports Facility Zone. He encouraged me to take the day off, but I didn't want to sit in my aunt's apartment and just stew. He could tell something happened between Luca and me. I'm just not sure if he realizes it's more than he thinks. Unfortunately, I have a shitty poker face.

Work has been the only thing getting me through the last couple of weeks. Fortunately, the terrible terrors, my interns, convinced the GM they needed the month off to study for midterms. Arianna has forced me to socialize, much to my dismay. I'd prefer to stay holed up in my aunt's apartment as long as I can, but I've come to learn that Arianna doesn't take no for an answer. She's introduced me to her closest two friends, who I absolutely adore. Natalie and Claire are around our age. They are as different as night and day. Natalie is exotic and voluptuous, with chocolate brown hair and bright green eyes that seem to glow with mischief. Claire, in contrast, has Icelandic white blonde hair and light blue eyes. Her subdued nature also contrasts to Natalie's boisterous personality. The fact that they accepted me immediately makes me love them both so much.

The four of us have hung out often over the past few weeks, effectively keeping my mind off of Luca being a wall away. It boggles my mind how often Arianna drives from Eternity Springs to Denver. All three women have apartments on the west side of Denver, but Ari still has to drive to her hometown for her job. The mandatory fun sessions with the girls have also helped me to stay in denial about the first road trip I'm scheduled to go on. Fortunately, the team didn't expect me to travel with them for the away preseason games, so I have a couple more weeks before I officially begin traveling with them ... and Luca.

It's hard enough to think about Luca being right next door at night. The thought of us both being in hotel rooms, and even in the close quarters of an airplane or bus, makes me break out in hives.

*I*t's now preseason. Luca being away for a few days at a time has not been as much of a relief as I thought it would be. I find myself stalking hashtags to find pictures of him. He doesn't have any social media that I know of. And since I'm in charge of the team social accounts, I see all the pictures coming in. There's rarely anything with him. Luca is very clearly avoiding the limelight right now, and I don't blame him.

Interestingly, he's begun texting me random thoughts.

Luca: Do you know what a Juicy Lucy is?

Me: Um, no?

Luca: It's a burger stuffed with cheese.

Me: Isn't that just a cheeseburger?

Luca: That's what I said!

Me: Where are you?

Luca: Minneapolis.

Me: So they have a version of a cheeseburger called a Juicy Lucy?

Luca: Yep. And there's an argument over who created it first.

Luca: Ever had a three-way?

Me: Luca!

Luca: Get your mind out of the gutter, Beauregard. It's a FOOD, not the sex kind of three-way.

Me: No, I have not had a food three-way. What is it?

Luca: Cincinnati chili on top of spaghetti noodles, and topped with cheese.

Me: Chili on top of spaghetti?

Luca: Yep.

Me: Is that weird?

Luca: I liked it. The chili is kind of sweet.

Luca: Just like you.

Luca: Any idea what the biggest export for Colorado is?

Me: Can't say that I do.

Luca: Guess.

Me: Beer?

Luca: Funny.

Luca: It's beef.

Me: Really?

Luca: There's this place on 44th that serves the most amazing bison Indian tacos. You need to try it.

Me: I'm not sure I could eat bison.

Luca: It doesn't taste much different from the ground beef you eat from a cow.

Me: That's true. I'll have to look it up sometime.

Luca: I wish I could take you there.

Me: I know. Me too.

*he therapist that Uncle Bennett recommended is not affiliated with the team, so I feel comfortable telling her about my almost-relationship with Luca. She told me we'd 'put a pin in that conversation' so we could focus on giving me coping strategies to help with my fear of flying. For the last two weeks, I've been tasked with watching YouTube videos of planes taking off and landing. We've also done some 'field trips' to Denver International Airport to watch the runways. That airport is massive. I've flown in and out of Atlanta all my life, but somehow, this airport feels bigger. Watching the airplanes take off and land was actually quite relaxing.

I made the mistake of Googling the airport, and seeing all kinds of conspiracy theories and details about weird things that have happened there. Also the weird horse statue with the glowing eyes ... what the hell is up with that?

With the season opener in Denver, we have a full week of events leading up to the first game. Adding in our media days where the players have their pictures taken, interview local media, and do soundbites for in-game material, it's been a whirlwind. I've been working sixteen hour days, and even slept at my desk once. I didn't mean to sleep there, I was just so exhausted I put my head down for a minute. Six hours later, my desk phone rang and scared the shit out of me.

I've only seen Luca a couple of times in the past few weeks. We had one meeting where I had to ask him a few questions for an article I was posting to the team website, and fortunately he was with other teammates. I think we both kept it professional? I really don't know. I'm struggling. And honestly, I hope he is, too.

The day of the first game, I'm at the arena at seven in the morning. It's a full day for me with press, interviews, and whatnot. Plus, it's my first 'real' hockey game. At the home preseason games I've spent the majority of each game posting on social media, and couldn't watch the entirety of the games. I never realized how draining creating social media content actually is. The team expects immediate updates on scores, penalties, and fights across every social media platform we have. Now I realize what a poor time it was for the terrible terrors to take a month off. It would be so much faster if we each were responsible for one social media channel to update throughout the games.

Admittedly, I've Googled Wolves videos. Well, specifically, I've Googled Luca. If I thought he was sexy before, seeing him in action was enough to put him on a pedestal no other man will ever be able to reach.

Three hours before the start of the game, I'm in my arena office. It's basically a little closet in the basement, but it works for the few times I'm here. My office at the Sports Facility Zone, where I spend the majority of my office time, is much nicer. But here, I'm supposed to be shadowing the team more often than not. So the office space doesn't really matter.

I've got my back to the door when I hear someone open and close the door. As I spin around, I see Luca in his game day suit. Wow. Suit porn is a real thing.

"Hey," he says.

"Hi," I whisper.

He reaches behind his head and scratches the back of his neck. I've noticed he does this when he's uncomfortable or nervous.

"Do you need something?" I ask. He shakes his head.

"I just ... I just had to see you, Han. How are you?"

"I'm, umm, I'm great. Of course, I'm great. Love this job. Love the team. Love the Denver," I stammer. A hint of a smile washes over his face. "How are you, Luke?"

He winces as I call him by his hockey name. "It's Luca to you. Always Luca. And it's wonderful knowing you love the Denver."

Heat crawls up my décolletage and onto my face. "I meant I love Denver. I'm enjoying living here."

"I'm glad," he says softly.

We stare at each other for a moment. His back is resting against the door and his eyes slowly peruse down my body. My heart rate increases and I take in a deep and shaky breath. I subconsciously catch my lower lip between my teeth, and Luca's eyes zero in on my mouth. His eyes dilate as he watches me for a long moment, before he drags his gaze slowly down my body. I swear I can feel him. I gasp as heat floods my core, my thighs clenching together as his slow perusal returns to my face.

Luca's left hand slides down and grabs the door handle, locking the door. Simultaneously we both step toward one another and our lips meet in a clashing of need. Of want. Of denial. I whimper into his mouth as his hands slide down to grab my ass, and he groans in response. Luca turns us so my back is against the wall, deepening the kiss as he pulls one of my legs up to his hip. I feel him against me and I shamelessly grind into him.

"Fuck, Hannah, fuck. God, I've missed you," he whispers as he trails kisses down my neck and onto my shoulder.

"Luca," I moan quietly. He takes my lips again in a searing kiss.

Voices outside the door make us break apart as someone knocks on the door.

"Ms. Beauregard? You in there?" a voice calls out. I think it possibly sounds like Gabe Dawson, but I'm not sure. Luca's jaw clenches as he rests his forehead against mine.

"Got a thing for the coach's niece, Daws?" another voice says with a tease.

"Nah. Just figured she'd be a good quick fuck," he answers. Luca's entire body stiffens as he lunges for the door, but I pull him back and put my hand over his mouth. His eyes find mine. Full of fury and anger. Tension is emanating off his body in waves.

"Coach would have your balls, man. Not worth it," the other guy answers.

"Yeah, I know. But I like a challenge," Gabe answers.

The voices drift away and Luca exhales heavily against my hand.

"Thank you," I whisper, as I let my hand drop from his mouth and settle on his chest. He furrows his brow.

"For what?"

"For trying to go to bat for me. You were ready to fight, even if it meant getting yourself in trouble. It's admirable, Luca. But please, don't risk your own career for me, okay? I can't have that on my conscience," I tell him softly.

"That's the thing, *bella*," he says quietly, "I'm beginning to think you're worth the risk."

I squeeze my eyes shut tightly as I lay my head on his chest. I wish it were that easy.

"I have to go, baby. Can I text you after the game?" Luca says against the top of my head, and I nod against his chest. I know we shouldn't. I know this is going to end badly. But I can't say no. I'm so drawn to him. Like a fucking moth to a flame, ready to destroy everything for a few moments with this man.

Luca leans down and places a soft and tender kiss on my lips, his right hand wrapped around my neck with his fingers in my hair. He holds me safely, like I'm the most precious cargo in the world. He makes me feel so cherished.

"Let me go out first, and I'll make sure you can leave," I say quietly and he nods. I grab my things and open the door, checking to see if the coast is clear. I motion for Luca to follow me. As I'm closing and locking my door, he walks past and drags his knuckles across the back of my hand.

How on earth a simple touch like that could rock me to my core is beyond me.

*y first full hockey game is intense and exhilarating. I flit around the arena throughout the game, grabbing great pictures and videos from as many angles as I can. I may have also pulled out my personal phone and snapped some pictures of Luca. He plays with such determination and focus.

I snuck down to the first row, right behind the glass, and got a bunch of pictures. It was at that moment when Luca got into an altercation with some douche on the other team, and he managed to look up right as I snapped a pic. The intensity in his stare as he looked at me? Holy fuck. The man just exudes sex and confidence. I made a mental note to send that photo to myself after downloading all the pictures.

The Wolves won, three to one. The owners, the Crawford family, have requested all employees attend a celebratory party after the first game. I'm incredibly exhausted and would love to just go home and crash, but I know I have to make an appearance. It'll be great content for the team socials.

Coincidentally, the place they've chosen to host this party is called Aurora's Castle. It's actually just a building in Denver, but has a huge open floor plan with breathtaking stained glass windows. The space has been decked out in massive hockey ice sculptures and floral arrangements that look like hockey players. It's weirdly aesthetically pleasing.

I'm not the best at parties. Or any event with tons of people, for that matter. So I'm trying to keep my spot warm against a back corner wall and nursing a glass of wine. I've already made rounds and taken some pictures, and now I'm deciding if I want to try and sneak out.

Another employee walks over to me with a cautious smile on her face.

"Hi, are you Hannah?" she asks tentatively, and I nod. "Great. Your uncle told me to come talk to you. I'm Elsie. I'm one of the physical therapists for the team."

I reach out to shake her hand.

"It's nice to meet you, Elsie. What else did my uncle tell you?" I ask her. She laughs lightly.

"Oh, just that you might need a friend at an event like this. Big crowds freak me out, so I was all too happy to come over and talk to you," she says.

"Oh, thank God! I'm a nervous wreck. I don't do well in these kinds of places," I tell her nervously. "How long have you worked for the team?"

"Just a year. It's been amazing. I love when I get to travel with the team. I didn't get to travel much growing up, so this has been a dream come true," she tells me. I brighten when I hear she'll be traveling too.

"Oh, that makes me so happy! I'm freaked out about traveling. I don't fly well," I confess.

"I won't be on every away trip, but I'll be on quite a few. Away trips we don't take the whole PT team, so we take turns," Elsie explains.

A ruckus draws our attention to the door as the team all come in at once. Everyone claps and cheers.

Luca is near the back, and I can see him scanning the crowd. When his eyes land on me, he smirks and gives me a subtle head nod as he reaches up and touches his lip. My entire body tingles thinking about the kiss in my office only a few hours ago.

"Holy hell, that was hot," Elsie whispers. My head whips to hers.

"What?" I ask nervously. My face feels hot and I can tell a sheen of sweat has appeared on my forehead. I'd fan myself if it wouldn't give me away.

"The way Luke looked at you," she says, her eyes wide. "Are you guys a thing? I mean, I don't think it's technically against the rules, but I figured it was frowned upon to fraternize with the players."

"Oh, no, it's nothing. He lives next door to me," I tell her nonchalantly.

"That's what they're calling it now? 'Nothing?' Hmm. Guess I need to find me some 'nothing' too," she teases. I'm about to correct her again when my uncle sidles up to us.

"Ladies," he says, and Elsie's posture completely changes. Uncle Bennett gives her a look, and Elsie's eyes drop to the ground. Oh, I think she's already found her 'nothing.'

"Hi Uncle Bennett. Thanks for sending Elsie over to save me," I tell him. He gives me a crooked smile.

"I figured you two would have some things in common. How'd you enjoy your first full hockey game?" he asks.

"You've never seen a hockey game?" Elsie asks incredulously. I shrug.

"Well, I mean, I'm from Georgia. Hockey isn't exactly big there. Plus my last job was with a college football team," I explain.

"Oh. Well this is *so* much better than football," she tells me passionately. I sneak a peek at my uncle, and he's watching Elsie with a heated look as she explains why hockey is better than football.

"Okay, I get it. I do. I'm still learning about hockey, so cut me some slack," I tell her, laughing.

"I'm sorry. I just love hockey. I grew up with it, even played on some teams myself," Elsie says with a sheepish shrug.

"I know you said you've been working for the team for the last year. How old are you, if you don't mind me asking?" I ask.

"Oh, I'm twenty five," she answers. She turns and looks over her shoulder at a couple players whooping it up by one of the ice sculptures, and I make a very pointed look at my uncle. He's thirty five. He refuses to look me in the eyes.

"Well, I've had an incredibly long day, I'm going to head out. Uncle Bennett, can you give Elsie my contact? I'd love to chat with you more when I'm not about to fall asleep on my feet," I tell her. She nods enthusiastically. I give my uncle a hug.

"We're gonna talk later, mister," I whisper in his ear.

"I figured."

I sneak around the edge of the party and quietly head outside. Pulling up the Uber app, I see a bunch of drivers nearby. It's only a few blocks to the apartment building, but I'm exhausted. I just want to get back to my aunt's apartment quickly.

As a car pulls up and I confirm it's my driver, I slide into the backseat and begin to close the door.

The door is yanked from my hand as a voice says, "Room for one more?" as Luca slides into the seat beside me.

Chapter 12

*L*uca

I can't help it. I watched her as much as I could at the party. When I saw her sneak out, I followed. I don't think anyone saw me, but honestly at this moment, I don't really care.

I'm done fighting this.

I want Hannah.

Been thinking about her since the moment she pounded on my door. And the few kisses we've had have been the best of my life. I'm done putting my job before her. Hell, the coach has it out for me anyway. I'm probably done after this season. But a girl like Hannah only comes along once in a while. I'm not avoiding this anymore.

Hannah looks at me, her eyes wide.

"It's okay. No one saw me," I whisper.

The Uber driver looks at me with his eyebrows raised.

"We're going to the same building, might as well share a ride," I tell him. I'm tempted to haul Hannah into my lap, but I think that might freak her out. We have a lot to talk about.

Hannah is quiet on the quick ride back to our building, and we don't speak as we walk side-by-side into the lobby. We enter the elevator in silence.

I'm beginning to second-guess my decision to follow her when I feel her hand softly slide into mine. I let out an exhale of relief as she leans her head against my arm.

"Will you stay with me tonight?" she whispers.

"Nothing I'd rather do, Pixie," I tell her with a wide grin.

My heart is beating a million beats per minute as we get to our floor and I follow Hannah to her apartment door. I can't help but stand right behind her as she unlocks her door, my hands sliding around her waist and letting her feel me. I notice her hands trembling as she attempts to unlock the door, and I carefully place one hand over hers to calm her.

"I'm nervous," she admits, as she manages to unlock the door. I push her inside and close the door. Hannah turns to me in the dark apartment and steps into my embrace, standing on her tiptoes as I bend down until our lips mash together.

I slide my hands down the backs of her thighs and pick her up as she squeals, then walk over to the couch. Sitting down, Hannah straddles me with her hands locked in my hair. As soon as we are seated, my steel length pushes against her heat and I groan.

"Luca," she murmurs against my lips. Our kiss turns carnal as my hands pull her shirt out of her waistband so I can touch her bare skin.

"*Bella.*"

"Luca, I need ..." she trails off.

"What do you need, baby?" I ask as she grinds against me. Bet I could make her come like this. Not even touching her. "Do you need to come? Do you want my fingers, my mouth, my cock? What do you want?"

She stops and stares at me with wide eyes, her pupils so dilated I can barely see the irises.

"Wait," she breathes. "What ... what does this mean? Nothing's changed, what are we doing?"

She begins to look hysterical as her eyes dart around. I grab her chin and force her to look back at me.

"I refuse to fight this anymore, Pix. Never felt like this before. I'll be damned if I'm letting some stupid maybe-rule impact whether or not we're together. I want you, Hannah. I've never wanted anyone like this. I'm not ignoring it anymore," I tell her fervently.

Hannah's mouth is open as she stares at me in shock.

"It's okay, baby. I'm fine with taking things at your speed. That is, if you want to do this with me," I say.

"I don't understand ..." she says.

"Okay, let me make this a little clearer for you. I can't stop thinking about you, Hannah. I've never felt this way before. Never felt the need to brush a woman's teeth, or hold them all night. There's this visceral need deep in my soul to take care of you, Pixie, and that tells me this isn't just another fuck. I could easily fall for you, and I'm not going to let anyone else tell me that it's not okay. If you want to be with me, then let's do it. If you don't, you need to tell me now. I won't pressure you into this."

"Umm, okay. Wow, that's a lot to unpack after a hockey game," she mutters, and I chuckle.

"Yeah, I'd say I'm sorry for unloading this on you, but I'm not. I haven't stopped thinking about you. Never had this happen before, which is why I know I can't let you go. Not unless you don't want me," I say quietly. Her head snaps back to mine.

"I do want you, Luca," she whispers with a small smile, and my heart leaps in my chest. "I'm worried, though. I don't know how we should handle this."

"Here's my thought. I'd like to talk to my agent about it, if that's okay. He should be able to give us some advice on if we should tell the team, how we should handle it, and all that crap. As for anyone else, I'd kinda like to keep it just between us," I tell her, and I see a quick jab of pain in her eyes. "Wait, let me explain. I just want to enjoy dating you. Spending time with you. I don't want anyone else to interrupt that bubble and get in our space. Do you understand?"

"Can we just ..." she trails off.

"What?"

"Can we just be us for a little while? No agent. No friends. I'd like to get to know you better before anyone else gets involved," she whispers.

"I'm cool with that," I tell her with a smile. "So we're secretly together?"

She nods, but still looks uncomfortable.

"What's on your mind, Pixie?"

She takes a deep breath and then says, "Would we be *together, together*? Like exclusive? I just want to be sure ..."

I interrupt her immediately.

"I don't share, Hannah."

Her eyes widen at my tone. I'm dead serious.

"I don't fucking share. You're mine. End of story."

"How very alpha of you, Luca," she teases. I give her a small smile.

"In this situation, yeah. Guess I'm taking on a possessive role here, but baby? I'm yours just as much as you're mine. It goes both ways. I'm your man, okay?" I ask her, and she gives me a beaming smile and a nod. "But this — this is new for me. I'm not entirely sure what I'm doing. And we need to be careful at work. Will you trust me? And be patient with me? I'm probably going to fuck up a bunch of times, and I don't want you to run for the hills as soon as you get an opportunity."

"I promise I'll be patient. And you need to be patient with me. My past relationships haven't been the best, and I'm a little trigger-shy."

I tense, wondering what she means by 'not the best.' But as I'm about to ask another question, she yawns.

Shit. It's almost midnight. I don't know what time she's been up since, but it's been a long day for me, so it's probably been as bad or worse for her.

"You need sleep, *bella*," I tell her, and she nods sleepily.

"Would you ... I mean, will you ..." she trails off, uncertain.

"Yeah, baby. I'd really like to sleep here, if that's okay," I say softly, running my hand along her cheek. "Let me go grab my tooth-brush and I'll be back, okay?"

I give her a quick peck as she stands up from my lap, and I jog over to my apartment. I left all of my stuff at the arena in my locker, since I knew I'd be going straight to the party. I make a mental note to remember to go get my things tomorrow. It's nothing pressing tonight, just the item that became my superstition once I made my NHL debut. Arianna gave me her favorite Barbie the morning of my first game, and when I scored, she said it was because of the doll. When I scored the following game, I wondered if she was correct. Barbie has faithfully attended every game, both home and away, since then. Once my teammates got wind of my unique superstition, however, they took advantage. Let's just say Barbie is now rocking half a mohawk, some interesting clothing choices, and quite a few Sharpie tattoos ... mostly of dicks. We might be men, but we're all the equivalent emotional intelligence of fourteen year old boys. Also, don't mess with a hockey players superstitions. Ever.

I grab my toothbrush and head back to Hannah's apartment. She left the door ajar for me, so I close it and lock up, turning off the kitchen light before walking toward her bedroom. She's in the bathroom washing her face, and I walk up behind her and lean down to kiss her shoulder.

I know this is her aunt's apartment, and it's clear they have different tastes. Caroline is bougie. All the best clothes. Designer everything. There isn't a thing out of place in this apartment. Hannah ... Hannah is comfort. She's a cool breeze on a hot summer afternoon. The first sip of an ice-cold limoncello after an amazing home-cooked lasagna. Caroline may be defined as refined and elegant, but Hannah is class and poise. I'd be shocked to know they're related, but I know how different my own siblings are, so I understand how personalities differ.

We brush our teeth together, and it's weirdly comfortable and domestic. I've honestly never felt this connection with anyone where I've wanted to spend as much time together as possible. Every time I catch her eyes, she giggles. It's like a melody straight to my heart.

I remove everything but my boxer briefs, and Hannah strips

down to a tank top and panties. As soon as we're both under the covers, I pull her toward me and kiss her deeply. My tongue slides into her mouth as her nails drag up my spine, making me shiver. I break off the kiss to look at her.

"I just needed another kiss before we go to sleep, baby," I admit sheepishly. She giggles.

"Highly doubt I'll ever say no to a kiss from you, Luca," she whispers. I reposition us so her back is to my front and I wrap my arms around her tightly. She sighs in bliss.

I fall asleep the fastest I've ever fallen asleep.

Chapter 13

*H*annah

✦ ⁘⁘⁘⁘⁘⁘⁘ ✦

*W*hile it was great to establish some parameters for whatever was going on with Luca, it was pretty dang hard to move forward when our schedules were complete insanity. I thought college football teams had harsh schedules, but they don't even touch what Luca and the team go through.

Luca skates almost every day of the week. Non-game days have him attending morning meetings, and a morning skate, sometimes doing interviews, any social media assignments, and personal appearances, or charity work. He heads back to his apartment for a couple hours, but then he's back on the ice in the late afternoon. Luca told me the afternoon sessions aren't required at all, but he puts in the time to improve his own skill, and to set an example for the younger guys. Then he naps before he's meeting with teammates to watch game tape, or spending time doing extra workouts in the evening hours.

Game days are even worse. All of that, plus a game, plus a quick post-game meeting with the coaching staff, and then he typically does a post-game workout to help with any injury or muscle soreness. I've barely seen the man in two weeks, because I've been as busy as him. Keeping on top of all the content going out across all

Wolves social media is definitely more than a one-woman job. Since my two interns, back from their month off, are more concerned with chatting with players than actually doing any work, I've been working fourteen to sixteen hour days trying to stay ahead.

Not only do I create and implement certain social media challenges and content, but I am also responsible for tracking comments to ensure nothing slips past that would raise red flags. Already this season I've had to handle an ex-girlfriend of one of the rookies who has an ax to grind with getting dropped after the draft, and a group of fans who call themselves Gabe's Girlies. They've attempted to start a commenting war attacking Luca. The nastiness and vitriol these people spew while hiding behind a computer, or phone screen, never ceases to amaze me.

The Wolves have been fortunate to have the first two weeks of the schedule almost solely at home, which Uncle Bennett says is pretty atypical. They only had two nights away, at San Diego and Los Angeles, before returning home again. But that comes at a cost: they're about to leave for a two-week series of back-to-back away games in Canada, and then the team heads onto the northeast for a games in Boston and New York.

I was originally scheduled to attend all of the games for this trip, but suddenly I was pulled. If I didn't think my uncle suspects something between Luca and me before, I certainly do now. When I approached him about it, he would barely make eye contact before muttering about social media and 'crazy ladies.' When I asked for clarification on what he was talking about, he faked a phone call. My thirty-five-year-old uncle faked a damn phone call to avoid talking to me.

The terrible terrors are way too excited about "traveling with the hotties," as they exclaimed giddily to me. I had to lay down the law that they were not to be anything but professional in this capacity, and I'd be keeping track of them at all times. Fortunately, Elsie is traveling with the team and ensured she'd keep an eye on Jessica and Lindsey.

Since the team is leaving tomorrow, Luca asked me if we could stay in tonight. He wants to cook me dinner before cuddling on the couch. His words, not mine. I'm sure hoping we do more than cuddling, though. I'm wound tighter than a line of firecrackers waiting to go off on the Fourth of July.

> Luca: Running late. Coach wanted to yell at me some more. Be there in twenty minutes.

> Me: Which coach?

> Luca: Take a guess.

> Me: My uncle?

> Luca: Sorry, Pix. He's got it out for me right now.

> Me: I wish I could talk to him about it, tell him to calm down. But he'll know immediately if I do.

> Luca: Pretty sure he already knows. That's why he's got it out for me.

> Me: I'm sorry, Luca. I hate that he's being so juvenile.

> Luca: Don't worry about me, Han. I can handle good ole Uncle Bennett.

I giggle as I toss my phone on the couch. With twenty minutes, I can do a quick refresh, and change into some sexier undergarments. I'm bound and determined to seduce Luca Santo tonight, and a quick visit to a high-end lingerie boutique Arianna recommended this week means I'm prepared to take him down.

I was tempted to purchase something out of my comfort zone. Something so seductive, so erotic, that it would be like I was a completely different person. But I just couldn't do it. My southern upbringing reared its ugly head as I contemplated between a bra and panty set with only about two inches of total fabric, or the innocently sexual white set I purchased. White lace bra with rhinestones adorning the cups, and a white lace thong. White sheer thigh highs and a white garter belt complete the ensemble. Other than the nylons on my legs, I'm able to put back on the dress I wore to work, and Luca won't be able to tell anything is out of the ordinary.

In a stroke of genius, I decide to remove the thong. Easier access. And somehow, going commando makes me feel like a badass bitch, and I know Luca will never expect it.

As soon as I slide my red Herve Lager cocktail dress over the lingerie, a feeling of power and seduction comes over me. The sweetheart neckline accentuates my collarbone, but still gives the illusion of sweet and innocent. Knowing I have seduction on my mind is making me drunk with power. I swear I'm standing taller as I stare at my reflection in the floor-to-ceiling mirror my aunt had installed in the closet. As I slide my heels back on my feet, making me almost four inches taller, I'm overcome with confidence. My man isn't going to know what hit him.

When a knock sounds at the door, I rush to fling the door open. Luca gives me a breathtaking smile as he kisses my cheek and walks into the apartment. He places his grocery bag on the counter, before turning and catching my head in his hands. His lips are on mine as he backs me into the wall. I gasp into his mouth, allowing his tongue to slide against mine, as my hands find his hair and hold on. I don't know what it is about this man and pushing me into walls, but I'm absolutely here for it.

"You changed," he whispers as he kisses down my chin and onto my neck.

"No, this is what I wore to work," I answer breathlessly.

Luca chuckles against me, the vibration making me shiver. "You weren't wearing anything on your legs, Pixie. I stare at your legs and ass every chance I get. I'd know if you had stockings on today."

I'm shocked. I had no idea he paid that much attention to detail. My ex-boyfriend, Jefferson, wouldn't even be able to accurately pick a pair of shoes to match a dress, let alone notice if I was wearing anything at all. We dated the better part of two years, then off and on for another two, before I finally ended things with him. My parents were horrified. The Collins family had all the good connections in southern Georgia. Just another example of my parents not caring about my happiness, and just using me for their own aspirations.

"I didn't — I just —" I stutter.

Luca's head pops up from where he was nibbling on my collarbone, his mouth tipped up in a small grin. "You got something sexy under there for me, baby?"

As his hands slide down to settle on my ass, I let out a loud sigh of arousal. There's no sense in lying about it now. "Yes."

Luca's eyes darken. "Seriously?"

"Yes?" I respond uncertainly.

"I figured you'd lie," Luca says with a laugh.

"I'm a horrid liar. I'd much rather be honest," I admit. Luca's lips find my forehead, where he kisses me tenderly.

"Kinda loving that about you, Han. But I don't think I'm going to be able to focus on cooking now, knowing you're right here, like a present I need to unwrap," he says against my skin.

"I'm not that hungry," I blurt out, causing Luca to throw back his head with a bark of laughter.

"No?" he asks.

"Are you?" I respond.

"Just for you," he answers. His lips find mine again as he picks me up, my legs wrapping around his waist. I'm glad the dress I wore today is an A-line, so I can still get as close to him as possible.

"Bedroom," I mumble against his mouth. "Now."

"Yes ma'am," he responds. Luca walks toward the bedroom, his lips never leaving mine. I expect him to drop me on the bed, but he sets me on a dresser instead. The height of the dresser makes us almost eye level. Luca tucks a piece of hair behind my ear, dragging his finger down my neck and into the valley between my breasts.

"Baby, I don't have a condom, but *fuck*, I want to see what you're wearing under this ..."

"I, uh, I have some condoms," I whisper, suddenly shy and self-conscious. The badass bitch from earlier has left the building.

"You have condoms?" Luca asks, one eyebrow cocked as he waits for me to answer.

"I picked up a box today," I confess, and I feel Luca let out a relieved breath.

"Thank fuck," he says, leaning his head against my shoulder. "I should have gotten some. But I didn't want you to think I expected this — anything — tonight."

"It's — it's been a while for me, Luca. You don't have anything to worry about with me ..." I trail off, realizing I'm insinuating I have to worry about him. He sighs against my skin.

"I haven't slept with anyone since well before we met," he whispers.

"Really?"

"Really. And the team tests us routinely. I just got tested a few weeks ago. All clean," Luca says.

"I just assumed — I mean, the night we met there were all those girls ..."

"I know. Nothing happened with them. I'm not even sure why I brought them back to my place. I've been miserable for a while now. I think, maybe, I've been waiting for you," he says quietly.

Oh my.

"Do you remember telling me that you don't share?" I blurt out.

Luca chuckles. "Yeah?"

"Neither do I."

"I'm cool with that, Pix. I want you, and only you. Sound good?"

"Yes please," I sigh as I pull his mouth to mine. I'm about to tell him to pull me off the dresser, but Luca reads my mind and yanks me back into his arms, letting me slide down his body. He steps away from me and stares down at me.

"Take off your dress, Pixie. Slowly," he commands, his voice seemingly deeper and huskier than just a moment ago. My dress has a series of buttons down the front, and my fingers shake as I slowly unbutton them, one by one. Luca's eyes are hooded as he watches, his breathing labored. "Show me your bra."

I pull the dress apart, letting him see just a hint of the white lace bra. He groans and closes his eyes momentarily, before adjusting himself in his pants.

"Take off your shirt," I whisper as I continue to unbutton my dress.

"Take —" Luca's voice cracks, and he clears his throat before continuing, "take off the dress. Now, Pixie. I need to see you."

While he yanks off his own shirt, showing me the most amazing set of pecs I've ever seen and what appears to be miles of bronze skin, I let my dress fall to the floor. I'm left in a bra, garter belt, stockings, and stilettos.

"Jesus Christ, Hannah," Luca growls. "Holy shit you're so fucking hot. Get over here."

I don't even get a chance to move before Luca grabs me and crashes our lips together in a brutal and erotic kiss. I gasp into his mouth as his hands find my bare ass, and he groans as he gently kneads it. As the kiss really gets going, I'm unceremoniously tossed onto the bed.

"I need to taste you, right fucking now. And don't even think about taking off those heels. I want to feel them in my back," Luca snarls as he yanks me to the edge of the bed, drops to the floor, and buries his head in between my legs. He's a mess of lips, tongue, and teeth as he maniacally attacks my pussy. Licking from my asshole to my clit, he leaves no inch of skin untouched. "Eyes open, *bella*. Watch me. Watch me eat you."

I open my eyes and lift my head, propping my elbows on the bed to see Luca's eyes the darkest I've ever seen them. I feel him penetrate my opening with one finger, slowly crooking it upward until he finds my G-spot, and I moan loudly. "I knew you'd be good at this."

"You thought about this?" he says against me as he takes my clit in between his teeth and nibbles.

"God, yes. Dreamed about it," I say breathlessly. "Fuck, Luca, I knew it would be so good ..."

"What did you dream about? Tell me, Pixie," he says gutturally as he slides a second finger inside.

"I knew you'd be good with your tongue. I dreamed you'd wake me up like this every morning. Then, after you got me off a few times, you'd take me to a different place in the apartment and fuck me. So hard. Always hard. Then we'd shower together. Sometimes a bath. Fuck, so good, don't stop," I whimper.

"A bath? Like when you got yourself off when I could hear you?" he whispers against me, his fingers picking up the pace as he adds a third finger.

"Yes. God, that was hot. Luca I'm so close."

"I know, baby. Come for me," he says, latching around my clit and sucking hard. My entire body stiffens, a wave of euphoria coasting over my skin as pleasure surges through my veins. I can't breathe, the feeling is so intense, until the wave crashes, and I shake harshly through the orgasm.

"Holy shit," I gasp, as his fingers don't slow. Luca circles his tongue around my clit as my body slowly returns to normal, then quickens his pace again.

"Another," he growls as my back arches and I scream. White spots dot my vision as I struggle to catch my breath. "I need to be inside you, Pixie. Where are the condoms?"

I mumble something incoherent and point in the direction of the drawer they're stashed in. My body feels liquified as I vaguely register Luca opening the box and ripping open a condom wrapper.

"You okay, Pix?" he chuckles.

"Uh-huh," I murmur. I feel Luca slide his arms around my waist, picking me up and sliding me toward the center of the bed. "Can't have you on the edge for this. I need room to work."

"Room to work?" I ask, giggling.

"Yeah, baby. Gonna ruin you for any other man now, okay?"

"Oh. Okay," I tease, my eyes still closed in the post-orgasm haze. Ruin me. Okay. Sex is enjoyable, but it's not *that* good ...

Luca holds one of my legs at a ninety degree angle and pushes into me hard. So hard that I scream. Should have kept my damn eyes open so I saw the beer can coming at me, apparently. My entire body locks up at the intrusion.

"Relax, Pix. You said you wanted it hard. Fuck, I'm sorry. I should have waited, got you wetter. Shit," Luca says. He starts to pull out, and I'm so afraid he'll leave that I wrap my legs around him and dig my heels into his back.

"No!" I shout. "Don't leave."

"I wasn't going to leave. I was going to give you a minute ... Jesus, Hannah, you squeezing me like that ... fuck. You feel so fucking good ..." Luca trails off as he groans when I shimmy my hips slightly. The pain from before has morphed into a blissful line flirting from pain to pleasure.

"Luca, move. I need you to move," I whimper. Luca's hips shift, just an inch, but enough to hit places inside me that have never been hit before. "God, yes! Please!"

Luca moves more, finding a groove as his groin pushes against mine. Each time he bottoms out, he hits my sensitive clit, sending a zing of exquisite bliss into my bloodstream. His hands slide up my arms until our fingers are intertwined, and he lifts his head to look at me. "Open your eyes, Pix. I need your eyes."

When our eyes meet, everything fades away, except for this beautiful man. The connection I feel to Luca is unlike anything I've experienced before. It's physical, yes, but I feel like our souls are connected. Like we were always meant to meet.

"Luca," I whisper, emotion clogging my throat as tears fill my eyes.

"I know. I feel it too, Hannah," he replies. His pace speeds up, his thrusts shorter and less measured, as he gets closer to his orgasm. "Don't close your eyes. Okay, baby? I want you to watch me come."

"Okay, baby," I reply, and he groans as he viciously hammers into me. I come again, a rarity I can count on one hand happening in my entire adult life, considering I've only ever given myself multiples a couple of times, and my orgasm triggers his. He shouts as his cock spasms inside me.

"Holy shit," he gasps as he collapses on top of me. "Who'd have thought you calling me baby would make me come so hard?"

"That's what did it?" I ask, stroking his back slowly as I try to catch my breath. "No one has ever called you baby before?"

"Full disclosure? Yes. But not like you. Not like this. With you, it's different. With you, it means more. So much more," he says as he leans up to kiss my lips tenderly.

Well, Luca was right about one thing. He definitely did ruin me for any other man.

Chapter 14

*L*uca

One of the nice things about hockey is the fact that teams typically have overnight flights. Coaches like to have us fly out right after our games, so we can sleep in the next city, and wake refreshed.

So explain to me why the fuck *our* coach *loves* to have us on morning flights. And I'm not talking about a flight after sunrise, where we'd have time to grab breakfast. No. I'm referring to flights that are so early, so ridiculous, that nothing is open. No one is on the roads.

If only there were ways to fine coaches for this kind of bullshit.

The Wolves ownership has a team plane. A plane that can fly any damn time of the day. So why are we flying at the crack of dawn? Who the fuck knows. The owners are, for lack of a better term, granola. Many people in Colorado are, especially in Boulder, where the owners live. I can only assume they probably make us fly this fucking early because there's less fuel burned into the atmosphere, or some shit like that.

I don't care how we fly, in all honesty. I go to sleep as soon as my head hits the headrest. I'm one of those people who can sleep anywhere. The loud hum of the flight lulls me right to sleep.

It's the getting up at the ass crack of dawn I could do without.

And leaving a naked, voluptuous Hannah in her bed so I could get packed into an airplane with a bunch of smelly guys? Not my idea of a good time. Especially after our night.

I don't miss the smirk Coach Davenport throws my way. Yeah, asshole. I know you're onto us. He's feeling way too victorious about separating us. I don't even know how he did it. He doesn't have any say with the social media team. I don't even know if he has pull with the GM. All I know is Hannah was supposed to be on this trip with us. Now she's not, and he's looking way too happy about it.

"Hey Santzy, why didn't you come out with us last night? Been a while since you've partied with us," a voice says as he sits next to me. I open my eyes to see Ryan McNichols, the goaltending coach, looking at me intently.

"The fuck you doing back here? You highfalutin coaches stick in first class," I tease him. Ryan used to play with me. He was the unofficial captain my first two years here, and was hired on when he retired a few years back. Goalies can't be captains, due to the logistical nightmare that would provide in the heat of a game, but he was always a leader everyone looked up to. He's one of the few — actually the only — coaches I like on this team. I would like Davenport, but even this minute, he's glaring at me from first class. Impressive, honestly, considering I'm well past the exit rows and in a window seat.

"Just wanted to see how you are," Ryan says, before clearing his throat, and then lowers his voice. "You didn't hear this from me, man, but there's a witch-hunt out for you. Woodward and Davenport are determined to get you off the team."

"I know," I sigh. I've kept my nose clean. Absolutely no bad publicity at all. But nothing appeases Coach Woodward.

"I knew Woodward didn't like you, but what'd you do to piss off Davenport?"

"Fuck if I know." I'm certainly not telling Ryan about Hannah. It's not that I don't trust Ryan, but I know it's his job to report back to the coaches. If it's between him staying loyal to me or loyal to the team, I expect him to choose the latter.

Ryan clears his throat again, his voice dropping to a whisper. "I overheard him talking about his niece living next to you."

"Okay?"

"Is it true?"

"Yes, she lives next door to me. It's her aunt's apartment, but she's staying there currently."

"Davenport suggested there was something ... there," Ryan whispers, looking around nervously.

"Suggested."

"Yeah."

"Use your damn words, McNichols. What the fuck did he say?"

Ryan clears his throat again, his eyes darting around.

"I swear to all fuck, Ryan, you clear your throat one more fucking time ..."

"He said he saw chemistry and assumed you were fucking her," he blurts out. "Say it ain't true, Santzy. I know you like getting your dick wet, but the coach's niece? You're really fucking with your career if that's the case."

Last night, when Hannah told me she was a bad liar, it made me think about the fact that I'm a good liar. Granted, I don't go around lying just for the sake of lying, but I know when needed, I can get away with quite a bit. So, I put on my Lying Luca hat, look Ryan straight in the eyes, and lie. "Not true, Man. Hannah's gorgeous, but she's not my type. Way too uptight for my taste. And I wouldn't fuck up my chances with the team like that."

Ryan audibly sighs, his posture dramatically changing as he relaxes in the seat. "Thank fuck. I was freaked I'd have to go back up there and tell them ..."

"Tell them what?" I say sharply. Ryan's face pales.

"Fuck, I wasn't supposed to tell you that. Shit, I'm sorry. Lowest guy on the totem pole here, Santzy. They made me come back here.

I'm sorry," he mumbles before launching out of the seat and charging back into first class.

I'm clenching my fists so tightly, I'm surprised my fingernails don't puncture straight through the skin of my palms. I'm fucking furious. I take a deep breath, hoping my face doesn't show how pissed I am. I refuse to look up, knowing Davenport is still watching me. Instead, I pull out my phone and fire off two texts, first to Hannah, and second to my agent.

> Me: Hey Pix, it was torture leaving you this morning. Let me know your schedule this week so we can figure out some times to talk. FYI: your uncle is definitely on to us. He just sent another coach back to ask if anything had happened between us. I lied. We'll tell him when we're ready, okay? But you might want to make sure my name isn't in your phone. Also, I left one of my keys on the counter for you, in case you want to sneak in and steal any of my clothes to sleep in. Missing you already. (Heart emoji)

Next, I text my agent.

> Me: What's your availability to talk about some concerns I have this week? I have a unique situation that may impact my time here, so I'd like to know what my options are.

Max responds immediately. I swear the man never sleeps.

> Max: What did you do.

> Me: Nothing that will require a press release.

> Max: Luca ...

> Me: Remember me telling you about Caroline's niece next door?

Max: I FUCKING TOLD YOU NOT TO

Me: Would it help if I told you it's not just sex with her? She's different, Max. There's something about her, man. She's worth it.

Max: Does Davenport know?

Me: I think so.

Max: What the fuck does that mean? And where are you, anyway? I thought you were flying out this morning?

Me: Delayed for fog.

Max: Answer the question about Davenport.

Me: I think he suspects. He doesn't know for sure, but he's doing everything possible to keep us apart. She was supposed to travel with us for this trip, and then suddenly, she's pulled off the trip. And he looked a little too pleased with himself when I saw him this morning.

Max: That's not exactly a good enough reason to assume anything.

Me: Then he and Woodward sent McNichols back here to question me about it. McNichols told me that Woodward and Davenport want me off the team.

Max: Jesus.

Max: You've got three options, I guess. One is you request a trade and get the fuck out of there before it gets bad. Another is you play it out and see what happens, but expect a trade at some point. And the last one is you just retire.

Me: Seriously? Nothing else? Trade, trade, or retire? Nothing keeps me here?

Max: You're fucking the AC's niece. You have a shitty track record with publicity. Your teammates are fine with you, or at least put up with you, but most of the coaches either don't like you much or straight up despise you. And the owners are apathetic at best, but might love to get rid of your contract and free up some money. So yeah, those are your three options.

Me: Should I even bother putting forth the effort right now? Doesn't seem like I've got anything going for me.

Max: Keep doing what you always do. Force their hand. They want to trade you, they're going to have to get a fucking beast of a trade if you're at the top of your game. Show them what they'd be missing. Prove them wrong, and prove me wrong. Prove that there's a fourth option: that they keep you.

Me: I'm starting to feel like it's not worth it.

Max: Maybe it's not. If it's not fun for you anymore, we'll get you out of there. You can decide if you want to take your talent elsewhere, or retire at the top of your game. You have the power here, Luca. Not them. Remember that.

"Sir? We're leaving. You need to turn your phone onto airplane mode," a voice pipes up next to me. I don't even acknowledge the voice other than to nod. I text Max telling him we're leaving, turn off my phone, slap on my headphones, and block out the world.

And dream about Hannah.

The only good thing about away trips is how fast the time goes. Yeah, there are periods of down time. But if I know Hannah can't talk, I keep busy. I've never worked out as much as I'm working out now. I'm sticking with whatever indoor facility I can access, whether that be the hotel gym or just running up and down stairs somewhere. That chick cornering me months ago in front of my building after a run is still at the forefront of my mind. And I'll be damned if I give the coaching staff more ammunition to trade me.

I'm noticing I'm getting less and less playing time in games. It's difficult to do when you play as a pair on defense, because you go on the ice together. At first, I was told it was to give the rookies on-ice experience. Now, however, they aren't giving any reasons. In fact, Coach Woodward looks at me and just waits to see if I say a word. They're baiting me, and I don't know what to do about it.

With only two games to go before we return home, we've arrived in Boston a night early, giving us a much needed night off. We're all exhausted. Regardless of playing time, a two-week road trip is as mentally exhausting as it is physical.

Typically, we share a room with someone from our line. This portion of the trip, I'm somehow lucky, and get a room all to myself. I'm looking forward to FaceTiming Hannah and being able to say anything I want without a teammate possibly listening in.

So when someone knocks on my door at just after eight in the evening, I curiously open the door.

"What the fuck?" I exclaim, as I stare at Hannah. "Holy shit. Get in here."

Hannah giggles as I grab her arm and yank her into my room. "Surprised?"

"Fuck yes, Pix. How did you get here? You flew? By yourself? Holy shit, baby, I can't believe you're here. Did anyone see you?"

"I flew by myself. I was determined, but free champagne in first class helped. And no one saw me. I have a ticket to tomorrow night's game. I'm way up in the rafters," she says as she wraps her arms around my neck.

"I was going to be home in two days, you know," I say softly as I lean down and nuzzle her neck.

"Too long," she sighs. "Way too long."

I trace my tongue up her neck and across her lips, dipping into her mouth to duel with hers. "God I've missed you. This is the best surprise ever."

Hannah gasps as I reach down to grab behind her thighs and pick her up, then toss us both onto the bed. "What time is morning skate?"

"It's not mandatory tomorrow. I don't have to report until noon."

"You're mine until noon? Really?" she whispers, a slow smile spreading across her face as her eyes sparkle.

"I'm yours," I respond, clearly leaving off the time. I'm hers, for as long as she'll keep me. This thing with Hannah ... it's different than I expected. She gives me a peace I didn't know I needed.

As I'm about to kiss her again, another knock on the door jars both of us.

"Who is that? Do they do room checks?" Hannah hisses, terror covering her face.

"No, they typically just call and ask where we are. Go hide in the bathroom," I whisper. I untuck my shirt to cover the obvious bulge in my sweats, and wait until Hannah is hidden in the bathroom before opening the door. A barely clad woman leans against the door frame.

"Hey, sexy," a woman says as she gives me bedroom eyes.

"Uh, you got the wrong room," I stammer.

"Luke Santo, right? I'm here for you," she says as she takes a step toward me.

"The fuck you are," I snarl. "I don't know you. Get the fuck away from my room."

The woman blinks at me. "You — you don't even have to do anything. Just let me make you feel good."

"No."

"Why not?"

"Because I have a girlfriend."

"So? Like that has stopped you before," she huffs.

"I've never had a girlfriend before, so it wasn't an issue. But now I do, and I won't fucking do that to her. You need to leave," I state.

"What's your girlfriend's name?" she asks. What an odd question.

"Why do you want to know?" I ask.

"It's just a question," she shrugs.

I stare at her, cocking my head to the side. "There are only two reasons you'd want to know her name. Either you're a reporter, or I've been set up by someone. Which one is it?"

I see the look of fear cover her face before she schools her expression. "Neither one. I just want to know her name."

"Tell me what your name is, darlin,' and I'll think about telling you what her name is."

She smiles, thinking I'm coming around. "My name is Michelle."

"Hi, Michelle," I say, giving her my best panty-melting smile. Her smile widens even more, as she inches closer to me. I know I've got her, and go in for the kill. "Alright, gorgeous. Tell me. Reporter or set up?"

"Set up," she answers, before gasping and covering her mouth with her hand. "I didn't mean that. Shit."

"Cool. You need to leave," I tell her, before closing the door in her face. Locking the door, I push open the bathroom door to find Hannah with her phone pointed toward me. She motions for me to be quiet as she pulls me into the bathroom. Pointing the phone toward the mirror, she closes the door.

"Luca, say the date and location," she whispers. I do as she asked, slightly confused. "Now summarize what just happened."

"Uh, some chick came to my door and said she was here for me, and finally admitted someone was setting me up," I whisper. She stops recording and slips her phone in her pocket.

"Do you know who would be setting you up?" she asks.

"I have my suspicions."

"Who?"

"Hannah, we don't have to do this ..." I trail off.

"Is my uncle one of the suspects?"

I sigh. "Yes. But I think it was most likely Woodward. He's had it out for me since the end of last season."

I rub the back of my neck before looking at Hannah. She's staring at me with a cute smile on her face. "What?"

"Am I your girlfriend?" she asks.

I chuckle. "Do you want to be my girlfriend, Pix?"

She nods. "I do."

"Can I be your boyfriend, then?"

"Yes, please," she says giddily. I lean down and softly kiss her. No matter what happens, as long as I have Hannah, I have faith everything will be okay.

Chapter 15

Hannah

I have no idea how Luca will play today, because we didn't sleep. At all. Honestly, I had every intention of just trying to sneak in a kiss somewhere during the day. I just wanted to see him. Watch him play. Be in the same building as him. Getting an entire night with him was much more than I expected. I never thought I'd miss him this much. And when he texted me that he had a hotel room to himself for the night, I knew it was kismet.

Because the team will leave directly from Boston's arena to head to New York for their final game of this away trip, Luca checks out of the hotel midafternoon. Since I traveled with just a backpack and no extra clothes, I'm thrilled when he gives me one of his T-shirts to wear. I find it extra special to wear something of his to his game tonight, knowing I can't wear his jersey. Not only because I can't be recognized, but also because the Boston fans are apparently quite brutal to visiting fans. I can't take any chances that I make the news. Uncle Bennett cannot find out about this trip. I'll tell him about my relationship with Luca on my own terms, and not because I'm forced into it.

Luca has afternoon requirements before he's planning on

napping at the hotel, so I take a tour of Boston. I've never been here, and I find I'm enjoying myself too much. I'm well off the beaten path, steering clear of the arena, in hopes I don't get spotted by any Wolves staff. After a phenomenal lunch at an Italian bistro, I found a local bookshop full of unique books, knickknacks, and Boston-centered paraphernalia. I get so invested in scouring the shelves, I miss a slew of texts from Denver. The terrible terrors are on the warpath. How dare I take a sick day and leave them to their own devices?

I sigh as I begin responding to various other staff requesting assistance with something Lindsay or Jessica messed up. Lord, they are awful. Just awful. Somehow a video of the two of them arguing about which player was the hottest was uploaded to the team's Instagram account. It only shows their feet, but I recognize their overpriced stilettos, and their vapid voices. A million views in an hour. I ignore a phone call from the GM, letting it go to voicemail, because I obviously can't answer it while on the streets of Boston. Everyone thinks I have a debilitating stomach bug. The GM's voice message is less than ideal. Evidently social media staff aren't allowed to take sick days. Ever.

Someone from the marketing department texts, letting me know one of the interns flooded the women's staff bathroom at the Sports Facility Zone and blamed it on the mascot. Yes, the mascot.

A different staff member texts to ask which of the interns may have been responsible for adjusting the thermostat to the arena, somehow making some of the ice melt. I responded and asked how the hell either one of them had access to the thermostat in the first place. Furthermore, what kind of setup are we rocking if one fucking thermostat controls a whole damn arena? Aren't there any other ways to cool the ice? The response I get is that the entire heating and cooling system is a gigantic computer program, and somehow, one of the interns guessed the password before jacking the temp of the building up to eighty degrees. Fortunately, it was caught before too much damage was done to the ice.

Knowing the men who run this organization, I'd bet on the password being wolves, stanley, chalice, or some other hockey related term. I'd also bet that one intern kept people away from the room where the computer is so the other intern could guess the password.

And finally, I get a text from Aunt Caroline. She's sorry to do this to me, but she's coming back from Europe a few months sooner than expected, and how soon can I clear out of her apartment?

Well, that's just lovely.

I treat myself to a rather indulgent early dinner near the arena, allowing myself to wallow in the misery of knowing I won't live next to Luca anymore. Not only that, but I have no prospects for apartments at all. I don't know what the hell I'm going to do.

After my third glass of cabernet, I whip out my phone and decide to tell my aunt exactly where she can fuck off to.

> Me: When are you coming back?

> Caroline: In a day or two.

> Me: I'm essentially subletting your apartment, which means I need more time to find a suitable alternative. I have nowhere to go, Aunt Caroline.

> Caroline: I'm sorry you feel that way. You can stay for a week or so after I return, but you'll need to find a place.

> Me: I understand that. You just dropped this bomb and expected me to be okay with it.

> Caroline: You're right. I didn't think about that. I'm sorry. It was a long night, and I'm exhausted.

> Me: I'll start looking for apartments this weekend.

> Caroline: Okay, Hannah. You'd love it here. I'm still in Italy. It's gorgeous.

Me: Maybe I'll make it there one day.

I toss my phone back in my backpack and sigh. My aunt lacks a sympathetic filter when speaking in person, and it's even worse via text. I should have given her the benefit of the doubt that she wouldn't boot me out of her apartment immediately. She does have *some* heart ... just not much.

I sneak into Boston's arena with only minutes to spare before the puck is dropped. I climb up to the very last row, so far up that the players look like little ants zipping around the ice, but the feeling is still electric. I spot Luca immediately, and he tilts his head up to look at my section, as if he knows I arrived.

The arena staff zoom a camera in on him, which allows me to see him rub across his sternum before placing two fingers on his lips. I lose the ability to breathe. Was that a sign for me?

Then the game starts, and I forget all about the possible signal from Luca. Holy moly, this game is so fast. I can barely keep track of the puck, but even way up in the rafters, I can feel the pulse of the crowd. The energy moves like ocean waves from right behind the glass and all the way up to me. I find myself forgetting to contain my enthusiasm for the visiting team, and after getting more than a few nasty looks from people around me, I sneak out at the beginning of the second period. I knew I wouldn't be able to stay the entire game, as my red-eye flight doesn't leave me much time to get to the airport and through security, but I stand at the bottom of the stairs to take one last long look at Luca. Again, it's as if he knows where I'm at, and his eyes meet mine.

And he rubs his sternum, right over his heart, while staring at me. As he nonchalantly rubs his lips immediately after, I gasp, and I see him smirk. I shake my head, chuckling, as I clutch my own hands to my chest in the shape of a heart, before waving quickly and turning away.

If I had waited five more seconds, I would have seen my uncle spot me.

*T*he following day, I'm back at work after my 'sick' day. I'm essentially a waste of space, sitting at my desk at the Sports Facility Zone, so exhausted I can't truly function, when the terrible terrors walk in gleefully.

"We have a list of things we'd like to run with," Lindsay says matter-of-factly.

"About what?" I ask as I cover my mouth in a very unladylike yawn.

"Social media games and trends we can try," Jessica answers.

Because I'm too tired to argue, I nod. "Alright. Let's have 'em."

They both stare at me. "Seriously?"

"Uh, yes?"

"Wow. You typically turn us down," Lindsay says.

"You caught me at a bad moment. Would you like me to tell you to get out of my office?"

"No!" they both shout.

"Then hop to it."

"Okay," Jessica says, clearing her throat, "we want to do the 'what's in the box' game with as many of the guys that will do it. We've seen some sports teams do it where all of the items were things that had to do with their sport, but we'd like to do the opposite. So instead of hockey items, it would be all things figure skaters use."

Huh. That actually might get some traction. "Okay, get me a list of items by the end of the week that we could use."

"Oh, wow. Okay. We can do that," Lindsay says.

"What's next?"

"Well, Lindsey and I did a deep dive into the team's social media channels, and we saw something totes ridic."

"What's that?" I ask.

"No one ever posts live play-by-plays."

"Yes, I do. I always post the goals, penalties, and any fights," I defend.

"No, we mean like every little detail. Which players are out there. Who isn't doing well. It would be like a live broadcast in written form," Jessica explains.

"What are you suggesting?" I ask.

"Hire someone to live-tweet the games. It wouldn't even have to be someone who travels with the team. Just someone who has access to all of the games. And definitely not on the main Wolves accounts. Make secondary accounts that are just for live events. Not us, though," Jessica says.

"Why not you?" I ask, intrigued.

Lindsay giggles. "Oh, um, we don't really understand hockey."

I laugh. "That's valid. I didn't either, when I took the job."

"Really? Why did you take the job then? If you don't mind me asking," Jessica says.

"My experience up until this point was with social media for a college football team. I wanted a new experience, and wanted to get out of Georgia. When this position opened up, I was all too thrilled to apply."

Jessica and Lindsay look at each other, as if having a silent conversation. "So, um, it wasn't to get closer to the players?"

"No," I laugh, "not at all. I was around tons of players in Georgia, but definitely never dated one. My boyfriend back home was in finance."

"Are you still dating him?" Lindsay asks.

"No."

"Why'd you break up?" she presses.

I sigh. "I'd rather not get into that, ladies. Like I said, I wanted to get out of Georgia. He was one of the reasons. Suffice it to say, I realized he wasn't a very nice guy."

Lindsay chews on her lip. "Well, um, some guy asked about you at the front desk while I was walking in. I thought he had an accent like yours. Very preppy looking. Definitely out of place here."

I can feel my pulse skyrocket. "What color hair?"

"Blonde. Like super blonde."

Shit. That's Jefferson.

I immediately turn off my computer and stand up. "Listen, girls, I know we haven't always been on the same page. But I could really use your help right now. My ex ... he's not a good guy. I don't want to see him. I need to get out of here."

Jessica jumps up. "We got you, girl. Hang tight."

She and Lindsay run out of my office as I bag my belongings, before they return with one of the security guards, Hank.

"Ms. Beauregard, I hear we possibly have a situation with an ex-boyfriend. May I escort you to your car?" he says politely.

"Yes, Hank, that would be wonderful."

"Are you familiar with the employee-only tunnels to the back parking lot? I assume that is where you're parked," Hank says.

"Yes, I am parked back there. I didn't know there was another option for getting to the parking lot."

"I don't suggest it if you're walking by yourself, as you'd be stuck if someone snuck in and waited. But it's nice when the weather isn't cooperating," he tells me. He leads me to a back staircase, then down to a long hallway that parallels the rink. We walk quietly to the door, before he stops me. "What does your ex-boyfriend look like? I'll see if he's anywhere in the lot."

"A little shorter than you. Blonde hair. Skinny."

Hank steps out into the lot, scopes the perimeter, and motions for me to follow. "I'll walk you directly to your car. If he approaches, I'll detain him so you can leave. Go straight home. You're staying in your aunt's apartment, right? Tell whoever is working the lobby about him. Maybe even get them a picture. If he came all this way, he's not likely to settle on going back home, Ms. Beauregard."

I was afraid of that. Jefferson and I didn't break up on good terms. In fact, he completely lost his cool. He threatened all kinds of things, including sexual assault, if I didn't stay with him. He seemed to have forgotten the entire reason I broke it off with him was because he tried to rape me. I only managed to get away because he was incredibly drunk and couldn't fully get an erection. He lashed out, slapping me across the face hard, before he fell off the bed and knocked himself out. I had my locks changed while he was at work the following day, and began actively searching for jobs immediately.

Like I told the terrible terrors: Jefferson isn't a good guy. Just another Southern guy who grew up wealthy and assumed he could get whatever he wanted whenever he wanted, regardless of how he needed to get it.

Considering my father introduced me to Jefferson, and both of my parents were horrified when I explained why I had broken up with him, just shows how out of touch my parents truly are. They saw nothing wrong with him trying to rape me because his family has connections. That's more important than morality and being a decent human being.

The only way Jefferson found out I was here is probably because of my mother. She's really the only person who knows where I am. My father couldn't be bothered, and when I left Georgia, I ceased to exist to him. I highly doubt my uncle would have done this, even with his assumptions about Luca, because he knew how desperately I wanted out of Georgia. He didn't know everything, but I inferred enough for him to understand I was willing to move to Colorado without a job if need be.

As I thank Hank for walking me to my car, I quickly exit the parking lot and fly into downtown as quickly as possible. I'm thankful the underground resident parking lot is gated, but I still hustle up to the lobby so I can speak to the security staff there. They assure me that they'll keep an eye out.

Once safely in the comfort of my aunt's apartment, I'm all too aware of Luca being gone. God, I wish he were here tonight. He'd make me feel safe. Checking the time, I know his game has already started in New York.

After eating a bowl of cereal directly over the sink like a savage, I send Luca a quick text telling him I miss him, and then head to bed. I'm running on only a few hours of sleep over the past few days, and I'm horribly exhausted. I'll tell Luca tomorrow about Jefferson.

If only I knew things would never be the same after today.

Chapter 16

Hannah

The following day at work, I'm a bundle of nervous energy. Not only am I keyed up knowing my ex-boyfriend is possibly roaming around Denver, but Luca got home sometime overnight. I had early morning meetings and commitments, so we had decided while in Boston that he'd get a few hours of sleep in his apartment before I would try to sneak home during my lunch break to see him. Not even two full days apart, and I'm acting like he's coming home from war.

Just as I'm about to leave, I get a text from my aunt letting me know she's arrived back at her apartment, a full ten days early. Lovely. Then, to make matters worse, she tells me she's hoping I can find another place to stay within the week, because a friend of hers is coming for a visit.

Then, my uncle pops his head in my office. "You got a sec, Han?"

"No, I was just about to run back to Caroline's. She's back, did you know that?" I ask as I'm rummaging through my purse.

"Oh, no. I didn't know that. That's pretty early, isn't it? I thought she was staying for six months?" he asks.

"I don't know. She texted me yesterday to say she'd be coming back early, but then just texted to tell me she's in her apartment. I thought I had a couple more weeks to find a place."

"She's kicking you out?"

"Evidently."

"You know Caroline. Her ability to recognize when she's not being the most tactful person is paper thin."

I sigh. "I'm aware. What do you need, Uncle Bennett?"

"Uh, need you to come for a quick meeting in my office, actually," he says sheepishly, his neck reddening as he absentmindedly scratches at his chin. A sudden pit in my stomach tells me this isn't going to be a quick meeting, nor will it be enjoyable for me.

"Okay," I say quietly as I trail behind my uncle back to his office.

When I step through the doorway, I know it's bad news. Not only is Coach Woodward in attendance, but so is the GM.

"Take a seat, Ms. Beauregard," the GM says. I sit, interlocking my fingers tightly as I wait for whatever bomb to drop. What player did something awful? Who needs a social media cleanup? Or worse: what did my interns, the terrible terrors, manage to mess up this time?

I had no idea just how bad it could be, until I see Coach Woodward smile at me. The smile is full of malicious intent, and I know.

They know.

They know about me and Luca.

"Picked the wrong player to fuck around with, Ms. Beauregard," Woodward says with a creepy chuckle.

"Excuse me?" I say sharply.

"Santo. You could have fucked any of them. They'd all have been willing. A Georgia peach like you with that tight ass? All of them would have done it. But no, you had to go for Santzy. The one fucking troublemaker on the team. But, honestly, I'd like to thank you. I've been waiting for a reason to kick his miserable ass off the team, and I just got it," Woodward sneers.

My uncle's head swivels toward Woodward. "That was not what we agreed upon, Coach."

"I don't fucking care what you think you agreed to, Davenport. This is my team. That piece of shit needs to go," Woodward shouts.

The GM steps forward. "Coach, this isn't the time nor the place. Explain to Ms. Beauregard why she's here."

Coach Woodward grins, a leering smile that highlights his sinister eyes. "You're going to set Santo up, my dear."

"I will do no such thing!" I shout. My entire body shakes as I stare at these three men. The GM looks back at me with a stoic expression. My uncle won't meet my stare, and Coach Woodward looks on victoriously.

"If you want to keep your job, Ms. Beauregard, you will. If you want to have any job in any sport in this state, you'll do exactly as I tell you to," he snarls.

"This is absurd! There's nothing in the employee handbook that says we can't date. I looked. Why are we being punished?" I cry. "And why do you hate him so much?"

Woodward glowers at me. "Not your concern. He's a bad seed, and he'll take the entire team down with him. His contract was up at the end of the year anyway. You just managed to speed up my plans."

I look at the GM, who stares back at me. "How can you do this? How is this even legal? Are you seriously asking me to set him up?"

I see the GM's expression falter for a quick second as he glances at Woodward, and I know Woodward must have something on the GM. There's no way any of this is legal. If the NHL found out about any of this, all of them would be out of job. But why is my uncle here?

Before I can open my mouth to question him, Woodward speaks up. "Your uncle knows why he's here. If he can't keep you in line, he's out of a job too."

"Too?"

"Yes, Ms. Beauregard. If you don't do exactly as I say, you're fired. And if Santo gets even the slightest hint that any of this is going on, I'll bury both of you," Woodward says gleefully. He steps toward the door, stopping next to me and placing his hand on my shoulder. He leans down so his mouth is next to my ear. "Did you enjoy your

Boston visit, my dear? I certainly enjoyed the video I got from Santo's room. You are quite ... bendy. I'm sure your family would love to see the video if it accidentally goes viral across social media, should you choose to go against me."

His fingers slip dangerously low on my collarbone as he squeezes my shoulder tightly. A wave of nausea overtakes me as he and the GM walk out of my uncle's office.

"I'm sorry, Hannah," my uncle says hoarsely.

"Why did you let them do that?" I whisper, angry tears collecting in my eyes.

"He told me what he'd do if I didn't help him."

"Oh, really. And what was that?" I ask as I swipe the tears from my cheeks.

Uncle Bennett sighs. "He told me he has a video of the two of you, Han. I can't let that get out there. It would ruin you. I saw you in Boston. I knew you were there. I just didn't realize Woodward would set Luca up like that, and you'd be caught in the crossfires."

"You knew I was there?"

"I saw you at the game. I think you were leaving, maybe to come back here?"

"I did leave. At the start of the second period," I murmur. "No one knew I was going to Boston. How did Woodward know? Luca didn't even know until I knocked on his door."

"He had the cameras set up to see if he could get any videos of Luca. I guess he figured he'd leak anything, if anyone came to the room with Santo. Then you showed up, and Woodward realized he could use you to his advantage."

Great. If I hadn't gone to Boston, none of this would be happening.

"How did you know which room was Luca's?" my uncle suddenly asks.

"We were texting. He told me he had gotten the only single room for that game, so I looked up the hotel records," I explain.

"You aren't supposed to have access to that, Hannah. How'd you manage that?" he asks.

"Not revealing my sources. I won't throw anyone else under the bus. No one else might lose their job because of me today," I say stiffly.

"I wonder if somehow Woodward found out that you accessed the records? Him just conveniently hiding a camera in Santo's room is so coincidental."

"Luca told me about the single room *before* I accessed the records, though."

"Fuck, that's true. This all just doesn't make sense."

I look at my uncle, noticing his discomfort. "What else are you gaining here?"

His eyes widen. "Nothing. I swear. Woodward knows family is my weak spot. And he suggested he'd start firing tons of staff here too ..."

My brow furrows in confusion as I let his words marinate, until I remember a brief moment at the beginning of the season. A moment I haven't asked Uncle Bennett about.

"Did he threaten to fire that physical therapist? Elsie?" I ask. My uncle's expression changes for a split second. "Ah. Now I understand. Are you two together?"

"No. She's a sweet girl, but no. I'm not — I'm just ... not. She can get better than me. Someone her own age. I'm a dinosaur," he says with a brittle laugh.

"You aren't a dinosaur. How old is she again?"

"Twenty-five."

"Uh-huh." I can tell my uncle is stuck on the age gap between them, but I think it's nothing big. Age is just a number. If their souls are connected, it doesn't matter what decade she was born in.

"It's irrelevant. What can I do to help you right now? I don't know exactly what Woodward is going to make you do, Han. He really has it out for Santo."

"Do you know why?" I ask.

"Nothing for certain, but I've heard rumors."

"Of what?"

Uncle Bennett looks directly at me. "The rumor is that Luca slept with Woodward's wife."

I stare at him incredulously. "I find that incredibly hard to believe. Luca is a lot of things, but he wouldn't consciously sleep with his coach's wife."

"I'm just saying what the rumor is, Han."

"But you believe it."

"I never said —"

"I know you, Uncle Bennett. You believe the rumor. You told me on my first day to steer clear of Luca. You believe everything you've heard about him. I get it. He's made some shitty decisions in the past. I met him during one, believe it or not. But the Luca I know is caring and thoughtful. Sensitive. A family man. I bet he didn't know she was Woodward's wife, or he only found out afterward, or it never happened in the first place."

"Is he worth it, Hannah?" Uncle Bennett blurts out forcefully. "Is he worth losing your job over? Having a vile video leaked, destroying both of your careers? Are you okay if our family sees it? Take a moment and think about this. This is your life we're talking about."

"Who's to say Woodward won't release it anyway? And frankly, Uncle Bennett, who's to say he won't keep dangling it over my head to get me to do all kinds of things? Again I ask: is this legal? Can we go to the NHL? Doesn't the team have an attorney? This can't be okay!"

Uncle Bennett rubs his eyes as he sits on the edge of his desk. "I don't know, Han. I'm trying to protect you, but I don't know what to do here. Who is involved? Who is also in Woodward's pocket? If he'll blackmail us, he'll blackmail anyone."

I stand, walking over to my uncle, and give him a hug. "I know. I'm going to go see Aunt Caroline. Is it okay if I take the afternoon off?"

"Sure, sweetheart."

I lean in to my uncle's ear. "I'll text you later. Your office might be bugged."

Uncle Bennett's arms stiffen around me. "You think?"

"I don't know. Better safe than sorry," I whisper. I pat him on the back before stepping away and raising my voice slightly. "I need time to think about this. Please tell Coach Woodward he'll have my answer in the next two days."

As Uncle Bennett nods, I hold my head high and quickly walk back to my office. Upon arriving, I find a huge bouquet of flowers. My heart constricts as I think about Luca and everything I've learned over the past hour. Finding the card, I pull it open and gasp.

Roses are red,
Violets are blue,
You thought you escaped me,
But I just found you.
-J

As if I didn't have enough to deal with, now I have an abusive ex to throw in the mix. Fantastic.

What am I supposed to do? Should I go to the NHL myself? Will Uncle Bennett really lose his job? Will he ever forgive me if that happens? What about Luca? Will he still want me if he's humiliated by any video being released? I still have the video of the woman coming to his hotel door. Can I release that to counteract our possible video? Woodward could be lying about everything.

I'm second-guessing my gut instincts. It takes me back to telling my parents about Jefferson threatening to rape me, and the constant gaslighting he did whenever I expressed a desire to end our relationship. My parents blew me off every time. When he did hit me, my father asked what I had done to deserve it. Because, to them, Jefferson was well within his rights to assault me had I done virtually anything that could be deemed a disgrace.

If this goes public, who is here to support me? Would Aunt Caroline be there for me? What about Arianna and her friends? They've become my friends, but surely they'd support Luca if it came down to picking.

Luca.

Anything I do reflects on him. If a video is released, I don't know if he'd keep his position with the team. That publicity could hinder him getting picked up from another team. Luca and Arianna have both talked about their family and how close-knit they are. Would a public scandal like this affect them? My parents would be absolutely horrified. It would be my fault that someone planted a camera in Luca's hotel room. They would be the laughingstock of their country club, and that is simply unacceptable. Do better, Hannah Ann. Do better.

I don't know what to do. How to protect those that I care about. How I'm supposed to move forward now.

When I arrive back at my aunt's apartment, she's left a note for me that she's out for the evening. She also conveniently left me a pile of realtor cards. Seeing as my aunt is a realtor, the fact that she's trying to push me to work with someone else is concerning. We've never had a close relationship, but that still stings.

As I enter the guest room, I can hear muted music playing through the walls. Luca is there. Right there. So close, yet so far away. I know I can't go over there right now. He'll see right through my faux bravado. I won't be able to lie about anything. And I need time to think. To figure out if there's anything I can do. How to protect myself and Luca.

I whip out my phone and text the only person I can think of. Well, the only group I can think of.

Me: Y'all, I need help.

Claire: What's going on?

Arianna: Who do we need to murder? Wait. If it's my brother, I'd prefer to not be involved. I don't want to explain being an accessory to my entire family.

Natalie: You don't want to explain being an accessory to his murder, but you'd be fine explaining the murder?

Arianna: Well, yeah. Hannah's a level-headed gal. I doubt she'd want to murder him unless it was justifiable.

Me: Not wanting to murder your brother.

Arianna: See? We're good. Who are we murdering though?

Natalie: Can we maybe not murder anyone?

Arianna: WAIT! I need to add someone to this chat. Remember me telling you guys about my almost-cousin, Kate? She'll totally be on board with murder.

Arianna Santa adds Kate Reynolds to the chat

Kate: Hi, ladies! Who are we murdering?

Claire: Oh Lord. The almost-cousin is cool with murder.

Natalie: Hi, Kate. Claire and I are normal. Jury is still out on Hannah, since she's also new to our chat. But if you're friends with Ari, you must be nuts.

Kate: Yeah, kinda. So, who are we murdering?

Me: Lord almighty. WE AREN'T MURDERING ANYONE.

153

Arianna: I'm weirdly bummed.

Claire: Honestly? Me too.

Me: I need a place to stay. And maybe a job.

Arianna: Um, your boyfriend lives RIGHT THERE, and I'm pretty sure you already work with him, so what's going on?

Me: Listen. This stays in the chat. Luca can't even know, okay?

Kate: Ooooh, the boyfriend is Luca? No way! He's a hottie.

Kate: Since I know how a girls mind works, no, nothing has ever happened with Luca. He's my almost-cousin too, and I've only met him a handful of times.

I let out a relieved breath. I know Luca has a past. I get it. I can't be jealous over what he did before he met me. But I definitely don't want to be forced to chat with a past conquest.

Arianna: If you need a job, are you quitting? What happened? I thought you liked the job.

Me: I did. I do. I can't go into details right now. Some shit is going on, and I don't think I can stay in the job anymore. And my aunt came home from Europe early, so I need to get my own place. But I can't really do that if I don't have a job, so ...

Claire: My roommate just moved out. As long as you bring a mattress, you can stay with me. I'm way on the west side of town, though.

Me: I don't care where it is, since I doubt I'll be driving into downtown much now.

Arianna: Seriously, are you dumping my brother?

Me: It's complicated.

Arianna: That's bullshit, Hannah. He's crazy about you. What the hell is happening?!?!

Me: Nothing I'm doing is by choice, Arianna. I'm not the one pulling the puppet strings. I'm trying to protect him. Please, just let it go. Give me some time to figure things out.

A separate text comes in from Claire.

Claire: When do you need to move out?

Me: As soon as possible. My aunt showed up today. She wasn't supposed to be home for a few more months, then texted me earlier and said she would be back in a week. Obviously not. She wants me out quickly because she has a friend coming to visit.

Claire: Well, that's rude as fuck.

Me: I know. She doesn't really have the best scope of social expectations. I've never been that close to her, and I'm honestly surprised she even let me stay in her apartment this long.

Claire: You're more than welcome to come over today, but you'll have to sleep on the couch until you can get a mattress. My old roommate did leave a dresser, though, and the room has its own ensuite. We can discuss finances once you figure out your job situation.

Me: Thanks girl. I really appreciate it.

Claire: You know Ari isn't going to drop this, right? She's wicked territorial over Luca.

Me: I know. I just need some time to figure out what the hell is going on, and how I can protect everyone.

Claire: I don't know if you need help from the law, but my sister is a detective with Aurora PD. We can call her when you get here this afternoon.

Me: I think that would be a good idea. But please don't tell Arianna yet. I know she'll go right back to Luca, and I want to protect him as much as I can.

Claire: So he's involved? It impacts his career?

Me: Yes.

Claire. Alright, girl. Text me when you're heading over.

As I begin to pack my belongings, someone knocks on the door.

"Pixie? You home?" Luca calls.

I cover my mouth with my hand as a sob slips through. I desperately want to throw open the door and launch into his arms, but I can't. If he finds out what Coach Woodward is planning, he'll lose it. Lord knows Woodward is probably assuming I'll tell Luca everything, and he's waiting for Luca to attack.

The less Luca knows, the better.

I just hope I can keep everyone happy and safe.

Chapter 17

*L*uca

***

*S*omething is off.

I haven't heard from Hannah all day, which can be normal because of how busy she gets with work, but I feel it in my bones that something is wrong. She said she'd try to sneak home at lunch for an hour, but I never heard from her. I don't know what, but I have a weight sitting in my stomach telling me that something happened.

"Pixie? You home?" I call as I knock on the door.

No answer.

The problem is, I'm almost positive she's home.

I also know her aunt showed back up today.

Caroline Davenport is an odd bird. More than once, she's flirted with me. Her attempts at flirting are awful, but I recognized the attempt. Then she'd turn around and speak to me like I was the hired help. Other times, she'd be formal, as if we were work acquaintances who did the occasional happy hour function.

So when I saw Caroline as I arrived home early this morning, I figured Hannah would be kicked out fairly quickly. They're just so *different*. There's no way they could share a space peacefully. I intended to offer up one of my spare bedrooms to Hannah. Which meant she'd have somewhere to stash her things, and she'd be with me in my room. Because that's where she's supposed to be.

But I can't ask her, if she won't open the fucking door.

Why won't she open the door?

"Pixie," I say quietly, leaning my forehead against the door. "I know you're in there. I saw your aunt. Tell me what's wrong, *bella*. Let me in."

I swear I hear a gasp, or a small sob, but then I second-guess my hearing. Maybe she's not home. As I'm about to knock again, my cell buzzes with a text.

> Arianna: Emergency brother meeting needed asap.

> Me: Family or sister related?

> Arianna: Luca related. Come to my place, please. And bring food.

> Me: Can this wait?

> Arianna: What part of emergency don't you understand, big brother? EMERGENCY. Also it's equally an emergency that I'm hungry.

> Me: Hangry Ari is a mean bitch.

> Arianna: I know. Better get here quick.

Stuffing my phone back in my pocket, I try once more to get Hannah to open her door. "I gotta go to my sister's, baby. We'll talk later. Work through whatever you're working through, and then talk to me. Okay? I miss you."

I lock my door before getting on the elevator and heading down to the parking garage. As I suspected, Hannah's car is in the garage. I know she's there. I just don't know why she wouldn't answer the door.

As I drive to Arianna's place, I wrack my brain about what may have happened during the last couple of days. Hannah seemed fine when I saw her at the game in Boston. We texted the next morning as normal. But then it was radio silence. That's not completely atypical, as I know she can get extremely busy at work, but I have a nagging suspicion that something is wrong. Something happened.

Arianna lives about thirty-five minutes from me. She's almost halfway between downtown Denver and Eternity Springs. She absolutely loves her job, managing the spa and hot springs at my family's hotel, but she hates how small and quaint Eternity Springs is. She wants the nightlife and excitement of city living. Renting a place on the far west side of Denver allows her to get the best of both worlds.

As I pull into the parking lot of her complex, I see she's waiting at the door for me so I don't have to buzz her apartment. Her face is taut with worry.

"Alright, what did you do, and who do I need to hurt," I tease as I walk up to her and toss an arm over her shoulders.

"Let's go upstairs. I think we need some booze for this conversation," she says quietly.

"Shit, Ari. You're kinda scaring me."

"Yeah, well, this isn't a joke, Luca. So come on."

We walk silently up to her third-floor apartment. I'm pleasantly surprised to find my brother Leo inside. "Hey, man! What are you doing here? I thought you weren't going to make it back for a mid-tour."

Leo has been overseas for the better part of a year with the Army.

"I wasn't going to. They forced me," he says stoically. Leo has always been the strong and silent type. Military life suits him. He gets a task, he completes the task, and then he moves on to the next task. Planning and strategizing are core strengths for him. What exactly does Leo do in the Army? Fuck if I know. He just keeps telling us all, "it's classified," as if that gives us peace.

"How long are you home?"

"A week. Gotta head back before we ship out to our next FOB."

"What's a FOB again?"

"Forward Operating Base."

"What exactly does that mean?" I ask.

Leo sighs. "It's a base with very basic communication set up. We basically go and get everything set up for the soldiers coming behind us. Then we move on."

"And where are you going again?" I ask, wondering if he'll slip up and give us a location.

"Not happening, Luca. Nice try, though." His lips tilt in a very small smirk, which is as close to a smile as Leo gets.

"Alright, boys. Enough with the pleasantries. Luca, this is about you, not me," Arianna blurts out. Leo sits next to Ari on her couch, while I stretch out in a recliner.

"Huh? Me? What the hell did I do?"

"It's not what you did. It's something that is happening to you. I promised Hannah I wouldn't say anything, but I'm freaked out. Something is going on," she says.

"Wait. You talked to Hannah?"

"Yes. Well, no. Just some texts."

"What did she say?"

"That she needed some place to stay."

"Oh, that's nothing. Her aunt came back early. I was going to offer up one of my spare rooms. I'm actually surprised she didn't ask to stay with me."

"I don't think she wants to stay with you, Luca. She sort of insinuated something had happened between the two of you."

I stare at her incredulously. "That's news to me, Ari. I don't think anything happened."

Arianna opens her mouth before shutting it immediately. She chews on her bottom lip momentarily before finally saying, "she seemed to suggest she might also need a new job."

"What?" I shout. "Did she get fired? That's bullshit! She's the best social media coordinator we've had. Hold on. I'm calling the GM." I pull my phone out of my pocket, and open the contacts app.

"No!" Ari screeches, jumping from the couch and yanking my

phone out of my hand. "Look, Luca, something is fishy here. She said she needed to protect you. That's weird, right? Like, why would she need a new place to live, a new job, and feel like she needed to protect you?"

"In my line of work, that typically means there's something afoot in-house," Leo says. "Let's discuss some possible options. She could have been fired, or maybe she learned some secrets about staff, and doesn't want to get caught. Maybe someone hit on her, or touched her inappropriately ... Luca, sit the fuck down. We're not done talking this through."

I didn't even realize I stood up, my hands tightly in fists, ready to take on anyone who dared to touch my woman. Mine.

"But she said she needed to protect Luca, so wouldn't that rule out something happening to her?" Ari asks.

"Possibly. I doubt someone hit on her, or touched her in that case, though. Does she know about your coach hating you?" Leo asks, and I nod. "Have we ever figured out why he hates you?"

"He thinks I slept with his wife," I confess.

"Did you?" Leo asks.

"No!" I shout. "Jesus, Leo. I know I've gotten around, but I do have some morals."

"No judgment, man. People lie. Women go to bars without rings on, just as men do. She could have lied about it."

"I didn't sleep with her, ring or not. First time I met her was a few months after he was hired, at a team function. He was already a douche to me at that point, but I didn't know the reasoning. I only found out recently that he thinks I slept with his wife."

"How did you find out about that?" Leo asks.

"Heard a teammate talking about it. He didn't know I was behind him. No one believes me that I didn't do it," I explain. My blood boils just thinking about it. Typically, a hockey team is like a family. You're with the guys all the time. But I've been slowly and systematically forced out, and I can only assume Woodward is behind it.

"Have you tried to talk to him about it?" Ari asks.

"I have. He shuts me down whenever I bring up anything, and he's never alone with me. Hannah's uncle is almost always with him."

"Hannah is the girl? Who is her uncle?" Leo asks.

"One of my coaches."

"Could he possibly have given her an ultimatum?"

"I doubt it. He's only about ten years older than her, if that. I'm not even sure if he knows about us ..." I trail off. "Holy shit. He knows. Which means I bet the coach knows too. They must have gotten to Hannah and demanded something."

"Demanded something?"

"I don't know. Woodward hates me. He's been making comments all season about my contract being up. He wants me out of here, and I wouldn't put it past him to do something to ensure I leave."

"Do you want to leave?" Leo asks.

"Fuck no," I scoff. "I love being here. Love being so close to home. I don't want to be shipped off to another team just because my coach is an asshole. As for playing ... I don't know. I'm drained right now, man. It's not fun right now, and I don't know if that's going to change or not."

"So what do we do now?" Arianna asks.

"We don't do anything. You mind your own business and let Luca handle this," Leo says pointedly.

"But I'm invested now. And Hannah is my friend, too. What am I supposed to do?" she whines.

"You back the fuck up and lay low. Let Luca handle it. Give Hannah some space, too. If she's worried about Luca's life, or his career, then you need to respect that. Do you think Hannah would lie to you?" Leo asks.

Arianna shakes her head. "She's a really sweet girl. She's perfect for him, actually."

"She really fucking is," I murmur. From the first moment I saw her at my door in her silk pajamas, I've thought of no one but her. "Should I let her know Ari told me something is up?"

Leo shakes his head. "No. If she thinks you are going to get involved, she might bolt. We experience it all the time overseas with informants. You can't force them to do what you want them to do, because it's their life on the line if they get caught."

"You're comparing my girlfriend to an overseas informant," I say wryly.

Leo shrugs. "Until I know differently, I'm lumping them in my head as the same thing. And frankly, if Hannah is that concerned that she's trying to get out of there, I'd say you should be incredibly worried, too."

I let out a long exhale. I woke up this morning full of happiness. Thinking about when I'd see Hannah at lunch, and wondering how many orgasms I could give her before she had to go back to work. Never thought I'd end the day hanging at my sister's, discussing what's going on with my girlfriend.

*T*he following day, I have morning skate, then a scheduled visit to the VA Hospital to visit some injured veterans. Obviously with two brother's in the military, the VA is near and dear to my heart. I hate these pre-planned visits, though, because it's all about politics, publicity, and getting my picture taken. I'm here for them, not fans reading articles on the Internet. Once the media leave, I typically stick around for a few hours just hanging out and shooting the shit with the vets. They give me a little more insight into my brothers, especially Leo.

When I get back to my apartment, I immediately knock on Caroline and Hannah's door. I get excited when I hear the door being unlocked, only to sigh in defeat when Caroline opens the door.

"Hello, Luca," she says stiffly.

"Is Hannah here?" I ask. I'm not doing pleasantries. I just want to talk to Hannah.

"No, she is not."

"Do you know when she'll be back?" I ask, irritated.

"I assume she won't be. She moved out."

"What?" I ask sharply. "You seriously kicked her out, with nowhere to go? Jesus, Caroline, that's a shitty move, even for you."

"I told her she had the remainder of the week to find a new place. She chose to move out last night," Caroline huffs. "She didn't even leave a thank you gift or anything. I let her stay here out of the goodness of my heart, and all she did was stain a couch cushion and kill my plants."

I roll my eyes at her. "She's your niece, for Christ's sake. She wasn't a tenant. It's no wonder the two of you don't have a good relationship."

"What?" Caroline gawks. "Who told you that?"

"Mrs. Willowby, of course," I sneer. "Who the fuck do you think told me? Hannah did. At least she has a better relationship with her uncle. Guess I can just lump you in the same category as her parents, Caroline. A fucking waste of space."

I turn, heading to my door, and unlock the door. Caroline clears her throat and calls out to me. "She's too good for you."

"Don't I fucking know it," I mutter as I enter my apartment and slam the door. I pull out my phone and open my text chain with Hannah.

> Me: Pixie, I don't know what happened. All I know is something is up, and I can't help you if you don't talk to me. Please, Pix. I miss you. Just tell me where you are, and I'll come to you.

I'm surprised when I see the three dots telling me she's typing.

Pixie: It's complicated, Luca. I can't be with you right now. Please give me space.

Me: What the fuck happened between Boston and today? Who got to you? Woodward? Your uncle? Do they know?

Pixie: Does it matter?

Me: Yes.

Pixie: Fine. They know.

Me: Did they make you break it off with me?

Pixie: No.

Me: Then why are you?

Pixie: Because I'm trying to protect you! Please, just let me go for now.

Me: For now?

Pixie: I don't know. Maybe.

Me: That's bullshit, Hannah. Kinda seems like you're keeping me on the line while you can do whatever you want.

Pixie: Whatever you need to think to help you sleep at night, Luca.

Me: That's the thing. I'm not fucking sleeping. Because I can't sleep unless I have you in my arms. You gonna help me out with that?

When five minutes elapse without a response, I throw my phone down in disgust. Whatever happened, it clearly rocked Hannah to her core. And this has Woodward written all over it.

Chapter 18

*H*annah

⸻✦⸻

I resigned the following day.

I'll be damned if Coach Woodward is going to use me to take Luca down. If he releases the video of us having sex, then I'm suing him for anything I can. There's no way what he did was legal in any way, and threatening to hold it over my head breaks all kinds of laws.

I hated insinuating to Luca that I might date other people. And I hate that we're new enough in our relationship that he doesn't know I'd never do that. I've never even been able to talk to two men at the same time, much less date them simultaneously. Frankly, if Luca and I can't make this work, it's going to take me a long time to get over him. I don't foresee any dates for a while.

After a sleepless night on Claire's couch, I'm a grumpy mess as I arrive at the office with an empty box and my resignation letter. My first stop is my uncle's office. As soon as he sees me, he deflates.

"No, Hannah. Fuck. No. Don't let him run you out of here," he pleads.

"Who, Uncle Bennett? Be specific. Who exactly is running me out of here?" I ask, popping my hand on my hip in frustration and defiance. "Because I swear if you say it's Luca, I'm liable to jump over this desk and ... and ..."

"And what?" he asks, a hint of a smile on his face.

"I don't know. I wasn't raised to fight. But I'd so something!" I shout.

Uncle Bennett chuckles. "I wasn't going to say Luca. I figured it was because of Woodward."

"I won't let him hold this over me. This is just the tip of the iceberg. He won't stop. He'll just keep using me to do his dirty work for him."

"You don't know that."

"Oh? Because he's such a good guy, and hasn't given me the creeps every single time I've interacted with him? Twice now he's touched me, Uncle Bennett, and it's been *completely* inappropriate. I wouldn't put it past him to suggest my job was on the line if I didn't sleep with him."

My uncle rockets to his feet, a thunderous expression covering his face. "He touched you? What? Where? He fucking touched you?"

I hesitate, again second-guessing myself. Did I overreact? Was it inappropriate? "They've been borderline. Like squeezing my shoulder, but letting his fingers dip a little too far down onto my chest. Not really touching anything, but still crossing a thin line."

Uncle Bennett is seething. "That motherfucker!"

As he rounds his desk and stalks toward the door, I step in his way. "I don't know what you're planning, but it needs to stop right now. You can't do anything that will put your job in a compromising position. You can't, Uncle Bennett. One of us needs to be here to protect Luca, and to protect all the other women who work under that bastard. I can guarantee I'm not the only person he's acted inappropriately with. We need to mount a defense. Catch him in action, and get him out of here."

"You're right. I fucking hate that I can't go pound his face with my fist, but you're right. How are we supposed to do anything if you aren't here, though?"

"We'll figure it out. But I can't sit here and act like it's okay that he is blackmailing me to do this job. He's already forced me to end my relationship with Luca. I won't let him mess with my job. Me quitting is my decision, not his."

"You ended it with him?" Uncle Bennett says softly. "Christ, Han, I didn't think you'd end it."

"What was I supposed to do? If Woodward gets wind of us still being together, I don't know what he'll do to Luca. I'm trying to protect him," I whisper.

"What are you going to do for work? Where are you staying? Caroline texted that you moved out."

"I'm staying with a friend."

Uncle Bennett's eyes narrow. "Are you secretly staying with Luca and just telling me you're not with him anymore?"

"Seriously? How do you think I'd cover that up, living right next to Aunt Caroline? I'm staying with my friend Claire. She lives west of town. I met her through Luca's sister, actually. She has a spare bedroom, and all I need to get today is a mattress. Then I can find another job."

"I'm worried about you, Han. You left Georgia to get away from a set of problems, and you landed yourself right into a new set of problems here."

I laugh bitterly. "That's just life, though, isn't it? Nothing is perfect. I'd rather be here alone than in Georgia with Jefferson anyway."

"You can always stay with me. If things don't work out with your friend. Okay?" Uncle Bennett reaches up and pinches my cheek, just like he used to do when I was a kid and he was a gangly teenager.

"Thanks, Uncle Bennett," I tell him. He gives me a big hug before patting me on the back.

*A*fter dropping my resignation letter off in Human Resources, I begin cleaning out my personal effects from my office. When the door bursts open, I expect to see an angry Luca. Instead, I find the terrible terrors, with looks of shock on both their faces.

"You did not quit!" Jessica shouts.

"I did in fact quit," I answer.

"No! You are so good at your job! You can't quit. Who is going to train us now?" Lindsay wails. "Seriously don't leave us. If you aren't here, the creep will probably bother us more."

I stop loading things into the box, turning to stare at them. "The creep?"

Lindsay nods, before looking at Jessica. They quietly close the office door before turning back to me.

"Well?" I ask.

"We can tell you, since you're leaving," Jessica whispers, "but it's one of the coaches. We call him 'the creep.'"

"Which coach?" I ask quietly. While I assume it's Woodward, I'm apprehensive they'll say it's my uncle.

"Can we get in trouble if we tell you this?" Lindsay asks.

"Get in trouble for saying some man in an authoritative position was pervy with you? I would hope not," I answer.

"I — we need these hours to graduate. And he seems like the kind of guy who would make our lives miserable for the fun of it," Jessica says.

"Aren't you related to the owners? I'd say you could just go to them, ladies. You have better connections than I do," I remind them.

They look at each other before Jessica speaks up. "Our grandpa owns the team. He's old school. He didn't want to let us intern here, and we had to promise never to come to him with any complaints or issues. We think he'd probably side with the coach and claim we'd brought it on ourselves."

I grimace. Way too many sports teams are owned by rich white men who think they're above everything, including the law. It's disgraceful.

"He just gives us the creeps, Hannah. And we saw him with one of the admin assistants a few weeks ago. She looked so uncomfortable," Lindsay adds.

"Okay. Tell me which coach, and I'll see what I can do," I tell them.

They look at each other, both nodding, before turning to me and whispering in unison. "It's Woodward."

Holy hell.

The tangled web of Coach Woodward and his antics just got more involved.

$\mathcal{A}$fter emptying my office and taking my things to my car, I fire off a text to my uncle asking for a dinner this week. I need to get him on board with me moving forward with a case against Woodward. I'm not entirely sure of who I should reach out to, and I figure my uncle will know best.

Before I can leave the parking lot, I receive a phone call from Arianna.

"Hey! Are you definitely looking for a job?" she asks.

"I am. Just turned in my resignation today," I answer.

"My hometown has an opening. The special events coordinator at Everlasting Inn and Spa is pregnant, and she wants to stay home with her baby. I think you'd be perfect for the job."

"Oh, that might be fun. What kinds of things would I do? Seems like it's a far cry from social media for sports teams," I say.

"Well, yeah. But there aren't that many options for that here. At the hotel, you'd be responsible for all kinds of events. Lots of weddings. Company events. You'd do some social media, as the hotel does have a Facebook and Instagram page, but you'd spend more time working in the trenches instead. There are some neat family-friendly events Gia created recently that she's hoping will continue in her absence as well."

"Gia? Is that the pregnant coordinator?"

"Yep."

"How do you know her?" I've never heard Arianna talk to me about a friend named Gia.

Arianna clears her throat. "Friend of the family."

"Oh. Okay, well, I guess I'm interested. Is there a website where I can submit my resume?"

"Actually, the website is currently down for maintenance. The CEO is available to meet with you today, which is why I'm calling. I really touted you for the position," Arianna explains.

"Do you even know any of my qualifications?" I ask, a smile covering my face.

"How different could social media and events be? I mean, it's all social, for crying out loud. Plus, you'd get to work with me!"

"What?"

"Oh, yeah. I work there too. I run the spa and the hot springs."

"Oh, hot springs? I've always wanted to see hot springs! In the south, that's just the water temp in the summer."

"Just you wait. Hanging in a hot spring while snow is falling around you is absolutely blissful. So, can you meet the CEO? Like, now?"

"Now?" I shout.

"He's in town, so it's crazy convenient. I mean, what are the chances?"

"You say 'I mean' a lot," I remark.

"Yeah. I know. You aren't the first person to tell me that. It's kinda my trademark at this point," she jokes. "But seriously, can you meet?"

"I guess. I'm in my car, ready to head back to Claire's apartment. I have nothing else to do."

"Great! I'm going to send you an address to the restaurant where he's meeting you — I mean, all the applicants. Cuz there's more than just you. For the position. The job," Arianna stammers.

I'm beginning to feel like I'm getting set up, but I can't figure out with what.

Twenty minutes later, I'm in the booth of a charming hole-in-the-wall pizza place with Dominic, CEO of Everlasting Inn and Spa. He's devastatingly handsome in a polished and refined way, but tension ripples under the surface of his crisp suit. Throughout our interview, he is professional and respectful, but he didn't smile once. I wonder if he's that unimpressed with me, or if he's just not a smiley guy. He seems ... stoic. Borderline depressed. And incredibly tired.

"Do you need a place to stay as you transition from your previous job? And can I ask why you resigned from the position with the Wolves?" Dominic asks.

"Can I be frank with you, Mr. ..." I trail off, realizing I don't know Dominic's last name.

"Just Dominic, Ms. Beauregard."

"If I'm calling you Dominic, then you need to call me Hannah."

He gives me a very tight smile with a nod. "Very well, Hannah."

"If I'm being frank, I was approached by someone in a position of authority, who threatened me with personal information if I didn't help him — I mean them — with ruining the reputation of someone else employed by the Wolves. I felt that the personal information would most likely be used again and again to blackmail me, and I couldn't stand to be part of that. I also couldn't take part in damaging the reputation and career of someone I lo — of another person."

Dominic's entire demeanor changes throughout my explanation. "So you're saying you were approached by a superior and essentially blackmailed to destroy someone else's career?"

"Yes."

"Was this superior a coach?"

I don't answer immediately. "I'd rather not answer."

"You basically just did, Ms. Beauregard."

"Oh, we're back to that again, Mr. ..."

"Apologies. Hannah. In any case, the coach put you in one hell of a position. I commend you for choosing to remove yourself. May I ask what kind of information he held over your head?"

"You're assuming it was a male."

"I'm familiar with the Wolves organization. All of the coaches are male. In fact, other than a couple of female physical therapists, almost the entire coaching and training staff are male. All females working for the Wolves are back office, admin, and marketing."

I stare at him, nausea overtaking me. "Are you going to report me? Please, please don't. I'm trying to figure out what to do, and how I can help the other person who is possibly in trouble there. I can't — I don't —"

"I'm not reporting you, Hannah. I'm a hockey fan, and I know some people in the organization. I won't put you in a worse situation than you already are. I can, however, advise you on moving forward. I'd suggest retaining an attorney if you plan to file any criminal charges."

"I can't afford an attorney," I whisper.

"We have an attorney on retainer for the hotel. I'm sure he can help you out. I'll have him give you a call once you're cleared with HR." Dominic says as he begins to slide out of the booth.

"Cleared with HR?"

"Yes. You're hired, Ms. Beauregard. If you're available, you can start tomorrow."

"Seriously?" I shout.

Dominic chuckles, finally showing me a very small smile. Devastatingly handsome with a frown, blindingly gorgeous with a smile. "Seriously. It was a pleasure to chat with you, Hannah. I'll see you at work tomorrow."

As he walks out of the restaurant, I realize he reminds me of

Luca. And I'm suddenly overcome with emotion, tears clogging my eyes. I so wish I could reach out to Luca and explain everything. Tell him about my new job. My new apartment. Everything.

But it's better to keep him out of the crossfire. If I move forward with criminal charges, I don't want Luca to get caught in the middle.

Chapter 19

*L*uca

"*J*esus Christ, Santzy, lighten up a little," Dawson mutters after I shove him hard into the boards. "This is a fucking practice, not the Cup. Chill."

No. No I will fucking not lighten up.

I'm pissed at the world.

I really only have myself to blame. Why on earth would I ever think I deserved a shot at love? I've made so many bad calls in my life, it's no wonder the karma train rolled right through and took me the fuck out.

I can't even look at Woodward. I'm seething mad. My body literally vibrates with animosity whenever he's near me. I want to wipe the stupid smirk off his face every time I see him. But I can't.

After texting my agent that I thought I needed out of Denver, he did some digging. They're definitely shopping around trying to unload me. The GM has reached out to a handful of other teams to see who would be interested in a trade. What's interesting is how they're waxing poetic about my skills to other teams, but dragging me through the mud locally. Multiple untrue stories have come out in the media over the last ten days, and Max thinks they're all coming from in-house. Essentially, Woodward and the GM want to get top dollar for me, and they want the public to turn on me so they'll welcome whoever comes in to replace me.

Enough with that shit.

I told Max I'm done. I'm fine with going out on my own terms. I don't want to play elsewhere. The last year has left such a foul taste in my mouth that I don't even want to play hockey anymore. It's no longer fun. I'm physically and mentally drained. I don't want to get traded, possibly to a team a couple thousand miles away from my family, and spend the rest of my career unhappy.

So when I told Max I intended to just fuck up the Wolves chances of making it to the playoffs, he initially laughed, as if it sounded hilarious. Then he realized I was serious. What better way of flipping the bird to your team one last time? Immature? Yes. Warranted? Fuck yes. Because I've thought back to how I've been slowly ostracized over the past couple of seasons. None of the guys reach out to me anymore. I've become the team pariah, through no fault of my own, all due to Woodward's leadership and coaching. I have no doubt he's been slowly poisoning the team's opinion of me. Probably on the down-low, but possibly straight up blackmail. So I figure, what the hell do I have to lose here? Friendships? Nope. A long career? I've already had that. A stable environment? That ideal left the building months ago.

Which is how I ended up seeing how many fights I could start in a week. Honestly, I wish I could try to beat the all-time goal of penalty minutes in a single game, which is sixty-seven, but these days, they eject you when you have a handful of penalties. Woodward was furious. When I was ejected twice, he scratched me for a full game. It was obvious why, considering the front page on the Denver Times was about how out of control I was, and what could have possibly set me on this path.

An "unnamed source" said tensions were high in the locker room, and Coach Woodward was "concerned" about my mental stability to continue with the team.

He can take my mental stability and shove it right up his ass.

Penalty minutes may not seem like a big deal, but they are. Especially for a player like me, because I'm lethal from anywhere on the ice. I'm not just a defensemen. I have amazing aim and precision, no matter where I am, and I do an excellent job of protecting my goalie. So not only does it mean the opposing team has a power play without me on the ice, but it also means I'm not out there scoring.

We haven't won a game since Hannah left me.

Fuck. *Hannah.*

God I miss her.

We weren't even really together that long, but I feel like part of my soul is missing. It's complete bullshit that we're apart. I don't even know where she's staying. I've asked Caroline, and she claims she doesn't know. Coach Davenport won't look me in the eye, only holding me off the one time I almost punched Woodward after he commented that I was way too wound up, and should probably call my skank to service me. Davenport looked me in the eye, albeit briefly, and said, "don't do it. You'll regret it. Let all of this play out, Luca."

He called me Luca.

I could be looking too deeply into things, but that subtle name change gives me hope. Does this mean he supports my relationship with his niece? I hope I'm not being stupidly optimistic in hoping it means something is going on behind the scenes. Maybe Hannah is working on something. Is she okay? Is she thinking about me as much as I'm thinking about her? Who knows.

"Santo! Get the fuck off the ice, you piece of shit," Woodward yells. Sure would be nice if my coach didn't refer to me as a piece of shit, but whatever. At this point, I'm surprised he hasn't started calling me Italian slurs.

As I pass him, though, he clearly mutters, "can't wait to get rid of you, you fucking prick. Your whore of a mother should have aborted you when she had the chance."

I whip around to face him. He did not just call my mother a whore. "The fuck did you just say to me?"

"You heard me, *Luca*," he sneers. "Get the fuck off my ice before I make you."

That's it.

This shit ends now.

"Oh, yeah, Coach? How exactly are you going to make me?" I skate to within inches of him, towering over his meager frame. I'm a few inches taller than Woodward normally, but my skates add a few more inches. You ever hear that expression those who can't do, teach? Well, those who can't make it in the NHL become coaches. And Woodward hasn't played one game as a professional hockey player. He didn't have the speed or the stick skills. But he had tenacity, and he had the drive to start at the bottom and work his way up. Considering what I know now, though, it makes me wonder how he rose to head coach so quickly.

"You won't touch me, Santo. You don't have the balls," he says deeply, but a slight tremor is detected in his tone.

"Obviously, I've gone mental, right? Isn't everyone concerned about my wellbeing?" I taunt.

"That's enough, Santo. Hit the showers," Davenport says, stepping between us and effectively stopping what would have undoubtedly ended my career immediately. I'm acutely aware of the letdown I feel. I'm just not sure if it's due to me really wanting to be done with hockey, or if I really just want to knock Woodward around a little.

I hear Woodward spouting off nonsense about me as I stomp into the locker room, and I roll my eyes in annoyance. Ripping off my practice jersey and pads, I throw them across the locker room.

"What the fuck were you thinking, Santzy? Are you trying to get yourself blackballed out of the league?" Davenport seethes as he follows me into the locker room. "I told you to lay low. Let things play out. This isn't laying low, asshole."

I turn to him as the adrenaline of the almost fight leaves my body. My back hits the wall next to my locker, and I slide to the floor. Jesus. I'm so fucking tired.

"Are you okay, man?" Davenport asks.

"What do you think?" I murmur.

"Hey, Coach!" Dawson yells from the doorway. "Since Santzy here is a ticking time bomb, and obviously can't show your niece a good time, can I have her number?"

What the fuck?

I'm off the floor immediately and in Dawson's face. "You so much as look at her, Dawson, and I'm ending you. Do you fucking understand me? Don't even think about it."

Dawson smiles victoriously. "Told you guys he was fucking her."

I look behind him to see most of the team, including Woodward, as they all look at me with varying expressions of disappointment and disgust. "I'm not fucking her. Davenport's niece is too good for us. Even me."

I walk away from Dawson. Technically, it's not a lie. I'm not currently fucking her. Would I like to be currently fucking her? Hell yes. But since that clearly isn't going to happen, I'm certainly not going to allow any of these jack wagons access to her, most of all Dawson. He's a weasel, and I wouldn't trust him with Hannah.

After ridding myself of all my practice gear, I dress quickly and leave the arena. Typically I shower here, but I need to be away from these people. I've never felt so alone. Our practice today was at The Sports Facility Zone, which means I'm driving back to my apartment when my phone rings.

When I see it's Davenport calling, I almost send it to voicemail. Almost.

"What? I didn't hit any of them. I can't be in that much trouble," I begin.

"I wouldn't have said a word had you hit Dawson. I would have been right behind you. But that was clearly a setup."

"You think?" I say sarcastically.

"You just need to keep calm right now. Let things play out."

"You've said that now multiple times, and I don't have a fucking clue what you mean."

"Things are being handled. Behind the scenes. Trust me."

"Seriously? You want me to trust you? You've wanted me gone from the moment you knew I was involved with Hannah," I tell him.

"And I was wrong for doing that. She's a grown woman, and I need to be respectful of that. If she wants to be with you, I won't stand in your way."

"That's moot."

"What do you mean?"

"She doesn't want to be with me. She broke it off. It's fine. I wouldn't want to be with me either."

"She wants to be with you, Santzy. She's just working through things right now."

"Working through things? I really wish you would stop with the vague terminology, Coach. She doesn't want to be with me. Pretty sure she blocked me on everything."

"She did block you on social media, yes. But she didn't block your phone number."

My mouth drops open as I pull into my underground parking. "She didn't?"

"No."

"How do you know that?"

"I had dinner with her last night. I asked her, after I caught her scrolling through your text messages."

"I don't see how it matters. She doesn't want to talk to me. I doubt she'd answer a text."

"Texts are a paper trail, Luca. But I bet she'd answer a phone call."

I clear my throat as I ponder his words. "Do you — do you know where she's living?"

"I do."

"Would you be willing to share that information?"

"I might."

I sigh. "Is this going to be like pulling teeth to get the information out of you?"

"It's actually quite simple."

"How so?"

"You have something I want."

I chuckle. "Is that so?"

"Yep. Your mom made lasagna for the team last year. I want two dishes of it, so I can eat one now and freeze one for later."

"Seriously? That's it?"

"Have you eaten her lasagna? It's fucking perfection. I'd say it's an even trade."

"How's your niece going to feel about you trading her for lasagna?"

"I'm trading an address, jackass. Not her. Get your facts straight. If you tell her I traded her, I'm making you run suicides for an hour tomorrow."

"Well played, Coach."

When he doesn't respond, I end the call. I'm suddenly feeling rejuvenated. Optimistic. Hopeful. And when a text comes in with an address on the far west side of Denver, I'm ecstatic.

*A*fter a quick shower, lunch, and answering some emails, I venture out to the area of town where Hannah is staying. I'm not sure how she ended up way over here, but I'm relieved she's not in a bad area of town. She's not too far from my sister, Arianna, and probably only twenty or so minutes from my hometown.

I decide to park near the apartment building and wait. It takes me a while to come up with something to say. There are so many things I want to tell her. Things I want her to explain. As I drum my fingers repeatedly on the steering wheel, I realize I'm so fucking nervous. I've never had this many nerves about a woman before.

It's close to six before I see Hannah's car pull into the parking lot. As she gets out of her car, I grip my steering wheel as tightly as possible to keep myself from sprinting over to her and kissing the daylights out of her. It's only been a few weeks since I've seen her, and I feel like it's been an eternity.

She's wearing a long coat over a patterned dress and knee-high boots. She looks absolutely breathtaking, her blonde curls pulled into a low bun, a few loose tendrils dancing haphazardly around her face as she quickly walks into the building. I wait about ten minutes before I take a deep breath and call her.

I bet her uncle is wrong. She won't answer.

She doesn't want to be with me.

She deserves better.

"Luca," Hannah says breathlessly.

Holy shit. I didn't even hear her answer the phone. "Hey, Pixie."

"Are you — is everything okay?"

I debate on how I want to answer. I could say yes, everything is fine. I could tell her I'm doing okay, but I wish I could see her. Or hold her. Or anything. But instead, what comes out of my mouth is, "I fucking miss you, Han."

She sighs and her answer is breathy and soft. "I miss you too."

"You do?" I ask, surprised.

"Of course I do! Did you really think I wouldn't?"

"I don't know. Everything happened so fast, and I didn't know what to think. I don't understand it all, to be honest."

"I know," she whispers.

"I just ..." I trail off, clearing my throat. "I needed to see you, Pix. You look beautiful."

"Wait, what?"

Shit. "Oh, um. Well, yeah. I'm kind of in your parking lot?"

"You're here? Right now? How did you find out where I live?"

I hate that she says she lives here, not that she's staying here. "I don't know if you'll believe me, but your uncle gave me the address."

"Seriously? Uncle Bennett?"

"Good ole Uncle Bennett," I chuckle. "And yes, I'm serious."

"Wow," she giggles. "Never thought I'd see the day that you'd be in cahoots with him."

Her giggle is music to my ears. "We've come to an understanding, I guess."

"Are you really downstairs?" she asks.

"I am."

"Apartment 3108."

I'm out of the car before I even check to see if she's ended the call.

Chapter 20

*H*annah

※※※※※※※※※

*H*e's here.

He came for me.

I can't believe he actually came for me.

And when I throw open Claire's apartment door to see Luca, for the first time in weeks, I almost cry. My heart is screeching at me. *This is it! This is our story!*

We stand still for a moment, staring at each other. Luca's eyes are bloodshot, with dark bags under his eyes. He looks as haggard and lost as I feel.

"Hi, Pix," he says quietly with a lopsided smile, and I lose it. A sob breaks through, and I crumble into a mess of tears, sobs, and a flurry of incomprehensible words. Luca jumps into action before I can fully slide to the ground, scooping me up, kicking the door closed, and carrying me over to the couch. He sits, positioning me in his lap, as I sob.

I owe him an explanation, but I don't even know where to start. How do I explain all of this? If he knows everything, will he hold it together and stay away from Woodward? If Woodward gets wind of this, will he release the video?

I've been in touch with the attorney Dominic suggested, and he's currently reaching out to some of his contacts to determine a course of action. He's advised me to keep Luca at arm's length, but I can't do it anymore. Luca has slowly infiltrated my heart, and even through my tears and hysterics, I know I've never felt more at peace, and at home, than I do at this very moment.

Once my sobs subside and I can breathe normally, I raise my head from where I had it buried in Luca's neck. He reaches up and wipes away my tears.

"It's okay, baby. It's okay," he whispers as he caresses my cheeks.

"I'm so sorry," I say brokenly.

Luca studies me momentarily. "What are you sorry for?"

"For pushing you away. For not explaining everything to you. For thinking I could do this by myself. But I can't, Luca. I can't. Because …"

"Because what?"

I look into his deep brown eyes, and know it's now or never. Maybe I can't tell him the entire truth about what Woodward is planning, but I can at least tell him my truth. "I'm in love with you, Luca. I love you. I'm lost without you. And that scares the shit out of me, because I probably ruined my only chance with you, and I wish I could go back and change how I pushed you away —"

My speech is interrupted by Luca smashing his lips against mine. I moan immediately as his familiar taste, what I've tasted in my dreams, floods my senses. His tongue slides between my lips and circles mine as one hand reaches around my neck to latch in my hair. I manage to maneuver my legs so I'm straddling him, wrapping my arms tightly around his shoulders.

Luca breaks off the kiss breathlessly, resting his forehead against mine. "Tell me again, Pix."

"I'm sorry," I respond.

He chuckles. "Not that part. The other part."

It takes me a moment to realize what he's referring to. "Oh. I love you, Luca."

He squeezes me tighter as a groan vibrates through his body.

"Fuck, Pixie. No woman has ever said that to me before. Well, other than family. I didn't realize what that would do to me."

"What does it do to you?" I ask softly.

Luca smiles against my lips, and I swear it's the most exquisite feeling in the world. "I've never been this happy. I've missed you so much."

"Does that mean you forgive me?"

"I don't think there was ever anything you needed to be forgiven for, but we definitely need to talk about what happened. I figure you did what you thought was best in whatever the situation was."

I sigh. "I did. I was just trying to keep you safe."

"Safe?" he asks. "Am I in danger?"

"No, not exactly. Safe isn't the correct word. I wanted to keep you as far from the situation as possible. I knew if you got wind of anything, you'd try to protect me, and that would get you into even more trouble."

"What can you tell me about whatever is going on? Who is involved?"

I stare at him, riddled with doubt. I'm worried about putting him in a compromising position with the Wolves. Concerned about the video being released. I haven't even met his family yet; what will they think of the slut in the sex tape? Now that I think about it, I never saw the tape. Is it even real? Could Woodward be bluffing the entire thing?

"Coach Woodward insinuated he had a camera hidden in your hotel room in Boston. He saw us together, and threatened to release the tape to the media if I didn't help him get you kicked off the team," I blurt out.

Luca stares at me incredulously, his mouth agape in shock. "Are you fucking serious?"

I nod, chewing on my lip, worried he won't believe me.

"That motherfucker!" he shouts, carefully sliding me off his lap before jumping up and beginning to pace the length of Claire's apartment. "How many laws did he break here? And he admitted it to you? Jesus, he's a dumb fuck. Was anyone else there when he admitted it?"

"My uncle and the GM."

Luca turns, his glare glacial. "Your uncle?"

"Yes. Woodward assumed Uncle Bennett would help take you down, but my uncle says he's only going along with it because he doesn't want me to be embarrassed if the tape does get released."

"Did you see the tape?"

"No. I was actually just thinking about that. Could he be bluffing?"

"I wouldn't put it past him. He'll do anything to get ahead," Luca says as he runs his hand through his hair exasperatingly. "Can we trust your uncle?"

"Yes, I promise. He knows he's on thin ice with me already," I tell him, then giggle at my pun.

"Thin ice? Really?" Luca teases.

"It slipped out, I swear," I say. "Are you mad? At me?"

"What? No, of course not. None of this is your fault, baby. This is all on Woodward," Luca says.

"Oh. It's just, as soon as I told you, you got as far away from me as possible, so I assumed ..." I trail off.

"Shit. No, Pixie," Luca says, coming to kneel in front of me. "I'm not mad at you. Not at all. I'm just really pissed we're in this predicament."

"Me too," I say quietly. Luca slides back onto the couch, pulling me into his side. I sigh as his arms tighten around me. "I should have told you from the beginning."

"Maybe, but maybe not. I don't know what I would have done in your shoes, Han. You were put in an impossible situation, and you reacted as you thought was best at the time."

"My new boss put me into contact with an attorney, who is looking into what laws Woodward broke and how we can move forward with criminal charges. My uncle is very inconspicuously asking around to see if anyone else was put in a compromising position with Woodward as well."

"Wait. A compromising position? Did something else happen?" Luca asks.

"Not exactly, but a couple of times he would touch my shoulder or neck and let his hand linger. It was creepy. Once his hand skirted way too low on my shoulder to be considered professional. Uncle Bennett thinks other female employees have probably had similar situations happen, and we just need a few to be willing to come forward."

I feel Luca's entire body stiffen next to me as my words sink in.

"That fucker touched you?" Luca growls.

"Well, yes. But nothing like what you're thinking right now. Trust me, I know the difference," I joke, and Luca's stricken expression meets mine.

"What the hell does that mean, Hannah? The difference between a nonconsensual grope and what?"

Luca and I have barely skimmed the surface of our dating histories, and he knows nothing of Jefferson. Nothing about Jefferson's temper, and how he'd get handsy with me. Woodward is nothing compared to Jefferson. But seeing Luca's chest rise and fall in quick succession, I'm hesitant to reveal all of this information right now. I fear Luca might burn all of Denver to the ground if he finds out Jefferson has been here looking for me.

"I had," I say, clearing my throat as I slide back into his lap and straddle his legs, "an ex-boyfriend who would get a little handsy while he was drinking. It never culminated in rape, but it got close a couple times. More than once I woke up with him already inside me, and I was definitely *not* a fan of that. Since our relationship ended, I've come to realize that Jefferson actually raped me. But that's how I know the difference between what Woodward did and what my ex did."

Luca's eyes narrow as his entire body goes taut. "Give me his last name. Right fucking now."

"No."

"Hannah, you will give me his motherfucking name."

"Luca, I will not give you his motherfucking name."

"Don't tease me, baby. I'll find out one way or another, and I suggest you choose the easy way of just giving me his name."

"Oh yeah? What's the hard way?" I taunt.

"I recognize and support your attempt at redirection, Pixie, but let's stay focused," he says, his determined gaze not veering from mine.

"Luca," I sigh. "It doesn't matter what his name is, or what our past was. It's the past. I refuse to focus on that. Yeah, I should have reported him. But I just wanted to get away from him. I hope that you can be my future, and we never have to speak of him again."

He rests his forehead against mine as we sit quietly together. My heartbeat has slowed, finally in tune with his, as I make a relieved exhale. Just being here in his arms has made everything worth it.

"God I've missed you," he murmurs, his hot breath dancing across my skin. Luca leans down to press a tender kiss against the crook of my neck.

"I've missed you too," I respond. "I didn't know what to do, Luca. I didn't know who to trust or who to approach."

"Why didn't you come to me? You could have trusted me, Pix."

"I didn't want Woodward to release the tape. Your family — I haven't met them, and I didn't want their first memory of me to be a sex tape. And the thought of me embarrassing you ..." I trail off.

Luca raises his head to look at me, but I close my eyes and avoid him. He grabs my chin gently with his thumb and forefinger. "You could never embarrass me, Pixie. Never."

"You've talked about how the public perceives you, and I didn't want to be responsible for another negative storyline. I wanted to figure out a way to save us both," I confess.

"We're stronger together, baby. Promise me you'll trust me from now on with everything, no matter what."

I nod as my head drops to his shoulder. "I promise, but just for fun, what would happen if I didn't trust you in the future?"

Luca chuckles against me. "You'd be punished, of course. Like the hard way you just asked about."

"Oh yeah? Explain."

"Well, while very much fun for me, it may not be much fun for you."

I tilt my head to the side, studying him. "Why is that?"

"Well," Luca says, his voice suddenly an octave lower and husky, "it involves edging you to the point of hysteria. Making your ass red with my hand, so red in fact, that you can't sit for a week without remembering how I own you. Choking you with my cock, and covering you with so much of my cum that you smell like me for days. Marking you as mine in every fucking way possible."

"That way, I choose that way," I say breathlessly.

Luca barks back a laugh. "I never said you'd come in that example, Pixie."

"I don't care, I choose that way. Please. Please, Luca," I whimper. He rests his forehead against mine as his hands clutch at my neck, holding me tightly against him.

"I would love nothing more than that, Pixie, but I have barely slept since Boston. I'm so fucking beat," he confesses.

"Luca, that was weeks ago!"

"Can I just hold you? I promise, I'll do what I said another time. We've got a game tomorrow night, and I just want to sleep," Luca says. I begin lightly scratching my fingernails up and down his back, and he sighs softly as his head drops to my shoulder. "God, I've fucking missed you, Pix. You're not allowed to leave me again."

"Okay," I whisper. As Luca's body begins to relax, I realize he's seconds away from falling asleep. As much as I don't want to wake him up, I don't think Claire needs to walk in on me and my maybe-boyfriend on the couch. "Come on, Luca. My bed is more comfortable than the couch."

"Okay, baby," Luca murmurs contently.

I stand, pulling him through Claire's apartment and back to the guest room. I'm suddenly nervous, though I don't know why, so I make a big show of pulling open the dresser drawers and rifling through them. "Bathroom is through there. I think I have a spare toothbrush somewhere —"

"Hannah."

"Hmm?" I respond, awkwardly searching through the dresser as if a toothbrush will magically appear in between my bras and underwear.

"I don't know what got you suddenly so nervous, but I literally just want to take a nap with you," Luca says quietly. He comes behind me and wraps his arms around me tightly. "I wasn't lying when I said I've slept like shit. I only got to have you in my arms a few times, but it was clearly a life-altering experience. I don't think I'm going to be able to go back to sleeping alone."

I sigh as I reach up to grab his forearms. He nuzzles my neck with his nose, sending goosebumps trickling down my arms. "I can still look for that toothbrush."

"I don't need a toothbrush, Hannah. I just need you. Please. Get in bed, Pixie." He slowly removes his arms and gives me a gentle nudge toward the bed as he walks into the ensuite. Still feeling nervous, I remove my boots, and sit on the side of the bed to pull off my tights. I'm not even remotely acclimated to Colorado weather, and the cold seeps through to my bones. I've been told by Arianna and Dominic that it isn't even that cold yet. I laughed, thinking they were joking, and almost had a heart attack when I looked up the average low temperatures in the winter.

"You okay if I get comfortable? Again, no ulterior motive here, Han. I just typically don't sleep fully clothed, and well, you know that, so, umm ..." Luca trails off, and I realize I'm not the only one with nerves.

"I'd like to get comfortable too. It was a long day at work," I say quietly.

"Oh, yeah. I haven't even asked about the new job. Are you

enjoying it?" Luca asks. I watch out of the corner of my eye as he reaches behind his head and whips his sweatshirt off. The smirk on his face tells me he heard my quick intake of breath. He's just so stunning.

"I think you're stunning too, Pixie," he murmurs. I feel a wave of embarrassment heat my face when I realize I spoke those words aloud. "Come on, Hannah. We have no reason to be this nervous. It's just a nap."

"It's not just a nap," I whisper.

Luca walks to the bed and sits beside me. "No. It's not just a nap. I don't know about you, but I'm hoping it's the beginning of a lot of naps for you and me."

I rest my head against his shoulder for a moment before standing to walk to my closet. After removing my dress and putting on a tank top and shorts, I walk back into the bedroom and find Luca buried under the comforter. "Come here, baby."

As soon as I slide under the covers, he yanks me toward him. Once his arms circle around me and he breathes against my hair, I relax. I've missed this. In such a short time, Luca became home to me.

As his breathing deepens and I can tell he is asleep, I realize why I felt so nervous. I laid my heart on the line. I told him I was in love with him.

But Luca never said anything back.

Chapter 21

*L*uca

~~~

I had every intention of taking a quick nap, ordering some dinner, and then convincing Hannah to let me make love to her. Or at least making out a little. But once I had her in my arms, I fell into the deepest sleep I've had in weeks. I wasn't exaggerating about the sleep issue. Getting three hours a night was a good night. So it shouldn't have surprised me when I slept for sixteen hours straight.

When I woke up alone, I was incredibly bummed. Rolling over, I breathe in Hannah's scent. I see a paper on the nightstand and grab it.

> *You looked too comfortable to wake up, but I had to go to work. My roommate leaves around eight each morning. Help yourself to anything you need.*
> *-H*
> *PS: I needed that sleep, too. I've missed you.*

The ear-splitting grin on my face must be comical.

I can't believe how quickly my little Pixie got under my skin and became my salvation. From this moment, everything I do is for her.

Grabbing my phone, I realize I missed morning skate. Oh well. They'll either fine me, or scratch me for the game tonight. Boo-freak-ing-hoo. Could not care less. I grab a quick shower, spending way too much time sniffing all of Hannah's products to see which one smells the most like her, before heading out. Since I'm so close to my home-town, I decide to make a surprise stop.

While Eternity Springs is about an hour from downtown Denver, depending on traffic, I don't get home as often as I'd like. Hockey season gets pretty chaotic, and it's difficult to manage a quick visit when I have so many obligations in Denver. Even with it being a weekday, the main street through town is bustling. When I see my brother's friend, Stone, outside his barbershop, and an open parking spot right in front, I veer into the spot and jump out. Stone owns the only barbershop in town, aptly named Stone Cold Cuts, and my shaggy mane could use some trimming anyway.

"Look what the cat dragged in," Stone calls out. He's been friends with my brother Alex since they were in elementary school, and I'd bet he spent more time with my family on holidays than his own. Stone's home life wasn't as idyllic as mine. "Can I even talk to you, or will you high stick me and get thrown in the sin bin?"

"Whatever," I chuckle.

"You've been on a tear, my man," Stone says, slapping me on the back and giving me a quick man-hug. "What's the deal? You thinking you want to break the record for penalty minutes in a season?"

"Just doing what I can to fuck with the head coach," I tell him, then quickly look around to make sure no one overheard me. "Shit. I didn't say that. Okay? You didn't hear me."

"Alright, sure. You want to tell me what's going on?" he says quietly. Stone has always been like an older brother to me. Even with his miserable upbringing, he has a calm and peaceful presence. But the less people who know about Woodward's antics, the better.

"Nah. Just dealing with some shit. You don't need to worry about it. Things are looking up. Hopefully, I won't be raking in the penalties," I tell him.

"You gonna let me touch this monstrosity of a haircut? Did Edward Scissorhands touch you up recently?" Stone shudders. He pushes me toward his chair and immediately throws a smock over me. "How you get women looking like this is beyond me."

"Please. They don't care what I look like. Just how much is in my bank account and how I fuck," I tell him.

"Ain't that the fucking truth," he murmurs.

"Besides, I got a girl now. No more playing the field," I say proudly.

Stone stares at me incredulously. "No fucking way. Mr. Hotshot Hockey Star has found a woman? I don't believe it."

"Believe it," I boast. "Best fucking thing that has ever happened to me."

"Damn. Another one bites the dust," Stone teases.

"What? You don't think about settling down? You're getting up there, old man. Gonna put you out to pasture here soon."

Stone rolls his eyes. "No pasture for me. I have no interest in settling down."

As he begins to cut my hair, I see a flurry of activity at the door. "I thought that was you!" Arianna rushes in with a big smile on her face, but the smile turns to a frown immediately upon seeing Stone. "Oh. You."

"Hello, Princess. What do we owe the pleasure of your company for?" Stone taunts.

Arianna throws a hand on her hip as she glares at Stone. "Nothing for you, old man. I'm here for my brother."

"I'm not a fucking old man," Stone mutters.

"Stop calling me princess, and I'll stop calling you old man," Arianna says.

"No."

"I'm not a princess."

"You certainly act like one, Princess. Tell me, what shopping have you done today? Did Daddy give you his credit card?" Stone seethes.

As I watch the insults get volleyed between Stone and Ari, I'm suddenly aware of the ridiculous sexual tension that oozes between them. This is fucking foreplay. And I'm horribly uncomfortable. Have I blocked this out, or have they been this way for a while?

"Okay, umm, let's redirect here," I call out. "Ari, what are you doing here?"

Arianna stops glaring at Stone to look at me. "Oh. I was picking up door prizes for the Children's Hospital fundraiser we're doing in a few weeks."

"With Gia on maternity leave, are you running the event?" I ask.

"No, we got a replacement. I'm just helping out." Ari turns to Stone. "It's all the shopping I do."

"Clearly," he mutters.

Ari turns back to me. "You should come have lunch with me. I'd love to introduce you to the new special events coordinator."

I notice a wicked gleam in her eyes. "I was headed that way anyway. Just saw Stone and figured I'd grab a quick cut."

I almost said I was going to kill two birds with one *Stone*, but I'd bet anything the only person who would laugh at my pun would be Hannah.

"What's that smile for?" Arianna asks.

I shrug. "Nothing. Just thinking about something."

Thinking about my girl.

But I'm not ready to tell Arianna that Hannah is back in my life. Because, honestly, Hannah and I still need to talk. Lay all our cards on the table, and make sure we're on the same page.

Jesus, the puns.

I'd be sick of myself if I wasn't so damn happy.

As Ari steps out to take a phone call, Stone leans down. "Reason you don't want Princess to know about your girl?"

"She's friends with Hannah. I want to be sure Hannah is one hundred percent on board before we tell friends and family. I'd hate to jump the gun and spook her."

"Dude, if you spook her by getting excited to tell your sister, she's not the right girl for you. Just saying."

I ponder Stone's words before replying. "Yes and no. There are other circumstances at play here, and I just got back with Hannah yesterday. Once I speak with her, I'll be shouting it from the rooftops. Until then, I'm being respectful. But enough about me. Why *do* you call my sister Princess?"

Stone chuckles bitterly. "Because she is a princess. Baby of the family. Got everything handed to her. Shopping is an extreme sport for Arianna. I bet all she has to do is tear up and your parents give her whatever she wants."

"Well, I don't like to see any of my sisters cry, but you're wrong on a lot of things there, Stone. She's not the spoiled princess you've made her out to be."

"She's the one who told me she was a princess, Luca."

"When?"

"Shit, I don't know. Fifteen years ago, maybe?"

"Jesus, Stone. She was a kid. Most little girls think they're princesses, or hope to be one. She was like ten. Which means you were around twenty. What the hell were you doing chatting with her anyway?"

Stone sighs, running his fingers through his perfectly quaffed hair, giving him the effortless tousled look that women love. Yeah, I know. I'm a guy, but I notice shit. "Dom dragged me to something. Hockey game for you, maybe? Princess parked herself next to me and bragged about how she had all the men in your family wrapped around her little finger."

That part isn't wrong. Arianna has always had a way of sucking you in. She's beautiful, a ray of sunshine, and her glass is always half-full. No matter the trials and tribulations that life threw her way, she remained optimistic. And Stone doesn't know a fucking thing about what my sister has been through.

As I see Ari walk back in the door, I speak quietly so only Stone can hear. "You're wrong about her. I'm not stupid. I can cut the sexual tension between you two with a piece of paper. Just know if you fuck around with her, Dom will murder you."

"She's jailbait, man. Besides, I'm not interested. Never gonna happen," he murmurs.

Lies.

Pretty sure I said that about Hannah, and look where that got me.

I'm going to enjoy watching this train wreck happen. Arianna is going to chew him up and spit him out, and if I had to guess, I'd say Stone begs her to do it again. She's going to break him, and I can't fucking wait to watch.

"*Cocco!*" I hear my mom call as I walk through the front entry of Everlasting Inn and Spa. Mom sweeps out from behind the concierge desk, her knee-length cardigan sweater billowing behind her as she slides over to me. Sofia Santo doesn't walk or run. She glides. It's remarkable, really. I've never seen a woman hold herself so regally. My mom has an effortless quality that I've never seen repeated ... until I met Hannah. My southern belle is all grace and strength. Until this moment, I never realized how much she reminds me of my mom.

"Hey, Mom," I say as she pulls me in for a hug.

"This is a surprise. Don't you have a game tonight?" Mom asks.

"I do. I was on the west side of town, so figured I'd come say hi and see if I could take my favorite mom to lunch."

"Your favorite mom, huh," she teases. Her smile makes me chuckle. Generally I look like my dad. I definitely get my height from him, and I'm the tallest of all my siblings, but not by much. Leo and Dom both are only about an inch or two shorter than me. But my eyes and my smile are both from my mom. And while my dad has a stoic and distant personality, my mom is a social butterfly. Clearly I get that from her as well. "What are you really doing here, Luca?"

"Can't I come visit when I want?"

"Yes, but this is unusual for you." She studies me carefully, and I try to keep my expression as benign as possible. As her eyes narrow, I know I did a shitty job. "This involves a girl."

I let out an outlandish guffaw and roll my eyes. "What? Why would you say that? That's absurd, Mom."

"I know you, *Cocco*. No one knows you better than me. Do you want to tell me about her, or would you rather I find out myself?"

"What now?" I ask.

She giggles wickedly. "Oh you sweet stupid boy. You think I don't have my ways?"

"Scaring me a little bit, Mom."

"Good. I like keeping all my babies on their toes."

"Your littlest baby is twenty-six, Mom. I think it's safe to say we aren't babies anymore."

She sighs, a sweet smile on her face. "If you are given the privilege of becoming a parent, Luca, you'll understand. Regardless of age, you'll always be my baby."

"Okay, I guess," I murmur as Arianna joins us.

"Did she tell you?" Ari asks giddily.

"Tell me what?" I respond.

"About our new special events coordinator."

"No? Should I care?" I ask, confused.

My mom and sister smile knowingly at each other before Ari walks away. My mom turns to me. "Remember what I said about always knowing about the women in your life, Luca?"

"Yes?"

"I always know, *Cocco*. Go get your girl," she says as she pushes me toward the dining room. "Go on. Trust me."

I don't even take two steps before I stop dead in my tracks.

What the fuck?

I only see the top of her head, but I'd recognize those blonde curls anywhere. As her entire body comes into view, I see she's carrying a stack of files, viciously typing away on her phone, and unaware of my whereabouts. A pencil skirt showcases the ass I can't see, but is imprinted in my memory, and her red stilettos show off her calves perfectly. But most of all, there's an aura around Hannah. I feel myself calming, just being in her space.

"Pixie?"

Hannah's head snaps up, and when our eyes meet, she gives me a beaming smile. "Luca, what are you doing here?"

I still haven't moved. "What are you doing here?"

Hannah's smile wavers, and she awkwardly chuckles. "I work here?"

"You work here." She nods. "At my family's hotel?"

Hannah visibly pales as her fingers stop typing. "Your family? Your family owns this?"

"Yes? Did you seriously not know that?"

She shakes her head emphatically. "Arianna got me the interview, and I never researched the family who owns it, and I just hit the ground running with back-to-back events, and I only briefly mentioned the new job, but didn't tell you anything about it, and I never thought you'd have a connection here, but why are you here anyway?"

God I love this woman.

I fucking love her.

This rambling, chaotic, sweet, emotional, protective woman. She is perfection. Absolute exquisite perfection.

As Hannah bites down on her bottom lip nervously, I realize I've been staring at her for an unknown period of time, making her anxious and unsure. That ends now.

Striding up to her, I cup her face and lower my lips to hers. She sighs against my lips as her taste explodes on me. I groan as her tongue tentatively skirts out to feather against my lips. And while my dick is telling me to deepen this kiss, my heart is telling me to slow. Worship her. I'll have so many other opportunities to have my way with Hannah, but at this moment, when I know without a shadow of a doubt that she's my future, I have all the time in the world to revel in this kiss.

Hannah breaks away breathlessly, unaware she's dropped all the files so she could grip my shirt tightly in both hands. As our eyes open simultaneously, I smile at her. "Now I know what my mom and sister were alluding to."

"What?" Hannah whispers.

"I didn't know you had a job here. Arianna was way too excited about me spontaneously showing up here, and my mom asked all kinds of questions about whatever girl had me tied up in knots."

"I have you tied up in knots?" Hannah asks, her eyes wide with wonder.

"Yeah, baby. You do."

"I don't think I've ever tied someone up before," she jokes, then she gasps in horror. "That's not what I meant!"

I chuckle. "I know what you meant. But if you'd like to be tied up, I can help with that."

Hannah's eyes grow hooded. "Promise?"

God dammit.

This woman.

Resting my forehead against hers, I nod. "Yeah, baby. I still owe you on the promise from last night anyway."

"I get off at five. Wait. I leave work at five."

"I'll get you off at five, too. Shit. I can't, I have a game tonight," I say, wincing. Fuck. I almost wish they'd scratch me. I'd rather be with Hannah tonight anyway. "Any chance you'd come to my game?"

Hannah looks torn. "I don't think it's wise for me to be at the arena right now. I'd like to get a plan in place where I can sneak in and out without Woodward, or the GM seeing me."

I sigh. "I understand."

"I'll watch the game on tv though," she says. I perk up. Better than nothing.

"You will?"

She nods. "Of course I will."

Before I can even think, I blurt out, "I love you."

Hannah's mouth drops open as her eyes fill with tears. "You do?

You didn't say anything yesterday, and I thought maybe I scared you off, but then I didn't really give you any time, and you were really tired, and —"

I cut her off with a kiss, sliding my tongue into her mouth as I pick her up and hold her against me. Her feet dangle a foot off the ground, and I feel her giggle into my mouth. Breaking off the kiss, I say, "I'm sorry. I was so fucking ecstatic about you telling me, that I didn't realize I didn't say it back. Of course I love you, Han. You're everything to me. You're it for me. This is it. You and me, okay?"

"Okay," she whispers.

It's only then that I realize we're in the middle of my family's hotel, and we're surrounded by a good chunk of my family members, who are all clapping. Hannah buries her head in my chest as I lower her to the ground.

"I didn't mean to embarrass you, baby," I say quietly. She looks up at me, her eyes full of love, and I know I've never had anyone look at me like that before. And I know I'll do whatever I can to ensure Hannah always looks at me this way.

"I'm not embarrassed, but this is my place of employment, and I am actually on the clock," she admits. As I'm about to apologize again, her eyes soften as she cups my cheek tenderly. "You could never embarrass me, Luca. And I love your family. I just wish I had known they were your family ... dammit, Dominic is your brother? I knew he looked somewhat familiar!"

As if he knew she mentioned him, my brother strolls up. "Hannah, I don't think we've properly met. Dominic Santo."

"You could have led with your last name during the interview, you know," Hannah says wryly.

"I could have, but where was the fun in that? Plus Ari told me not to. We were all on strict orders to not mention our 'famous' brother," Dom says with air quotes.

"Still here to have lunch with your favorite girl, *Cocco*?" Mom teases.

"I believe I said favorite mom, not favorite girl."

"Ahh. Touché, my sweet boy. Go have lunch with your favorite girl, then," Mom says with a wink.

Turning to Hannah, I grab her hand and bring it to my lips. "What do you say? May I have lunch with my favorite girl?"

Hannah absolutely beams. "As long as you tell me what *cocco* means."

"Our parents have Italian nicknames for all of us. They've called me *Cocco* for as long as I can remember. It means sweetie. Although just a few minutes ago she also called me a sweet stupid boy, so she likes to add terms of endearment in English too."

"I'll try to refrain from referring to you as a sweet and stupid boy," Hannah giggles.

"I will allow it if you change 'boy' to 'man.' Actually, as long as you say I'm your man, I don't care what you call me," I tell her as I slide an arm around her and pull her against me.

"Mine?" she whispers.

"Yours."

"Are you sure you're willing to take this risk right now? We can hold off, wait until the season ends or something," Hannah murmurs. After retrieving all of the files from the floor, I quickly kiss her lips.

"I told you a while ago that you were worth the risk, Hannah. And I have never been more certain about anything in my life. The only regret I'll have right now is if I *don't* take the risk with you."

"Then let's get some lunch so you can get back into town for your game," Hannah says with a smile.

As we walk toward the dining room, I stop. "Hey, Han?"

"Hmm?"

"Can I spend the night again tonight?" I ask her tentatively.

"I'd love to have a Luca sleepover again," she responds with a light giggle.

Music to my ears.

Chapter 22

*H*annah

"*Y*ou piece of shit!" I shout at the television. "You miserable son of a bitch!"

Claire laughs from the couch as I pace the length of the room. Luca has been on the bench all night, the team is down by six goals, and Woodward has the audacity to look pleased with the entire debacle.

"I don't really understand hockey, but why are we yelling right now?" Claire asks as she flips through a magazine nonchalantly.

"Because that asshole thinks the sun comes up just to hear him crow!"

"I'm sorry … what now?"

"Huh?"

"Hannah. I don't speak Southern. What the hell did you just say?"

"What? Oh. Essentially I said Coach Woodward is a cocky jerk who thinks he knows everything."

"Ahh. He does look like he's peacocking quite a bit. What do you think he's saying to Luca?" she asks, and I narrow my gaze as I attempt to read his lips. While I don't know exactly what he's saying, I can gauge Luca's reaction to know it wasn't anything good.

I'm also not surprised when Luca somehow stands as he's finally called to go on the ice, and his stick whips out to hook Woodward's knee, sending Woodward to a heap on the floor. Claire gasps, but I cackle. Asshole had it coming.

"Is Luca going to get in trouble for that?" Claire asks, her mouth agape in shock.

"I don't know. But seeing the look of satisfaction on his face, I don't think he cares much," I shrug. Luca has been on one hell of a tear since Boston. I think he's had more penalty minutes than regular playing minutes.

I know, because I've watched every game. Every single one. I hated hurting him, and feeling like I was responsible for sending his career into a tailspin. I'm still not sure if it's a good idea for us to be together right now, but I can't fight it any longer. The few weeks we were apart, I was miserable. I felt like I left my heart at his apartment door, and I've just been going through the motions.

I'm not sure how Luca got under my skin so quickly. We've barely known each other for long, but the connection I have to him is unlike anything I've ever experienced before. Knowing he feels the same has made this all worth it.

"Dammit!" I hiss as Luca blatantly high-sticks an opposing player. What is going on with him? I thought if we got back together, he'd settle down. But it's almost like he's even more deter-mined to wreck things now — "Holy shit! He's doing it on purpose!"

"Who's doing what on purpose?" Claire asks.

"Luca. He's trying to make them lose," I explain.

"Why would he do that?"

"Woodward and the GM want to trade him. There's some ... drama ..." I swallow harshly as I refrain from giving out any details. The attorney Dominic provided for me was already pissed when I called him this afternoon to update him that Luca and I were together. Now I know it's the attorney the entire Santo family uses when needed, and it makes sense since Dominic is also protecting

Luca here. "Anyway, they want Luca gone, and he doesn't want to go."

"Won't losing make them even more determined to get him out of here?"

I sigh. "My guess is he's determined to make it so no one wants him."

"If he gets traded, will you go with him?"

"I don't know. We haven't even talked about that. I just started at the hotel, and I actually really like it. It'll look incredibly bad on my resume to have resigned from two positions so quickly."

"Following your partner because he had to move isn't exactly resigning, Hannah. I think anyone would understand that."

"Possibly. Damn, he got hit with another penalty! This is ridiculous," I seethe. I don't understand what he's doing here. What he thinks he'll accomplish, other than pissing off the entire organization, and thousands of fans. And seeing Woodward's look of pure unadulterated glee, I'd say Luca's penalties are having the opposite effect from whatever Luca wanted.

"You want a glass of wine? You need one so you settle down and quit the pacing," Claire asks as she stands to walk into the kitchen.

"Might as well. Looks like it's going to be a long evening."

*O*ne problem with staying so far west of downtown is the fact that it's well past midnight before Luca will get here. Since I knew it would be incredibly late, I opened up a second bottle of wine after Claire went to bed. When a knock sounded on my door, I assumed someone had let Luca in.

I should have looked through the keyhole.

"Hello, *pet*," Jefferson snarls, reaching a hand up and grabbing my neck. "You thought you could run from me? Think again, *pet*."

I always hated how he called me 'pet.' Not only is the name incredibly demeaning, but he's hissing it at me with such malice.

Looking back, it should have been a glaring red flag the first time he used it. But I was so accustomed to giving men the benefit of the doubt. And, according to my parents, Jefferson was a 'good catch from a good family.'

I try to scream out for help, but Jefferson's hand tightens. I know I only have a minute before I black out, and I swiftly bring up my knee between his legs as hard as I can. He groans and crumbles to the ground.

"Claire!" I croak, rubbing my throat. I doubt she hears me, as she sleeps with at least two oscillating fans and a white noise machine on at all times, so I know I'm on my own.

"You fucking bitch!" Jefferson moans from the floor. He's half inside the apartment and half out, one leg braced against the door, meaning I can't close it and lock him out. I run to the kitchen and grab a knife, then dash across the room to get my phone. Quickly dialing 911, I rattle off the apartment address before letting the operator know the situation. I'm surprised at my ability to remain calm in this situation. Maybe I've subconsciously known something like this would happen eventually with Jefferson, and therefore it isn't a surprise. Or maybe my fight-or-flight mode kicked in at just the right time.

I make the mistake of turning away from where Jefferson thrashes in pain on the floor for a second, and he takes the opportunity to lunge at me. The knife is ripped from my hand, and I scream in pain as the blade slashes across my palm. He has it up to my throat immediately.

"Hang up the phone, Hannah Ann," he snarls. Another red flag is how he always referred to me as Hannah Ann, just like my mother. I whimper as blood drips steadily off my fingertips, smudging my phone as I try to end the call. "Did you really think I'd give you up? I spent years training you, *pet*. I will not go back to square one and train someone else."

"Train?" I whisper.

Jefferson chuckles maliciously. "Yes, *pet*. Train. I fucking trained you. You were nothing before me. You waited at the door when I got home from work with my whiskey. You knew every meal I approved of, the restaurants I wouldn't go to, and even how much starch to use in my clothing. When you so much as thought about stepping out of line, I reeled you back in. Then you got this little harebrained idea of moving to Colorado and broke up with me. Did you really think I put up with your awful parents and your boring as fuck sorority sisters because I wanted to?"

"What do you mean that you reeled me back in?" I'm hoping I didn't fully end the 911 call, and the operator is still recording the call. I didn't realize it at the time, but I know what Jefferson is going to say.

"Reminded you who was in control, obviously. You didn't like it when I got physical with you, and you'd get back in line and do as you were expected to do."

"No, Jefferson, I didn't like when you hit me," I tell him.

"You fucking deserved it every goddamn time, Hannah Ann. Staying late at work? Being around all those sweaty athletes for fun? You were supposed to be at home waiting for *me*," he seethes.

"I worked for a college athletic program, Jefferson. It was my job."

Jefferson turns me, dragging the tip of the knife against my neck. "It's moot now. We're returning to Georgia, and you will not be working outside of my home."

"Your home?"

"Yes, *pet*, mine. It's mine until you show me you deserve to call it yours. With how disgraceful you've been, you'll be lucky if I let you sleep on the floor next to my bed."

I stare at him incredulously. His eyes are cold. His typically well-kept hair is limp and pallid, not looking like the all-American blonde I remember when we first began dating. His skin is pale and discolored, as if it's been weeks since he's washed it. He doesn't look a thing like the Jefferson I remember. It is acutely obvious how different Jefferson and Luca are. Jefferson is a weasel, and Luca is a lion.

"What happened to you?" I whisper.

Jefferson's eyes narrow. "You happened to me. You. I wasn't supposed to actually fall for you, Hannah Ann. You were just a means to an end. Then you left me, and everything fell apart. So you're coming back with me, and you're making things right."

He begins to turn me, obviously with the intent of dragging me out of the apartment, and all hell breaks loose. A loud crash jolts me as Jefferson grunts, falling forward and hitting the floor at my feet. I see Claire behind him, holding the heavy lamp from her room. At the same time, the police run into the apartment, Luca hot on their heels.

"Sir, stay back!" An officer shouts at Luca, but he pushes through and yanks me into his arms.

"Are you okay?" he whispers.

I take a stuttering breath before whimpering, "No. I'm not okay."

Sobs break as my body finally relaxes into Luca's embrace. "I've got you, *bella*. I've got you."

He picks me up, cradling me against his chest, and moves to the other side of the room, away from where Jefferson has awakened and the police are reading him his rights. Claire looks on sympathetically, still holding the lamp, as she answers questions.

Luca doesn't speak. One arm holds me tightly in his embrace, while the other rhythmically strokes up and down my spine. His breathing remains steadfast, and I feel my heart rate begin to slow as I focus on him.

"Ms. Beauregard," a voice says from above me.

"Can this wait? She's fucking traumatized," Luca snaps.

"I only have a couple questions that I need to ask now, Mr. Santo. Everything else can wait until after she's received medical care, or even tomorrow at the station."

"I don't need medical care," I mumble, my voice raspy and stuttering.

"You do, baby. You need stitches," Luca murmurs against my temple. I jolt, realizing I'm bleeding everywhere.

"Oh, Luca, your suit," I exclaim. One of his beautiful game day suits is covered in blood.

"I don't give a fuck about the suit, Pixie. All I care about is you," he says softly. I sigh, resting my forehead against his, as I struggle to rein in my emotions.

"Why don't we walk down to the ambulance, and I can ask my questions while they're getting you situated in the rig?" the officer says.

"Can't I drive myself?" I ask. Both the officer and Luca laugh.

"No, ma'am, we'd prefer you take a quick ride. Like your husband said, you've had some trauma tonight. Let us worry about the drive."

"He's not my husband," I mutter.

"Yet," Luca says. I look at him, and he smiles lovingly at me. "Yet, baby. I'm not your husband *yet*."

Leave it to Luca to make me smile during one of the most traumatic times of my life. *This man.*

After giving Claire a quick hug, Luca carries me down to the ambulance. Me telling him I was perfectly capable of walking — I think — fell on deaf ears. With it already being a late night, and my adrenaline crashing, I have to fight to keep my eyes open. I only somewhat recognize Luca climbing in the ambulance with me.

When I open my eyes again, bright lights make me squint. It takes me a moment to acclimate, and I realize I'm in a hospital bed. Luca is asleep in a chair he's pulled up next to the bed, his head resting next to my hip, my uninjured hand clasped tightly in his. I take time to study him. Even after everything, he looks so effortlessly chic and handsome. Only Luca can pull off hair sticking up in every direction. He sighs and moans quietly in his sleep, smacking his lips together and muttering some gibberish. I can't prevent the giggle that erupts from my lips, causing Luca to stir. When he raises his head to look at me, he gives me a lopsided smile.

"Morning, baby," he says, his voice deep and scratchy with sleep.

"I didn't mean to wake you."

"You didn't. At least I don't think so? I swear I heard someone talking."

"Well, you were muttering something in your sleep, but I don't know what."

"I don't talk in my sleep."

"Okay. But you absolutely do."

Luca rubs his eyes before looking at me. "How are you feeling?"

"Alright. My hand really hurts."

"I'd expect it does. The wound was deep enough you needed some internal sutures, as well as a shitload of external ones."

"How many?"

"I don't know how many internal ones, but the doctors said they did close to twenty externally."

"Why am I still here? If it was just stitches, why couldn't I leave?"

Luca chuckles. "You wouldn't stay awake. Even though you claimed you didn't have a head injury, they were apprehensive about letting you go. Plus Claire's apartment is a crime scene, so you couldn't go back there anyway. I got us a room at the hotel. As soon as you're cleared, we can go there."

"Don't you have a game tonight?"

"No. Your uncle pulled some strings and had them put me in as a healthy scratch so I could stay with you."

"Won't that cause more issues with Woodward?" I ask.

"At this point, I don't care. They can drop me today. If last night was the last time I played professional hockey, so be it. There are so many other things that are worth my time. Never thought I'd say that, but a little Georgia Peach steamrolled into my life and taught me what's truly important," Luca tells me, a hint of a smile on his face as he brings my hand to his lips and kisses is reverently. "Besides, someone has to help you right now. I'll have you know, I'm an excellent sponge bath giver."

"Exactly what I wanted to hear, Santzy," my uncle says dryly from the doorway, an expression of mild disdain on his face. "Hey, kiddo. Sorry I couldn't be here earlier. Coach wasn't exactly kosher about Luca being gone today."

I turn to Luca, worry etched in my expression. "I'll be fine. Just go. I don't want him doing anything else that could cause problems for you."

"No, I'm not leaving you, Hannah. I don't care what Woodward does. I don't even know if he actually has a tape to release."

"I'm worried about other things he could do, Luca. Ways to make you pay."

"Like what?"

"I don't know!" I shout, exasperated. "He's slicker than pig snot on a radiator! I don't trust a damn thing that comes from that man."

"I'm sorry — slicker than what now?" Luca asks.

Uncle Bennett chuckles. "It means he's a snake."

I pout. "My expression is better."

"I know you think that kiddo, but you're not in Georgia anymore. Some of those more regional sayings need to be left at the border."

"Seriously, slicker than pig snot? Is that what you said?" Luca asks, his face screwing up adorably as he visualizes it.

"Slicker than pig snot on a radiator. It's a fine saying, and y'all should use it more. Perfectly defines Woodward. He's a shady person, and I don't trust him at all."

Uncle Bennett clears his throat. "Hannah, do you have any reason to believe that your ex-boyfriend may have been in cahoots with Coach Woodward?"

"I wouldn't think so. They don't exactly run in the same circle," I respond.

"I don't want you to jump to any conclusions, but I actually think there is a connection between the two. You say you saw him at your work weeks ago, then he made no effort to visit you again. Suddenly he shows up at your new apartment? How did he manage that? Did anyone know where you were living?"

"No. Just you and Aunt Caroline ..." I trail off. Uncle Bennett's expression darkens as his lips flatten in a thin line. While my relationship with my aunt has never been the best, his relationship with his sister has been a roller coaster. "She wouldn't do this, would she?"

"I wouldn't put it past her, pot pie," Uncle Bennett says quietly.

"Pot pie? You *still* call her pot pie?" Luca teases, effectively diffusing the tense atmosphere.

"Technically my dad called her that, but I continued the tradition when she begged us to call her a pumpkin pie. What were you, around three?" Uncle Bennett says, a smile tugging at his mouth.

"I don't know. Maybe. You can stop calling me pot pie whenever. I'm twenty-eight, Uncle Bennett."

"Pretty sure I told you a good decade ago to stop with the Uncle bullshit, yet here we are."

"Call it even?" I ask.

"Deal."

$\mathcal{L}$uca

$\mathcal{B}$ringing Hannah back to the hotel is both a blessing and a curse. It's great to keep her away from anyone that may have been an accomplice with her ex-boyfriend, but it also means my family is constantly flittering in and out to check on her.

It's safe to say I'm not the only Santo family member in love with Hannah. I even saw my stoic father crack a smile when she joked about getting back to work quickly. My somewhat reclusive grandmother, Annamaria Santo, even came to meet her after Hannah was discharged from the hospital.

"Good hips," she announced.

"Nonna!" Arianna shouted.

"What? It's just an observation," Nonna shrugged.

"You can't comment on a person's physical appearance like that, Nonna," Arianna chastised.

"Eh. I'm almost eighty. I do what I want."

Hannah watched the entire altercation with a smile on her face, and later told me she loved my grandmother immediately. And once my grandmother found out that Hannah enjoyed making jam from scratch, she promised to teach Hannah all about Palisade peaches and Rocky Ford melons, two well-known fruits from Colorado, and to share her personal jam recipes that only a select few family members know.

Hannah has officially been welcomed into the Santo family fold.

While all that was wonderful, I just really wanted some time with my girl.

Alone.

Coach Davenport might have gotten me one day off, but he couldn't swing the next road trip. Knowing I was leaving for five days right after Hannah was assaulted had me sick to my stomach. When I suggested I would quit, Hannah demanded I stay on the team. The attorney was close to finalizing the report he'd be taking to the police, and if I quit, everyone feared the case would fall apart.

After I finally dragged a very content Hannah away from my family, I slammed the 'do not disturb' sign on the room door and shoved a chair under the handle.

"I don't think that's necessary," Hannah says as she watches me from the bed. "He's in jail."

"I know that," I huff. "This is about my family. I love them, but they don't understand personal space. At least one of them has a universal key to open every door. I'm not taking any chances."

"You really think they'd just barge in here?"

"Wouldn't be the first time. I leave in the morning, Pixie. We just got back together, and they've monopolized your attention for the past twelve hours. I just want to hold you. I *need* to hold you, Han."

"Okay, honey," Hannah says quietly, holding up her good hand and beckoning me to her. I kneel on the ground in front of her, making her a few inches taller than me. Laying my head on her chest, I let out a relieved breath as her natural scent surrounds me.

"I don't want to leave you," I mutter.

"I know."

I look up at her as her hand finds my hair. "Are you sure you're going to be okay?"

She rolls her eyes and giggles. "I really don't think your family will let me be anything but okay. Nonna has plans for me."

"Are you choosing to call her Nonna?"

"No. She demanded it."

I chuckle. "That sounds like Nonna."

"What happened to your grandfather?" Hannah asks.

"He died a while ago. Ten years ago, maybe? I don't really remember, to be honest. All I remember is thinking he was the polar opposite of Nonna. She's loud, rambunctious, and the life of the party. He was very reserved. Stoic, like my dad. Dom remembers him really well, as does Alex. They said they never knew how Nonna put up with him."

"Sometimes the most outspoken people need someone to remind them when to reel it in," Hannah says quietly.

I look up at her, and she's staring off to the side. "Is that how your ex-boyfriend was?"

"No, not really. Starting out, he was quieter, but seemed really optimistic and enjoyed life. Went with the flow more. I thought he was spontaneous and charming. I can look back now and recognize how he slowly flipped a switch, and I didn't even notice it. He became regimented and authoritarian. I slowly began to change to match his energy, because if he was happy, it was easier. Once I realized I no longer recognized the person I had become, I wanted out. Only then was it evident that it was an incredibly unhealthy and abusive relationship."

"Fucking hate that you went through that, *bella*," I murmur, lowering my head to rest in her lap as she rhythmically runs her fingers through my hair.

"I don't regret it, you know. The relationship with him. It taught me so much about myself. What I won't settle for, and what I expect with a partner. Getting out of Georgia may not have happened if I wasn't so miserable. And it brought me to you," she says softly. "Let's get ready for bed. You have to be up in a few hours."

That quick reminder of my job makes me truly hate hockey for the first time in my life. Wordlessly, I get up and pull Hannah to the bathroom.

"What's all this?" Hannah asks. Multiple shopping bags cover the countertop and floor.

"I wasn't sure when you'd be able to get back into your apartment, and honestly, I didn't want you to go back there while I was gone anyway. So I asked Arianna to pick up some things for you. She and Claire remembered some of your skincare and shower things, but they guessed on some. My mom sent over a week's worth of clothes that would be easy for you to remove while your hand is still wrapped."

Hannah tears up, pressing her good hand to her mouth. "I don't deserve this. I don't — I'm not. This is too much, Luca."

Cupping her face between my hands, I force her eyes to meet mine. "You deserve everything, Han. Anything I have is yours. Anything you want, I'll get it for you. You name it, baby. Whatever you need."

"I just want your heart," she whispers.

"It's yours," I rasp, my voice thick with emotion. Our lips meet in a kiss I intend to keep soft and sweet, but Hannah molds herself to me and thrusts her tongue into my mouth. My greedy girl yanks hard on my hair as she rises on her tiptoes to get closer to me. Picking her up, I push the bags out of the way so I can deposit her on the counter. Hannah spreads her legs and I step between them, wanting to get as close to her as possible.

Our kiss is carnal. It's sloppy, as if we can't bother slowing down for fear of the moment ending. I want more, but I can't seem to stop kissing her. I'll be gone for five days, and I want her taste embedded in my skin. On my taste buds. I want to wake up and smell Hannah every morning that I'm gone.

Because there's no way I can leave her again.

I'll go on this last road trip, but that's it. I can't leave her again.

"Luca," Hannah whimpers into my mouth.

"What do you need, Pixie?" I ask, breaking the kiss to bury my face in her neck. Her pulse is going wild against my lips, and I suck hard against it, hoping I leave a mark. My mark. A blatant sign to anyone that Hannah is spoken for. Considering Hannah lets out a loud and guttural moan, I'd say she supports me staking a claim.

"I need you to ..." she trails off. I stand to look at Hannah, noticing her heavily hooded eyes and blown-out pupils showing how turned on she is.

"Tell me."

"I want your tongue. I need you to make me come on your tongue."

Damn.

I love take-charge Hannah.

Well, I love Hannah all the time, but her telling me *exactly* what she needs? Fucking hot as hell.

"My pleasure," I murmur as I kneel in front of her once again. Stripping her of her pants and underwear, I'm all too thrilled to bury my face between her legs and get reacquainted with her pussy. I groan as her taste coats my tongue. I'd almost forgotten how exquisite she tastes.

Almost.

Latching onto her clit and sucking hard, Hannah's wild cries of pleasure reverberate against the bathroom walls as I take her higher and higher. Her hand is clamped down on top of my head as if she fears I'll suddenly stop. Not a chance, Pixie. I'm down here until you push me away. It's been too long since I've had her this way, and I'll be damned if she's only coming once this way tonight.

Hannah's first orgasm creeps up on me. I'm so focused on enjoying myself that I miss all her telltale signs that she's about to come. When her body bows and her hand tightens so much I fear she might actually pull some of my hair out, I double down on my efforts to extend the orgasm as much as possible. As her entire body shivers through the aftershocks, I don't give her any time to relax before I slide two fingers in and tap repeatedly on her G-spot. With this orgasm, she cries out, making me realize her first orgasm made her lose her breath.

Now it's my mission to make her silently come again.

Hannah is fully slumped back against the bathroom mirror, but she's not pushing me away or telling me to stop. As I lap away, slowly dragging my tongue from bottom to top, I collect some of her wetness on my finger and slide it back to her untouched rosebud. She stiffens momentarily, until I suck on her clit again, and she relaxes against the mirror.

I circle my finger, allowing her to get used to the sensation, and she begins to fidget, her hips rhythmically moving in time with my ministrations. Achingly slowly, I push one digit past the tight ring of muscle. She lets out a low moan as I begin to slowly push my finger in and out. I slow my tongue to match my finger, and Hannah's hips slow as well.

"More," she whispers.

"Where?"

"Everywhere. I want to feel you everywhere."

I slowly pull my finger out and add a second finger. She winces momentarily as I begin to push both fingers back in, her body stiffening immediately, until I flick her clit rapidly with the tip of my tongue. Hannah relaxes again, and I'm able to get both fingers in past the first knuckle. As soon as I begin pushing in and out, Hannah's hips match the pace.

"Anyone ever taken you here before?" I murmur against her. Hannah shakes her head. "You gonna let me take this ass, baby? You gonna let me have this last part of you?"

I look up at her to find her staring down at me with a look of divine pleasure on her face like I've never witnessed before. Hannah has never looked more breathtaking than she does at this moment. As I slide fingers from my other hand into her pussy and hit her G-spot, her body stiffens as her eyes roll back. A gush of wetness hits my chin and neck as Hannah comes harshly, her cries of pleasure like music to my ears. I continue to manipulate her pussy and ass as her orgasm lasts for a few minutes as I lap up every ounce of her cum. Once she stops shaking, I slowly remove my fingers and sit back on my heels. It's then that I realize the gush of wetness I felt was more substantial than I thought, and I'm completely soaked down to my waistband.

Hannah squirted all over me, and I've never been fucking happier.

Standing, I chuckle at the scene in front of me. My Pixie is half on the counter, half off, her legs dangling dangerously off the edge. She has slinked down across the sink, her chin resting against the cold water handle, and a good chunk of her hair is over her face.

"Hannah?" I ask.

No response.

"You okay, baby?"

Sigh. Mumble. Fart.

A ladylike fart. A perfect Pixie fart. But a fart nonetheless.

Did I push her into an orgasm stupor? Is she asleep, knocked out, or so blissed out she doesn't even know what's going on?

"Will you marry me?" Hannah mumbles.

"Huh?" I shout. No way I heard that correctly.

"Need to lock you down. You're not allowed to do that to anyone else," she sighs.

"Did you seriously just ask me to marry you?"

"It's the twenty-first century. Women can ask too," she murmurs.

"I'd like to do the asking, if that's alright with you," I respond.

"Mmhmm," she hums.

"Come on, Pixie, let's get you to bed," I chuckle as I begin to pull her into a sitting position so I can carry her to the bed, her hand immediately snakes down to cup my hard as a rock erection.

"Not until I get to return the favor, handsome," she says slyly as she attempts to slide off the counter. And as much as I would love to feel her mouth on me, if she's game for more, I'm coming in her pussy.

"Another time for that, Pix. I'd rather be inside you," I tell her as I push my shoulder into her midsection. Hannah shrieks when I stand and stride out of the bathroom, then she giggles gleefully as she pummels my ass with one hand.

"Not a bad view," she muses before spanking me again.

A zing of pleasure courses along my spine, and I'm taken aback at how much I liked Hannah spanking me. Shouldn't that be the other way around?

"Liked that, big boy?" Hannah taunts.

I unceremoniously dump her on the bed, and she bounces twice before coming to a rest. "Does it make me any less of a man to say I did like it?"

Hannah gives me a beaming smile. "No. It means you trust me to experiment with."

I slowly strip off my shirt, watching as Hannah's eyes slowly drag up and down my chest as she bites her lip. I reach forward and grab her chin, forcing her lip to pop out from between her teeth. "That's my lip to bite, baby."

"Then hurry up and do it, Luca. I need you," she whimpers. "Hurry up or I'll do it myself."

My sweet, dirty girl.

I'm gonna have so much fun with her.

"Sit up so I can get your shirt off," I tell her. Hannah sits up, holding both arms above her head with an innocent smile on her face, waiting for me to remove her shirt. Due to the wrap around her injured hand, she's not wearing a bra, because she can't clasp it, and I immediately bend down to take one nipple deep in my mouth. Hannah lets out a moan, and slides her hand into my waistband to grab my stiff cock tightly. Now it's my turn to groan as she painstakingly slowly jacks me. The telltale burning sensation that begins at the base of my spine alerts me to one of the quickest orgasms of my life, and I stumble away from Hannah.

"What?" she asks, worry covering her face.

"You were about to make me a two-pump chump, Pix. I need a minute," I tell her. Best way to pull away from an orgasm is to visualize an image that horrifies you. Which is why I picture Gabe Dawson's flat white ass.

"Why are you chanting Gabe's ass over and over again?" Hannah giggles.

"Shh, it's working."

"Should I leave? Give you and imaginary Gabe some time alone?"

"Hush, woman."

"I probably should be concerned, but I think I want to see how this plays out."

I groan as she smiles prettily at me. Tipping my head to the ceiling, I send up a silent prayer to whoever sent this woman to me. I've had a lot of sex in my life, but I've never been teased during it so amazingly. Fucking perfection.

"Trust me, baby," I murmur as I strip out of my pants and climb onto the bed so I'm hovering over her, "I'm about to rid you of the ability to speak, and you'll know you're the only person I'm thinking about."

"Promises, promises, L — holy shit!" she screams as I slam into her in one thrust. The scream turns to a loud moan as she digs her fingernails into my back.

"You okay, baby?" I tease, beginning a measured pace where I'm giving everything to her, but not fast enough to make her come. Keeping this pace allows me to focus on her, and not on my own pleasure. I know as soon as I speed up, or when she comes, it'll be game over.

"Luca," she mutters.

"*Bella.*"

Her eyes open, staring clearly into mine. Her expression takes my breath away. The love I see is mind-boggling. The support and acceptance. Understanding. This woman is my equal. My partner. The person who will stand beside me for the rest of my life. And that feeling is remarkably humbling.

I'm overcome with emotion, tears burning the back of my eyelids. I grab Hannah's good hand from my shoulder and link our fingers together above her head. Her injured hand is wrapped around my neck tightly, as if she fears I'll suddenly get up and leave.

I'm never leaving. I need her to breathe.

"I love you," I whisper. A tear cascades down the side of her face, and I lean down to kiss the path it took. Hannah's breath catches when I bring my lips to hers. I know she can taste the saltiness of her own tears, and the essence of her orgasms from earlier. It's a poignant and erotic moment between lovers.

I can tell I'm close to coming, but I want Hannah right there with me. Her eyes remain open, but they're glazed over, and when I feel her walls begin to flutter around me, I pounce.

Amping up the pace, I rut into her harshly, resting my forearm on the bed next to her neck, our hands still entwined. I slide my other hand between our bodies, both slick with sweat, and find her clit. All it takes is a quick one-two-three flick, and Hannah's body tightens as her walls clamp down on me. I can barely thrust through my own orgasm because she's gripping me so hard. I keep coming and coming, rope after rope of cum coating her walls. Pulling out, I rise to my knees and grab my cock. A few pulls and I manage two more ropes that dot her stomach, breasts, and face.

Hannah covered in my cum is the most beautiful thing I've ever seen in my life. "Damn, baby. You're fucking gorgeous like this."

"Like what?" she asks breathlessly, her chest rising and falling in cadence with mine.

"Covered in me."

The little minx looks me dead in the eye before swiping her fingers through my cum, bringing them to her mouth, and licking them clean.

"If I ask, will you wake me up every morning to do that?" she whispers.

"For the rest of my life."

Chapter 24

*H*annah

I wake up blissfully sore, but alone.

I knew I would wake up alone, but it still hurt my heart.

As I stretch my arms above my head, I wonder where Luca is in the world right now. I'm not even sure if I know where this road trip was going. West Coast? Canada? Who knows.

My brief tenure with the Denver Wolves allowed me to get a backstage tour of how the team works. Originally, I found it odd that the team tended to travel on early morning flights, but chalked it up to my only experience being with a college football team. Maybe all NHL teams did this, I surmised.

I've now learned that it's basically just Coach Woodward being a dick.

Most NHL teams will travel the night before so the players have time to sleep on the plane, and then again at the team hotel, before they're required to attend any team practices or function. Woodward likes to schedule activities after the games, then forces the team to travel in the morning.

Honestly, it's a surprise there haven't been more injuries at away games, because there's no way they're rested. I forcibly shake my head to rid my mind of horrid visions including Luca being hurt, potentially thousands of miles away from me. Lord knows Woodward would probably stand over him and laugh instead of help him in any way.

As my arms stretch above my head, I hear a beep as the door is unlocked. Even knowing it won't be him, my heart hopes it's Luca.

"Put the girls away, ma'am," Arianna shouts as she covers her eyes.

"What?"

"I didn't come here to see your high beams, Hannah." She points with the same hand, her eyes squeezed shut, and I realize the sheet has fallen from where I had it pulled against my neck.

"I'd apologize, but you barged into my room. You're lucky your brother isn't here, or you'd have probably gotten quite the eyeful."

"True," she muses, "but I do enjoy when I have something to hold over my brothers' heads. It's especially great at holiday events."

I roll my eyes as I try to shimmy up in the bed using only one hand, while also ensuring my sheet stays faithfully atop my chest. "Why are you here, Ari?"

"Oh. I figured you might want some help getting dressed, and I brought you a coffee. Also Luca told me to show up here since he wouldn't be able to."

"Well go put your nose in the corner by the door so I can run to the bathroom."

"Seriously? My nose in the corner?" Arianna scrunches up her nose as if appalled by the thought.

"You didn't have to do that as a kid?"

"No."

"How did your parents discipline you?"

She shrugs. "I don't know. I'm the baby of the family. I didn't get disciplined."

"That really explains a lot," I mutter. "Turn around! I'm not letting you see anything other than the high beams."

"Jesus, are you buck naked under there? Gross. Better tell house-keeping to really bleach these sheets," Arianna teases.

I decide two can play at this game. "You're absolutely right. Because I got some last night. All night long, actually. How was your night?"

"Touché, Hannah Ann Beauregard. Nicely played," Arianna comments with a grin. "I'll stand over here and I promise I won't peek."

I'm not taking any chances. I rip the sheet from the bed and make a run for the bathroom as soon as she turns around. Surveying the bathroom, I notice Luca has organized everything Ari purchased for me so it's easier for me to access. He's even removed all the tags from the clothing. I quickly put on underwear, pants, and a long sleeved shirt, foregoing the bra. I'm not asking Arianna to help me put on a bra, and frankly, I can go without. The high beams Ari spoke about are more like tiny lightbulbs on a moped. Not much to write home about on top, but I know I've got a banging ass.

As I walk out of the bathroom, I find Arianna staring at the bed with a wistful expression on her face. She looks almost lost. She lets out a big sigh, making me feel awful about teasing her.

"Thanks for coming to help, but I did okay. Y'all did a great job of buying me things that would be easy to put on. What do I owe you?" I ask as I take the coffee from her hand.

She snorts. "I didn't pay. Luca did. Good luck getting him to accept payment from you. He loves to spend money on the people who are important to him."

My heart flutters a bit thinking about Luca. I never knew a man, a partner, could be so caring and thoughtful. Even my own father never showed compassion, or love, toward my mother. Theirs was a business arrangement, plain and simple. In the short time I've been working at Everlasting, I've already seen that Luca's parents modeled a different dynamic for their kids. Nick Santo might appear callous and borderline cold, but when looking at his wife, his entire demeanor shifts. He softens. His love and adoration for her is evident. If Luca looks at me like that, I know I'll be the happiest woman in the world.

"Are you working today? My parents said you could take the day off," Arianna says.

"I'm going to see how much work I can do. I want to stay busy. I think I'll have to go speak to the police at some point, but other than that, I've got nothing to do. If I sit here, I'll just think about everything that happened, and miss Luca."

"Denial. Good choice."

"It's not denial. I know myself, Ari. If I have too much time to let the events marinate in my head, I'll become really depressed. I have every intention of getting a therapist to help me work through what has happened. I just don't want to spiral into a depressive episode, especially with Luca gone."

Arianna nods. "Okay. As long as you're sure. Let's head down and see what we can scrounge up for breakfast."

Heading downstairs, I get a wave from Sofia, Luca's mom, and a hug from Isabella as she's leaving to go back to her bakery. She supplies tons of desserts, breads, and other treats for the hotel while also holding her own as a business owner. As we're about to step into the dining room, I hear someone call my name.

"Uncle Bennett? What are you doing here? Why aren't you on the team plane?" I ask, obviously confused.

"I got fired on the tarmac this morning," he tells me. My mouth drops open.

"What? Why? Who fired you?"

"Woodward. Han, he knows you're working a case against him. He figured I was involved and fired me."

My stomach drops. During all the chaos from the past two days, I hadn't gotten an opportunity to respond to the lawyer yet about the case. He was ready to move forward with presenting everything to the police. I couldn't process that while trying to process Jefferson showing up, and I chose not to answer the lawyer yet. Now I regret it.

"What should we do?" I ask.

"You need to go to the police right now," Arianna interjects. "Where is the team headed on this away trip?"

"Seattle, Portland, and Vancouver," Uncle Bennett answers.

"Luca is in danger. You know that, right?" Ari says, her voice getting slightly louder. "Coach Woodward has a friend who is an assistant coach on the Seattle team. Actually, I think all three assistant coaches are friends of his. My gut is telling me something is going to happen to Luca at that game."

"I thought a team could only have two assistant coaches," I reply, clearly choosing to ignore the doomsday prophecy Arianna just claimed.

"There aren't set numbers. A team can have as many, or as few, as they want. But I agree with Arianna, Han. I think Luca's in trouble," Uncle Bennett says.

"What am I supposed to do about that? They're in another state. Luca keeps his phone off the afternoon of a game. I can't exactly text him and say, 'hey, honey, your coach is trying to hurt you, be careful and good luck' now can I?" My voice wobbles as I struggle to keep my emotions at bay.

"No, but if you show up there, and he sees you on the ice, he'll know something is wrong," Bennett stresses.

My phone pings with a text, jolting me with adrenaline.

> Attorney: We need to move on this, Hannah. I have a report that your aunt is assisting the coach in setting everyone up, including your uncle. Woodward is becoming more unhinged, and the earlier we let the police take over the case, the better.

I close my eyes in pain. My aunt? Really? It hurts my heart to know she's as cold-blooded and apathetic as my parents. I'm not that surprised she is in cahoots with Coach Woodward, but it makes me doubt everything that has happened so far. Her letting me stay at her apartment, and her unceremonious arrival back home that was timed so perfectly with the coach threatening to release a video from my time with Luca in Boston. Was any of it real?

Clearing my throat, I look at my uncle. "I need to meet with the attorney immediately, and then take all of the information to the police. After that, we can go to Seattle. Can you book us a flight?"

"Of course." Uncle Bennett looks uncertain. "This is a lot to take in. Are you okay?"

"Oh, sure," I tell him with a shaky smile. "But this week can suck it."

He chuckles. "Completely agree."

*T*he attorney was all too thrilled to hand over the entire investigation to the police. I wasn't sure if I did the right thing by not preemptively telling my uncle about my aunt's potential involvement, but the attorney agreed with me to let the police handle it. If Aunt Caroline did in fact set all of us up, including her own brother, then she needs to be held accountable.

One factor I didn't count on was the involvement of the terrible terrors. Lindsay and Jessica had both been incredibly helpful with getting information to the attorney. They had at least six other female employees who were willing to go on record that Coach Woodward had touched them inappropriately, and another few who said they were propositioned by Woodward.

A detail in the investigative report showed that a few players were approached as well. Luca's arch nemesis Gabe Dawson reported more than once that Woodward wanted him to set Luca up, and Gabe refused. The only thing he admitted was riling Luca up in the locker room on one occasion. I sincerely hope Gabe is a better person than Luca has always thought.

After handing everything over to Denver PD, we made our way to the airport for our afternoon flight. Uncle Bennett managed to get us two seats on a budget airline with a layover in San Francisco. We'd arrive in Seattle just before puck drop, and wouldn't get to the arena until the second period.

I only hope nothing disastrous happens before then.

"Hannah."

I look up at my uncle, who watches me with a hint of a smile. "Hmm?"

"You're shaking the entire row of seats, pot pie."

I didn't even realize I was shaking my leg, so lost in my own thoughts. "Sorry."

"You don't need to apologize, kiddo. I know you're freaked out."

"It's just ..." I trail off, trying to collect my thoughts. "If something happens to him, I won't forgive myself."

"This isn't your fault."

"I encouraged him to go, Uncle Bennett. He wanted to resign from the team. He didn't want to leave me."

"He really wanted to quit?"

I nod.

"Damn. I had no idea he was set on that."

"Had he mentioned it to you before?" I ask.

"No, but I could definitely see it. There's a point in every aging hockey player's career where shit just gets tiring. Every year there's a younger and faster guy trying to take your spot. I could see it in Luca's eyes when it stopped being fun for him."

"I don't want him to regret giving it up for me," I confess.

"He's not giving anything up, Han. He's gaining so much more than hockey. He's getting a future with you. You can't put a price tag on that."

I let my uncle's words marinate in my thoughts through our flight to San Francisco, and the hour layover. After taking off on the two-hour flight to Seattle, I finally speak up. "How will I know?"

"Know what?" Uncle Bennett responds.

"If I made the right choice. If Luca doesn't regret anything. Everything."

He chuckles. "Seeing as how I'm single with zero prospects for a woman, I don't think I can give you dating or relationship advice, Han. I can only say this: close your eyes and envision your future. Think about picking up your son from daycare, and going home to your cute house full of toddler toys, Georgia peach paraphernalia, " I giggle at that thought, "and your husband cooking dinner. Is it Luca at the stove? When you've had a bad day, who do you want to run to? Who will make your heart feel better? If Luca doesn't come up for all of those scenarios, then we can get right back on a plane in Seattle and head back to Denver. But if it is Luca in your dreams, then we're doing the right thing."

I think about picking up my child — a daughter, because Uncle Bennett is clearly wrong there — and going to my cute house in Eternity Springs. Only a few Georgia items, but lots of things that remind me of my husband. A room devoted solely to his hockey career, but with a smattering of toddler toys throughout the room as well. A beautiful juxtaposition to explain our unique dynamic. And Luca, with help from his mom, cooking lasagna at the stove. As soon as he turns to give me his breathtaking smile, I know. Luca is my destiny.

"He's it for me, Uncle Bennett," I say quietly.

He gives me a soft smile. "I know he is, pot pie. I just wanted to make sure you knew it, too."

J'm all too thrilled when we land twenty minutes early, and Uncle Bennett convinces the flight attendants to let us deplane first. I have no idea what he told them. He could have offered up my firstborn for all I know. But we were allowed to quickly move up the aisle and onto the jetway before anyone else. A cart awaited us to whisk us to the terminal, where an Uber was ready.

The fifteen mile route from Sea-Tac to downtown Seattle may have only taken twenty minutes, but I swear it felt like an hour.

"Do we have a plan?" Uncle Bennett asks.

"I texted a physical therapist with the team. She's snagged a couple team passes so we can sneak in and try to find Luca."

He clears his throat. "Uh, which physical therapist?"

I stare at him, my eyes narrowing with recollection. "Elsie. Remember? You introduced us months ago."

Uncle Bennett's face reddens. "Uh, yeah. Yeah, I uh, I remember that. I didn't know you kept in touch with her."

"Not incredibly often, but yes, we've kept in touch. You ready to tell me about her yet, Coach?" I tease.

He emphatically shakes his head. "Nope."

I roll my eyes. "Something clearly happened between y'all."

"I'm not discussing this with you, kiddo."

"You act like you're so much older than me. I'm still an adult."

"Yeah, well, she's basically not, so nothing can happen there."

"Why not?" I ask, thrilled to have this nice diversion from the anxious turmoil in my stomach.

"She's still a kid, Han."

"I'm fairly certain twenty-five is considered an adult in most states." I pause, sarcastically putting my finger to my chin, as if in deep thought, before continuing. "No, wait. She's an adult in *every* state, Uncle Bennett."

"She's still a decade younger than me. And we work together."

"Worked."

"What?" he asks.

"You worked together. You no longer work together."

"Shit. I forgot I got fired," he grimaces. "We're here. Where is Elsie meeting us?"

I quickly text her, and she gives me detailed directions to what entrance she's stationed at. When we arrive, she's not alone.

"Who the fuck is that?" my uncle growls.

"Not sure," I murmur. He's taut with animosity. He's staring at

Elsie with feral desire. Obsession. Even I'm surprised with how quickly he stalks up to Elsie and grabs her head, taking her lips in a deep kiss.

I look at Ben, the intern working with Elsie, and he chuckles as he shakes his head. Ben is gay. Obviously, Uncle Bennett doesn't know that. Was this a setup to get him to recognize what he'd lose if he didn't get over this age thing? I don't know. Whatever it was, it worked.

"Here," Uncle Bennett says, breaking off the kiss to shove a visitor badge in my hand. "Go. I'll be here."

It's my turn to chuckle. Evidently finally realizing he wants Elsie trumps my need to get to Luca.

"Come on, girl. I'll take you to where the Zamboni is," Ben tells me as he puts his arm through mine. "You ready to make an entrance?"

"Huh?" I ask him, confused.

"Elsie assumed you wanted to make an entrance. We've got you on board the Zamboni between the second and third periods."

"Um, no thank you," I tell him hastily. "I just need to see Luca and make sure he's okay."

"We were hoping you'd steal the show, girl."

"No. Not at all. I just need to speak to him and warn him about what's going on."

"I think he'd know something was amiss if he saw you on the Zamboni."

"But so would everyone else, including whoever is out to hurt him!" I don't specify that Coach Woodward is the main issue, because I want to keep this as close to a few people as possible. Elsie only knows I needed to speak with Luca urgently.

Upon our arrival at the Zamboni entrance, Ben points down a long hallway. "The locker rooms are down there. I snuck a peek at the Seattle one, and damn, it's crazy impressive."

"The actual room, or the boys?"

"Both, girl. Always both," he winks. "Seattle has the sexiest men in the NHL."

"Our boys hear you saying that, they're likely to be pissed."

Ben scoffs. "Please. A good fourth of our boys are at least bi."

I stop and stare at him. "Seriously?"

He nods. "Ask me how I know, my sweet Georgia peach."

"If you're planning to go into detail, I think I'd rather it remain a mystery."

"Ruin the fun for me, then. But cute that you still refer to the team as *your* boys, Hannah."

"They aren't the problem," I mutter.

Suddenly, Ben pushes me to the side. "Shit. Turn around and cover your face."

Confused, I do as he asked. Before I can inquire to the issue, I hear Woodward shouting at everyone. Ben just saved me from a very awkward run-in.

"Santo!" Ben calls. "I'd like to check your knee out before you go back on the ice."

"Hurry the fuck up!" Woodward snarls.

"Wait a minute, then go into the locker room, girl," Ben murmurs over his shoulder.

"Okay," I whisper. I turn slightly, watching as the team walks down the hallway toward what I assume is a separate entrance to the ice for the teams. As soon as Woodward is out of sight, I briskly walk to the locker room. I stand behind Luca, listening to him chat with Ben.

"Nothing wrong with my knee," Luca says.

"I know. You'll thank me in a minute," Ben replies. "You sure are getting your ass handed to you out there, though. Anything else hurt?"

"My entire fucking body." Luca tilts his head to the left, and I see his profile. I audibly gasp, my hands coming to cover my mouth, as I see welts, bruises, and dried blood dotting along his neck, onto his chin, and across his cheek.

"Luca!" I cry out. He swivels in shock and barely catches me before I launch into his arms.

"Pixie, what are you doing here?" he asks, his voice muffled against my hair.

I let out a stream of gibberish, my voice becoming more and more unrecognizable as my emotions catch up with me.

"Baby, you need to slow down, I can't understand you," Luca says quietly, grabbing my shoulders and pulling me away from him to look me in the eyes.

"Luca, your face," I say miserably, reaching up to gingerly touch his lips. He winces as I touch a fresh cut. One eye is swollen, and his nose looks broken.

"Not my best look, I know," he jokes. "Most minutes I've had on the ice in a while, though."

"There's a reason for that, honey," I tell him, my voice quivering. "Woodward might have reached out to friends on Seattle's coaching staff to really give it to you today. He wants to see you hurt."

I see the flash of pain cross his eyes. "I don't know why I'm surprised."

"I'm worried. My uncle is too."

"Where is he, anyway? Coach just said he wasn't traveling this trip."

I stare at him incredulously. "Luca, Woodward fired my uncle."

"You're shitting me!"

"No. Wouldn't let him get on the plane this morning. We think — we think my aunt has been conspiring with Woodward against the both of you."

"Jesus, Han. I'm so sorry," he murmurs as his arms come around me again. He rests his chin against the top of my head as I cling to him.

"I don't want you to go back out there," I blurt out.

Luca doesn't respond for a long moment. "Then let's go."

I back away from him, looking up at his beaten face in confusion. "What do you mean?"

He gives me a soft smile. "I'm done with this. Hockey. It's no longer fun. I don't even view it as a job anymore. I'm exhausted, and everything hurts. But worse than that is how it has impacted you. I just want to be with you, Pixie. I don't want hockey to pull us apart."

"It won't pull us apart. I'll support you with playing, if that's what you want to do," I tell him.

"That's the thing. I don't want to be apart from you. Ever. I want to go to sleep with you in my arms and wake up next to you. I want to cook dinner together, and talk about our days. I don't want to FaceTime you from a couple thousand miles away, then be so fucking depressed at missing you that I can't function. I'm not sad about being done. It's time. What have I told you more than once?"

A smile grows on my face as I remember his words. "That I'm worth the risk."

"You are, baby. So let's get the fuck out of here. I want to go home."

As Luca starts removing his gear, I stop him. "Wait! Won't you get fined?"

He rolls his eyes. "It's a stupid low number for leaving a game."

"Ten thousand bucks," Ben pipes up from the doorway.

I whirl to Luca. "That's not a low number!"

Luca laughs. "Baby, I made seven million dollars last season. I can afford ten grand."

My mouth drops open. "Seven — seven million?"

He nods.

"And that was for one season?"

"Yep."

"And you've been playing for how many seasons now?"

He laughs. "Quite a few. We're set, baby."

I nibble on my lip, my mind whirling with thoughts.

"What's going on in that head of yours, Pix?"

"Aren't you worried I'm only after your money?"

Luca lets out a loud laugh as he unlaces his skates. "Not even a little bit. You're the most genuine woman I've ever met. When we're together, you treat me as Luca, the guy who irritated you from next door. You don't look at me as Luke, the hockey guy with a padded bank account."

"I fell for you before I knew who you were," I confess.

Luca stands, cupping my face with both hands. "No, baby. You fell for me knowing exactly who I am."

"Oh? And who are you?" I ask, and Luca smiles.

"Yours."

Chapter 25

*L*uca

While I was surprised to find Hannah standing in the visitor's locker room at the Seattle Serpents arena, I wasn't all that shocked when she announced she felt Woodward was in cahoots with the other team. Not only was I on the ice almost double the amount of minutes I'd been allowed over the last few weeks, but the Serpents really had it out for me.

I knew it was bad when asshat Gabe Dawson was coming to my defense and ensuring I was okay.

I also knew I wouldn't be continuing on with the Wolves one more game.

Twenty year old players can take a beating, get completely shit-faced, and still make it to morning skate the following day. As a thirty-year-old hockey defenseman, I've seen my fair share of beatings over the years. But nothing like this, and definitely not one I can recoup from in a day or two.

Looking back, I'll realize this was Woodward's hope. Give me a brutal assault on the first day of the away cycle, guaranteeing I'd perform well below my ability for the rest of the games. Then I'd either bow out myself, or he'd be able to field low-ball offers for a trade.

As much as I'd love to stick it to him, I'm tired. And Hannah is way more important than any bullshit games with an NHL coach nursing his ego. Nothing I can say will convince him I didn't sleep with his wife. The fact of the matter is, she obviously slept with someone. I was the easiest scapegoat.

But, in all honesty, I wouldn't change a damn thing, because I have Hannah. My nonna, as crazy as she is, truly believes that everything happens for a reason. It's not exactly the same as karma or kismet, but it basically means that we learn from every situation. Every experience. From all of this, I learned that, without Hannah, my life is meaningless. I'd rather have her than all the Cups. Hannah is my Holy Grail.

"Do you want to take anything else?" Hannah whispers as I grab her hand and walk toward the exit.

"Nope. Got my skates, and got you. That's all I need," I tell her, bringing her knuckles to my lips.

"Santzy, yo! What the fuck?"

I look over and see Dawson staring at us. I try to get between him and Hannah, but my little Pixie beats me to it. She lets go of my hand, marches up to Dawson, and shoves him as hard as she can.

"Woah! Calm your terrier, man," Daws says as Hannah pummels him with her firsts.

"How involved were you in this shit, Gabe? Tell me the truth!" Hannah hisses.

"Baby, it's okay. Let's just go," I cajole her.

"Not until he answers me," she says stubbornly, crossing her arms over her chest and tapping her shoe impatiently. "Come on, Daws. Answer."

"I'm not entirely sure what you're asking, but Coach told me to come get you? He says you're in first line again," Gabe says slowly.

I sigh. "Sure does seem like he's playing me a lot, huh."

"It does."

"Did he tell you ahead of time he'd be replacing you with me?" I ask.

A crease forms between Gabe's eyebrows as he digests the information. "Not exactly, but I did overhear something with one of the Seattle coaches that made me wonder."

"Did he insinuate he wanted Luca hurt tonight?" Hannah asks.

Gabe nods. "I didn't put it together until you were really getting railed on out there. You okay, man?"

"I'll be alright."

Gabe nods. "I take it you're not returning? Does Coach know this?"

"Nope."

"You meeting us in Portland?"

"Nope. I'm done, Daws. I'm not doing this anymore."

"Fuck," he breathes. "All because of Woodward?"

"No. All because of her," I tell him, giving Hannah a soft smile. "She's worth everything, man. I just want to be with her."

"What are you planning to do about Coach?" Gabe asks.

"Not sure. I'll figure something out. But I'm done. Tell him they're taking me for concussion protocol so we get a head start to the airport, okay?"

"I can do that," he says, removing his glove and putting a hand out to shake mine. When I take his, he squeezes hard. "I know we haven't always gotten along, Santo, but even I recognize what Coach did tonight was over the top. If I can help with a case against him, let me know."

"Appreciate it."

"Gonna miss messing with you at practice," Gabe chuckles.

"I'm sure you'll find a rookie to fuck with soon enough," I tell him with a grin.

Gabe lets go of my hand, tilts his chin at Hannah, and walks back down the hallway toward the ice.

Sliding my arm around her shoulder, I lean down to give her temple a very light kiss. Jesus, my entire face is throbbing. "Come on, Pix. Let's get out of here."

Hannah looks up at me, love evident in her eyes. "I am so proud of you, Luca."

"Thanks, baby. Let's get going before Coach decides to try and find me. Is your uncle really here? Where is he?"

"I left him with Elsie."

"The physical therapist? He's got a hard on for her, right?"

"Yep."

"How's that going?" I ask as we round a corner and find Bennett with Elsie against a wall, a passionate kiss between them.

"Pretty well, I'd say, considering this is how I left them," Hannah comments. "Uncle Bennett!"

They break apart, a lovely pink shade of embarrassment covering Elsie's face as they both wipe their lips.

"What's going on? Is the game over? You're going to get in big trouble for leaving before the end, Luca." Bennett states.

"Is it really important right now? Can we leave?" Hannah begs.

Bennett turns to Elsie, who gives him a shy smile. "I'll text you."

"You better," she replies.

One last kiss before Bennett motions for us to follow him outside the arena. He stops when he notices I'm wearing my game-day suit and carrying my skates. "Just the skates? You didn't grab your bag?"

"Nothing I want in there. Just the skates."

"The rest of your things are still at the hotel?" he asks and I nod. "We can stop there to grab them. I'll book us flights in the meantime."

An Uber drops us off at the team hotel, and Hannah helps me pack up my things. I was expecting to sleep here tonight, since Woodward has us on a six am flight, and none of my things are packed. "Do you mind if I take a quick shower?"

"Go ahead. I'll pack," Hannah says. I jump in the shower, taking the quickest shower I can, and step out to find Hannah waiting for me. "I'm done."

"You're done?"

"Uh-huh. I'm an excellent packer," she says.

"So it should be super easy to pack up your apartment and move in with me?" I ask. Her smile fades.

"I don't think I want to live next to my aunt, Luca. I'm still not sure of her involvement. I can only assume she's sleeping with Woodward."

"Gross. I thought she had higher standards than that. Actually, that's kind of bullshit."

"What?"

"He's treated me horribly all season based on a rumor that I slept with his wife, but he's potentially cheating on her at the same time? That's ridiculous."

"I'm not surprised he's a hypocrite."

As I shove my legs back into my suit, I grunt. "You know I have a house in Eternity Springs, right?"

Hannah's mouth drops open. "Really?"

"Really."

"Can I see it?"

"Of course, Pix. It's pretty empty, but I think it would be nice to decorate it with you. I wasn't joking when I said you could move in with me."

Hannah studies me. "Can I think about it? It's been a chaotic couple of days."

I try not to let the hurt show on my face. "Sure, baby. The offer is open whenever you're ready."

"It's just ..." she trails off. "We've been dating for like less than a week, Luca. I'd like to actually go on a date with you. In public."

I chuckle. "I already know exactly where I'm taking you for our first date, Pix. It'll be the most perfect first date ever."

"Oh yeah?"

"Yeah. And since it'll be the last first date you ever go on, I'm going to make it epic."

Hannah giggles and shakes her head at me. "Come on, dreamer. Let's get this show on the road before the big bad wolf shows up."

If you would have asked me at the end of last season how I'd feel when my hockey career was over, I'd have either refused to answer you, or I would have told you it was years away.

Until Hannah.

Until I recognized my future, and could let go of my past.

I'm not even sad.

Do I know what the future holds? What may or may not happen to Coach Woodward? What I'll do with all of my free time? Nope. But I don't care.

Because Hannah is worth the risk.

Chapter 26

*H*annah

***

e're barely on the airplane before all three of our phones begin blowing up.

"Don't answer. In fact, turn them off," Uncle Bennett demands.

"Why?" I ask.

"Whoever leaked what just happened probably didn't do it with good intentions. It's bound to be a zoo at the airport," he mutters.

Luca turns to me. "You flew."

"I did," I beam.

His eyes widen. "Holy shit. You flew to Boston! I didn't even realize that. I should have mentioned it when you showed up, but I was too shocked."

"I was a little shocked at myself, if I'm being honest," I admit.

"Were you freaked out? Either time?" he asks.

"No, actually. Getting to Boston, I was so excited about seeing you, I couldn't sit still. Today, I think the thought of you being hurt made my fear of flying seem insignificant."

"Awe, baby. My sweet little peach," he coos.

I roll my eyes. "Let's not make that a thing."

"Calling you my peach?"

"Yes. I'm happy as your Pixie."

Luca chuckles as he slowly strokes my hand. "Noted."

Uncle Bennett clears his throat. "Can either of you give me the name of the attorney? I don't have it on me."

Luca rattles off the hotel attorney Dominic referred me to, and my uncle makes a muffled call. I rest my head on Luca's shoulder and let out a relieved sigh. Everything leading up to this point was worth it. Luca is worth it.

"The attorney is going to get us out of the airport when we arrive. It's bound to be a shitshow."

"Why?"

"Woodward is the leak. He spewed straight venom at the end of the game, telling everyone about your relationship and Luca quitting. The press is rabid for more details."

"How did anyone know we were flying?"

"No clue. They're probably assuming we wanted to get back to Colorado as quickly as possible," Uncle Bennett says.

"Is this a nonstop flight?" Luca asks.

"No, we have a layover in San Francisco. Seriously, were you not paying attention when we boarded?" Uncle Bennett teases. "Of course not. You two were all lovestruck and staring at each other. I had to pull you to the gate."

"Seeing as how I had to forcibly separate your tongue from Elsie's mouth, I don't think you have any right to poke fun at us," I tell him. He at least has the good sense to blush.

"Pix," Luca says quietly, "how about a little vacation in California?"

I turn to him, a wide smile spreading across my face. "I've always wanted to see the Golden Gate Bridge. And the Pacific Ocean. And those cute trolleys!"

"You in any rush to get back to Colorado?" he asks.

I shake my head. "Will I get in trouble with your family?"

"Pretty sure I have an in with them, bella. Let me handle them," Luca says with a wink.

I turn to Uncle Bennett. "Are you okay if we take a detour and you head back alone?"

"Sure. Although it would have been nice had you told me that in the arena. I could have hung with Elsie more."

"And been spotted by Woodward? I don't think that would have been wise."

"Ahh. True. But yeah, I'm cool with heading back to Denver without you. I can handle the press."

I turn back to Luca. "How long do you want to stay?"

He cups my cheek, his thumb stroking my bottom lip. "A day or two. Then I thought we could rent a car and drive back home."

"I've never been on a road trip!" I gush.

Luca chuckles. "Your parents were zero fun."

"I'm aware."

"Do you think they will like me?" he asks.

"No," I giggle. "But I don't care. Their opinion doesn't matter to me anymore. They're just ugly. Besides, I have your family now."

"They're ugly? Really?" Luca laughs.

"Oh, no. I mean their personalities. My parents aren't kind. They don't have compassion. They'd run their best friends over with their cars if it meant they gained an inch. I don't want to be around them. Your family is kind and genuine. Thoughtful. Empathetic. No comparison which family I'd choose."

"Amazing I came from them, huh," Luca says with a bitter laugh.

I study him. "Why would you say that?"

He shifts uncomfortably. "Well, I was known as the man-whore of Denver. Even my family joked about how much I got around. Just like you did when you first met me."

When his eyes refuse to meet mine, I grab his chin and force him to look at me. "Your past doesn't define you. Do you understand that? Yeah, the notches on your bedpost could probably line a football field. But that's such a small and trivial part of your life. You know how I'm feeling before I can even verbalize it. You stayed with Arianna for a weekend helping her when she broke her wrist, and I bet she was fully capable of taking care of herself. Even when Mrs. Willowby gives you attitude, you are nice to her every single time. And how you care for me? No one has ever loved me like you do, Luca."

I'm getting choked up as Luca leans forward to place a gentle kiss against my lips. "It's a privilege to love you, baby."

***

*L*uca and I spent two days exploring San Francisco. Well, mostly we stayed in our hotel room. We feared getting recognized, and thanks to Luca's obviously injured face, we didn't want to take that chance. Instead, we stayed in our little bubble and fucked like bunnies. When we weren't in the throes of orgasmic bliss, we talked. Laughed. Cried a little.

It was the most euphoric start to our life together.

The drive back to Colorado was ... interesting.

My sweet cinnamon roll of a man does not like taking directions from me. Literally. I realized quite quickly that Luca doesn't have the best sense of direction when he began heading south out of San Francisco. He got a little snippy with me when I corrected him, so I decided to shut my mouth and see how long it took for him to recognize the error.

Three hours. That's how long it took.

At that point, we were well on the way to Los Angeles, so we just continued on. Seeing the Hollywood Sign in person was also on my bucket list, so I figured we might as well. The press had zero clue where we were, and this was a wonderful opportunity to remain anonymous for a little longer.

Two days in LA, a forced usage of Google Maps, and another two days in the car, and we arrived back in Eternity Springs. We timed it so we'd arrive at sunset, thus making it more difficult for any press that might be loitering around the town or hotel to see us. It helped that we were in a rental car as well.

When Luca passed the hotel entrance, I wondered how bad his directional skills were. "Where are you going?"

"I told you, baby. We're going home."

"Huh?"

"Remember? I told you I have a house here."

"Will the press be there?" I ask.

"I doubt it. No one knows about the house, except for my mom and dad."

"Couldn't someone just search the assessor website and find the info?"

"We went to extreme lengths to guarantee it isn't attached to my known name."

"Is that your subtle way of suggesting you don't actually own the house?" I tease.

Luca laughs. "No, I own it. But it's technically right at the county line, and it doesn't fall in Eternity Springs city limits. The address is pretty vague, and people will assume it's a vacation home further in the mountains."

"Did you change the address or something?"

"Sort of. The information online only has a PO Box. The physical address is a county address. Eventually, someone will figure it out. But for now, it's our little escape. Oh, and I added a massive gate and fence around the entire property. None of these fuckers are getting in," he says wickedly.

"Are you even allowed to change addresses on things like that?" I wonder.

"We didn't really change the address. My siblings and I are co-owners of a corporation that is headquartered in Boulder. Any property we have is listed through the corporation to keep our family name out of it. The fucking gossip site does enough damage anyway."

I choke out a laugh. "A gossip site?"

"Yeah. I'll show you later. I'm pretty sure you've already been on it. Whoever runs it probably guessed which of us you'd end up with."

"What?"

"The gossip site really likes to focus on my family. Don't tell my sisters, but I read it. Most of it is pretty comical. It covers some typical newsworthy things like vandalism, or petty crime, but mostly it's all about the love lives of the residents. So when you have six out of seven kids still single in a well-known family, we get a lot of publicity."

"What's the name of it?" I murmur as I whip out my phone.

"*The Eagle Has Landed.*"

Within a minute, I have the site pulled up. "I can't believe I still have coverage up here — LUCA! They have my college sorority picture in here!"

"No way! Lemme see," Luca says as he yanks my phone away. "Damn, baby, you were hot even back then."

"I was seventeen in that picture, you creep," I mutter.

"How were you in a sorority then?"

"I skipped a grade."

"I would have only been nineteen then. Am I still a creep?" he asks hopefully, giving me that signature Luca lopsided smile.

I sigh. "I guess not."

"Good. Cuz thirty-year-old Luca is really wanting to do some nasty things to twenty-eight-year-old Hannah when we get home," he says with a gaudy wink.

"I don't think I ever said I'd move in with you, Luca," I chastise him.

"I know, Pix. But I also know you'll come around to it once you see it. Because this house? It's ours, baby. Not mine. Ours."

My heart skips a beat when he refers to it as 'home.' Our home. Together.

*O*ne tour of the mostly empty but breathtaking house later, and I'm officially in love with what Luca purchased. "Why don't you have any furniture yet?"

"I wanted us to pick it out together. I mean, I have a mattress. That's it. Not even a bed frame. And Arianna wanted to pick out more furniture, but I said no. I wanted us to choose what would be our first pieces together. Know what I mean?"

"I thought you just bought this a few months ago?" I ask, puzzled.

A slight wave of pink crests across Luca's neck as he gives me a lopsided smile. "I knew I wanted to get a house near home. As soon as I saw this one, I kept thinking about you. If you would like it. How would you decorate. What kinds of traditions we could create here. You were barely a blip on the radar, but I subconsciously knew you were different."

"Luca," I whisper. Overcome with emotion, I wrap my arms around his waist and bury my head in his chest. I feel his lips ghost across my hair as he squeezes me close.

"Without realizing it, I imprinted you all over this house, Pixie. And if you had decided you didn't want to be with me, I had every intention of selling it. I had too many dreams about what life could be like with you here. If that wasn't going to happen, I wanted no part of the house."

"What dreams did you have?" I ask, captivated by how Luca's eyes sparkle with love, yet his voice delivers a gritty and deep conviction I've never heard before.

"I dreamed of the places I'd make love to you. And the places we'd fuck. Cooking dinner together. Watching the snow, and waking up next to you. Christmas morning with our kids."

"Kids?"

"Yeah, *bella*. We need your genes to continue. Don't you think?" Luca says with a grin.

"I hadn't thought about that yet," I mumble, overwhelmed. I'm clearly having difficulty processing all of this information. Granted, when he told me he loved me, I figured he had interest in a future with me. But to hear him actually say he wants this to be our home, and he wants kids with me, is something I wasn't mentally prepared for.

"Uh oh. Did I scare you?" Luca teases, but I see an element of uncertainty in his eyes. "Your pace, Hannah. Everything is at your pace. I guess I'm a little stoked to get going, huh."

"This is a little unexpected," I admit, "but I'm not scared. I think I had myself convinced the future I hoped for wouldn't happen, you know? I was ready to hold my horses. I didn't think you were there yet."

"Hold my what?"

"Horses."

"Hold my horses."

"Yeah."

"Gonna need a southern translation again, baby."

"Be patient."

"Ah. So you expected you'd need to hold your horses until I caught up to you?"

I nod affirmatively.

"How do you feel now that you know I'm right there with you?"

A slow smile spreads across my face as I stare up at Luca. "Really good, actually."

His grin matches mine. "Good. Now how about we start christening this house? Kitchen, shower, or bed?"

I frown. "You don't have a bed."

"I didn't show you our room yet, Han. I have a mattress. It's on the floor, but it'll be fine for tonight. I wanted you to see everything else first, because I knew once I got you in our room, we weren't leaving again for the rest of the night."

"Oh. I like that plan," I giggle. Luca chuckles, then drops to shove a shoulder into my stomach, picking me up quickly. I shriek as he runs up the stairs and down the hallway before launching both of us onto a large bed.

"What if I had said shower?" I ask breathlessly as he peppers kisses across my neck and onto my collarbone.

"We'll get there next. I've got plans for you tonight."

As he looks down on me with a beautiful smile, I can't help but smile in return. "Ask me again, honey."

He looks puzzled for a moment before he chuckles. "Hannah. Pixie. Love of my life. Will you please move in with me?"

"Yes," I whisper, pulling Luca down to kiss his lips thoroughly.

It was the next morning before I finally saw the ensuite bathroom, but I was definitely not upset about being kept in bed with Luca all night.

*T*he following day, after Luca's family again encouraged me to take more time off, I awoke to find Luca's side of the bed empty and cool. Reaching for my phone to see no text messages from him, I wrap myself in a sheet and search the house for my man.

I honestly don't think I could have picked a more perfect house to blend our personalities together. The rustic nature of the large picture windows and exposed wooden beams suit Luca's style, but the open floor plan and pewter fixtures and accents suit mine. Modern lights trailing down from vaulted ceilings give and ethereal glow to the rooms beneath them. I can already envision comfortable couches, a large table perfect for entertaining Luca's family, and a perfect nook for toddler toys or a small art table.

Kids with Luca.

After Luca fell asleep last night, I realized one of the reasons I was so taken aback by Luca's nonchalance when mentioning kids.

I'm late.

My period was never structured perfectly with a calendar. It fluctuated within ten days, so I didn't think a thing about it being late.

Then all hell broke loose with Jefferson, my hand injury, and going to Luca in Seattle. My missing period was the last thing on my mind.

A quick look at my phone calendar when I woke up to pee in the middle of the night confirmed my theory. If I am indeed pregnant, it happened in Boston.

If I had figured this out only a few days ago, I'd be a nervous wreck to tell Luca. But now, knowing he's already thinking about babies, I'm only anxious to find out if I am pregnant.

As I pad barefoot down the stairs, I hear Luca talking.

"I don't see why they want me to come in. I'll pay the fines. Whatever. I'm done, Max. I don't want to play another minute of hockey."

Max responds, and Luca listens intently before sighing. "Why the GM wants to see me is ridiculous ... it's the owner who wants to see me? Max, give me some ideas here. Are they seeking some kind of legal recourse for me walking out?"

I creep silently toward Luca, unable to stay away from him. If the organization sues Luca, because of me, I'll never forgive myself. My arms slide around Luca's waist as I plaster my front to his back, terrified of what Max may say.

Luca stiffens slightly at my touch before relaxing into my embrace. When Max's voice comes out much louder than I anticipated, making me jump, Luca chuckles and shows me his phone on speaker.

"Mr. Crawford didn't tell me anything, man. He just said he wants you in his office as soon as possible. Oh, and he did ask you to bring Hannah."

"Me? No!" I blurt out, horrified.

"Why I thought you wouldn't be listening is beyond me. Hello, Hannah," Max says dryly.

"Hi Max," I whisper. My face heats with obvious embarrassment. I've never met Max in person, and I've only heard him speak on the phone once or twice. This is not how I expected my introduction to Luca's agent to go.

"It's okay, baby. Whatever it is, we'll figure it out. Together," Luca says quietly. "We're a team now. You get me?"

I nod, biting my lip to avoid blurting out that I think I might be pregnant. Our team may be getting a tiny bit bigger in the foreseeable future, and that's probably making me hormonally emotional about seeing the team owner today.

When Luca finishes his call with Max, he turns around and tugs me into his arms. "Mr. Crawford always seemed like a just and straightforward man. Very honest and understanding. I really don't think he'd call us in for a meeting if it was about something bad. He'd have his attorneys do that."

"Are you sure?" I ask quietly.

"I do. In fact, I wouldn't be surprised if he had good news for us."

"What kind of good news could he have?" I mutter.

"I know you've been enjoying a self-mandated social media sabbatical, Han, but I haven't. And there have been a lot of stories released over the past couple of days about Woodward and his lackeys, your aunt included."

My head whips up. "Seriously? What did they say?"

"That Woodward is under investigation for a couple things, and that the GM was involved. How he was having an extramarital affair with Caroline, and that she may have been essential in some of his more intense strategies when Woodward needed someone out."

"Any idea on how long she was screwing him?"

"Dawson told me it may have been a few years."

I feel the corner of my lip quirk up. "Dawson, huh."

Luca scratches at his scruff. "Uh, yeah. Turns out he's not such a bad guy. I mean, he's still a jackass, but not a complete douche."

"It's wonderful that you can promote him from douche to jackass."

"When it comes to the male hierarchy of disgustingness, I am a fair judge."

"Obviously I have to ask where you fall on the hierarchy."

"At the top."

I snort and roll my eyes. "As every humble man should be."

"Not even a little bit, Pixie. You want to know why I'm at the top?"

"Why?" I ask, already smiling. Whatever the answer is, I know it's going to make me love him even more.

"Because you took me there."

And as he sweetly kisses my lips, I know he's right. Whatever the female hierarchy is, I'm at the top because of Luca too. We make each other better, as the best partners do.

Chapter 27

*L*uca

*L*ike I told Hannah, I've never had a bad conversation with Mr. Crawford. Then again, I've also never chatted with him when I left mid-game and refused to return, nor when I had been part of an investigation into the coach and GM he employs. While I assured Hannah I was confident it would be a good reason for being beckoned to Crawford's imposing corner office at the Sports Facility Zone.

I've been lucky to have played my entire career here, so I don't have experience with other owners. I've heard gossip and stories, though. Many owners are hands off. Some are helicopter parents, always swooping around and putting their opinion where it doesn't belong. Crawford never operated as either of those owners. He seemed to trust his front office and the coaching staff to make the best decisions for success. Instead, he threw his focus into other programs. He spearheaded a pretty big charity, as well as creating one of the first all-encompassing mental health and rehabilitation facilities for pro athletes in the country. As an athlete himself, he recognized the mental strain professional sports take, and understood that struggle after injury requires even more maintenance. Now, any athlete who enrolls in the rehab program at CPA must undergo a series of evaluations and sessions with a sports psychologist before they are cleared to begin training again.

"Are you sure this is going to be okay?" Hannah whispers as we wait outside Crawford's office, her small hand trembling slightly encased in mine.

"I think so, yeah," I reply. I hope so.

"Mr. Santo, Ms. Beauregard, you can go in now," his receptionist calls out.

"Now or never, Pix," I whisper, squeezing her hand.

As we walk into Mr. Crawford's office, we both stop dead when we see Hannah's uncle sitting alongside Mr. Crawford wearing a big smile.

"Uncle Bennett?" Hannah asks uncertainly. "What are you doing here?"

"Couldn't let you two have all the fun, could I?" Bennett jokes.

"Please, come in. Hello, Hannah, I'm David Crawford," Mr. Crawford says, extending his hand to shake hers. Hannah shakes it warily, as if she's afraid he's going to physically lash out and hurt her in some way. "Take a seat. We have a lot to discuss."

I cast a quick glance at Bennett, and he smirks. While I don't enjoy feeling like I'm in the dark, I assume if Bennett is here, it's good news.

"Alright. Down to business," Crawford says, slapping his hands against his desk loudly as he slides into his seat. Just a hint of gray on his temples, he's not much older than everyone in this room. I've read some of the fan forums for him. Women are obsessed with his chin cleft, bright blue eyes, and wide shoulders. I'm strong enough in my own masculinity to admit he's an attractive man. Kinda blows my mind how these women don't realize he's a brilliant businessman as well. Granted, his family owned the team before he took over, but he's put forth a ton of time and effort into what we have today. Hell, the Sports Facility Zone didn't even exist until a year after I signed with the team.

"Hannah, you look like you're about to bolt," Bennett chuckles, jarring me from my thoughts. Looking at Hannah, I have to agree. She looks completely terrified.

"Ms. Beauregard, you have absolutely nothing to be worried about. In fact, I'd like to give you back your job, if you'll have it," Mr. Crawford says.

"No!" Hannah blurts out.

Bennett openly laughs. "You may want to explain why she can have her job back, David."

"Oh. You probably don't want to work with Woodward," he says, and Hannah nods emphatically. "That's understandable. He's been fired, so that won't be an issue."

Now it's my turn to stare. "Seriously?"

"Yes. The investigation that began after he propositioned Ms. Beauregard actually coincided with one of our own. I'd had concerns with his coaching style, and whether he was treating staff well. Unfortunately, it opened up into a much broader investigation than I thought it would. I had no idea the GM was involved. He's also been fired."

Wow.

"Were they just fired, or were there any criminal charges against them?" Hannah asks clearly.

"Oh, there are criminal charges. Definitely. But I can't speak to those. I did manage to snag a quick video of the police arriving to arrest the two of them this morning, though, and it just so happened to be timed perfectly with his normal scheduled press conference. While you'll find better quality on the news throughout the day, you won't get the sheer venom he spewed at me as the police dragged him down the hallway."

As Mr. Crawford turns his phone toward us, we watch as Woodward stumbles against the police, pulling his handcuffed wrists unsuccessfully. He spits nonsensical sentences about me and Hannah, even adding in a dig at 'that dumb bitch' Caroline for thinking she was worth more than a fuck.

"What happened with my aunt?" Hannah asks as the video ends.

Bennett clears his throat. "We've learned Caroline was much more involved in Woodward's plans than we originally thought. You were a plant, Hannah. Caroline never went to Europe. In fact, she's the one who brought Jefferson here. She called your mother and told her you were miserable, and that you wanted to get back together with him. Your mother was all too thrilled to give out your information to Jefferson, because she assumed he'd force you to move back to Georgia and be under her control again."

Hannah's eyes fill with tears. "My mother is responsible for all of this?"

"She was involved, yes. Caroline was mostly responsible, but I'm sure neither of them thought he'd hurt you."

"Mother knew he had hurt me, Uncle Bennett. She knew. For her to ignore that and send him here ... that's unforgivable. She's ... I'm done with her," Hannah whispers, frantically swiping at her eyes to wipe away the errant tears. "Who does that? Who writes off abuse like that?"

"A nobody, Pixie. She's no one. Nothing. You don't ever have to see them again, okay? I promise you, I'll never let them hurt you again," I tell her deeply. I hate that she's hurting. Hate that so many of her blood family took advantage of her like this, and didn't care about the results.

Hannah rests her head against my shoulder. "I know."

Bennett clears his throat. "Caroline was arrested as well."

"Oh. Are you — are you doing okay with that?" Hannah asks quietly.

"I had come to terms with my lack of relationship with my sister years ago. I had no idea she'd stoop so low as to set up family, but it is what it is. She made her bed."

"How long will it take to hire a new GM and coach?" I ask.

"The GM will take a bit. My family has always had an ideal for what we wanted in the GM role. But we've already hired a coach," Mr. Crawford says with a smile.

"Who?" I ask.

Mr. Crawford tilts his head toward Bennett with a brow raised. "The only one for the job."

Hannah gasps before jumping up to hug her uncle. "I'm so happy for you! Are you excited? Are you replacing your role then? Wait! Can you still date Elsie if you're the head coach?"

Hannah's eyes widen as she frantically covers her mouth with her hands, making Mr. Crawford bark back a laugh. "It's okay, I already know. Bennett disclosed the relationship as soon as I offered him the position. We have never had a strict no fraternization rule. As long as relationships aren't with direct subordinates, and they're disclosed to Human Resources, there isn't an issue. And anyone could see the two of them making eyes at one another for a while."

"Am I in trouble for how I left?" I blurt out.

"No. I'm sure if Woodward was still in control, you'd have been fined up the ass for every infraction he could think of, but this is my ballgame. If you want to come back and finish your year, or your career, we will welcome you back. But if you're completely done, we can retire you effective immediately. It's up to you. But I'm still waiting for an answer from Ms. Beauregard on returning to her job, and I assume your answer about returning is dependent on hers."

Hannah looks at me, and it seems like we have a nonverbal conversation.

I'm happy, she says.

Me, too, I respond.

Do you want to finish out the year? She asks.

Not really.

Me either.

Turning back to Mr. Crawford, Hannah speaks first. "I truly appreciate the offer, Mr. Crawford, but I'm really happy with my job at Luca's family hotel."

Mr. Crawford smiles. "I figured you'd say that. Mr. Santo, I assume your answer is the same?"

I nod. "I don't want to burn bridges or anything, and I'll come back if it's a big deal. But I'm happier than I thought I'd ever be. I'm okay with moving on from hockey."

"Generally there aren't many athletes who quit midseason, so I'll have to consult our legal and PR teams to determine how we move forward. But, honestly, I'd like to ask you to finish out the season. You've been with the team for quite some time. Hometown kid. The fans will be upset if they don't get to say goodbye to you."

"That's true," I murmur. I turn to Hannah, and she gives me a reassuring smile.

"It's okay, Luca. It's just a few more months. Besides, I never got an opportunity to cheer you on publicly. I wouldn't mind wearing your jersey while you're out there," Hannah says sweetly.

Sitting in front of a billionaire owner is not the best time for my cock to twitch, thinking about Hannah wearing *only* my jersey, but here we are.

"Focus, man," Bennett coughs. Yeah, he knew exactly where my mind went. And while I've definitely seen many women wear my jersey at games, I've never *wanted* someone to wear it before.

"How do we do this? Should there be an announcement as to why I've missed games so far?"

"I don't think we need to announce anything. If someone asks, we'll say it was a personal matter. No one needs to know more than that."

"Will I need to join the team on the trip?" I ask, a pit forming in my stomach. The team leaves tomorrow morning for a ten-day trip. The thought of leaving Hannah for that long makes me feel like vomiting.

"I don't think that's necessary. Enjoy your time together before the media really gets wind of it. While Woodward did make a spectacle, it hasn't yet been made widely known that the two of you are together. Enjoy that last period of anonymity while you still have it," Mr. Crawford says.

"Thank you, sir. I'd like to make the announcement soon that I will be retiring at the end of the season. Once we have a date set, I'll tell the team myself."

"We can work that out next week before the team gets back. I have meetings the rest of the day, but thank you for taking time to meet with me."

As his phone rings, he waves his goodbye before accepting the call. Bennett, Hannah and I quietly leave the office.

"You guys want to grab a cup of coffee? I'm sure you have more questions," Bennett says.

Hannah shakes her head. "I don't want to be in public. If they were arrested this morning, does the media know my name? If Luca and I are seen together, they'll put two-and-two together."

"That's true. Want to go to my apartment? I need to get a bag of clothes to take to the house anyway," I offer.

"You don't want to stay at your apartment anymore?" Hannah asks.

"Not if you're not there. I'm fine with staying at our house."

Hannah beams. "I like that you call it our house, but that's a ridiculously long drive to tackle every day. We can stay here too, you know."

"Okay, Pixie. I didn't know if you'd feel uncomfortable with knowing your aunt's apartment was next door ..." I trail off.

"No. Not at all. I like to think that everything happens for a reason. If she hadn't offered up her apartment, I wouldn't have met you. In a very salacious way, Aunt Caroline and Coach Woodward are responsible for bringing us together."

"Well, we aren't thanking them for it," I mutter. Hannah giggles as the three of us cross the street and head into my building. When we get into the elevator, I chuckle, realizing it's the same elevator we got stuck in when Hannah blurted out her bucket list. "Did we cross off every item?"

"What?"

"Your bucket list."

"Oh."

"You didn't answer."

"No, there are still plenty of items on my bucket list. I've added more as well," she says quietly. I sneak a peek at Bennett, who appears enamored by his phone, oblivious to the two of us.

"Oh yeah? Anything I could help with?" I whisper against her ear. She shivers involuntarily.

"Quite a few, actually," she responds. "Turns out I have a thing for elevators."

Arriving at our floor, I motion for Bennett to go before us, then call out his name. When he turns, I toss him my keys. "We're gonna be a minute or two. Help yourself to the good booze."

Hannah cackles as the door closes. I immediately hit the emergency stop button, and I push her up against the wall. I remember every moment of that unfortunate elevator ride where Hannah told me all of her hopes and dreams. I plan on making every single one of those wishes come true. Mountain climbing, Paris, sushi. All the orgasms. "You gonna come to my place tonight, *bella*? You gonna let me make you feel good? Say yes, Pix, please say yes. I'll make you feel so good, baby. Make you forget the rest of the world. Just you and me."

"Just you and me," Hannah replies breathlessly as I pick her up, her legs wrapping naturally around my waist. I give her a searing kiss before the elevator alarm goes off.

"Fucking cockblocking elevator," I mutter. Pushing the emergency button again, the car jerks and stutters before descending. I turn to Hannah, ready to make a joke about performance, but her face is green. "You okay, baby?"

"I don't think so —" she stops as she swallows harshly. "This is new."

"What is new?"

"Motion sickness, I guess?"

"You haven't had that before?"

"No."

"You were fine on the plane, and the entire drive back from San Francisco."

Hannah looks at me, a deep groove between her eyes showing her obvious distress. "Don't freak out, okay?"

I, of course, freak out. "What? What happened? Are you hurt? Did I do something? Do we need to get you to a doctor? The emergency room? What?"

"I said *don't* freak out," Hannah says with a light giggle. "Luca, I think I might be pregnant."

Time stops.

I don't know how long I stand there, staring at Hannah, but definitely long enough for the elevator to go down to the lobby and make it back up to my floor. Hannah has to forcibly drag me out of the elevator before I'm able to utter a single word. "What?"

"I worried this would happen," she sighs.

"Pregnant? Seriously?" She nods. "When did you find out?"

"I haven't actually found out anything, honey. My period is two weeks late. I was going to sneak out to get a test this morning, but then Mr. Crawford called us in, and we came here, and I figured I'd wait until tonight, or tomorrow, to take a test."

"Fuck that," I say, ripping my phone out of my pocket. "You can Instacart a dozen pregnancy tests, right?"

"What? Luca, no. A dozen? That's absurd. One will do. And can you Instacart that?" Hannah asks.

"Yep," I tell her, showing her the app. "Who knew?"

"Wait!" she shouts. "Shouldn't we add anything else? I mean, they're going to know it's you and me, should we try to pad the order so it isn't so obvious?"

I order six pregnancy tests and turn my screen off. Taking Hannah's face in my hands, I stare down at her. "I don't care who knows about us, Pixie. I want everyone to know that I'm taken. I want the world to see you as the one who completed me. But if you're not ready for that, we can make Bennett go get it."

Her eyes widen. "Oh shit! He's still in your apartment!"

I chuckle. "I'm sure he's enjoying all my good booze. It's fine. Should we go tell him the good news?"

Hannah beams at me. "You know, I guess you were right."

"About what?"

She carefully takes one of my hands, places it on her stomach, and covers it with both of hers. "We are definitely worth the risk."

Absolutely.

Chapter 28

Hannah

❧

As I sit next to Luca, his leg jiggling so fast he's shaking the entire bench, I realize he's incredibly nervous. "What's going on in that head of yours?"

He looks at me and gives me a sheepish smile. "Nerves, I guess."

"When is the last time you were nervous before a game?"

He chuffs. "Shit, I don't know. Actual nerves? Years ago. Generally I feel a ton of excitement to get on the ice, and adrenaline takes over. Feeling this nervous is different."

"Why are you nervous?"

He sighs, his eyes roaming across the ice. He asked to come in here early and have a moment. It's his first game back after everything that happened with Woodward. "I'm worried everyone will boo."

"Why would they boo you?" I ask.

"Maybe they'll think I let the team down or something. I don't know. Hockey fans are pretty passionate about things, and I missed a week of games. We lost every game too."

"You lost before that as well, Luca."

"Yeah, but then I was trying to get them to lose," he mutters.

"What?" I ask incredulously.

He gives me a sheepish smile as he scratches the back of his neck absentmindedly. When his eyes meet mine, I can see the anxiety and tension present. He's really spooked, and I've never seen him like this.

"When you broke things off, and I didn't know why, but I knew Woodward was involved in some capacity, I kind of went a little nuts. Fighting. Tons of penalties. I just wasn't a team player at all. I felt lost and alone, and the only thing I could do was lash out," he murmurs.

Oh, my sweet, sweet man. "I'm sorry you went through that."

"It's not your fault, Pixie. I just want to be honest with you, and tell you how I felt. I knew I was out of control, but I didn't care how it impacted anyone. I was bound and determined to go out in a blaze of ... something."

I take his hand in mine and rest my head on his padded shoulder. I'm about to tell him again how sorry I am, and how lost I felt during that time as well. But with our hands entwined, our arms together, I notice how it's hard to tell where Luca's arm ends and mine begins.

I'm wearing his jersey, publicly, for the first time.

"You're smiling pretty big there, Pix," he whispers as he rests his forehead against the top of my head.

"I just noticed our jerseys. When I'm holding your hand like this, it's like we're one person."

I feel him smile against me. "As long as we'd get to this point, Hannah, I'd do it all again. You're so worth it."

As we see fans beginning to file into their seats, Luca stands up. I felt tiny with him before, but when he's wearing skates, he's an absolute giant. Feeling weirdly inferior, I stand on the team bench, making Luca bark back a laugh.

"I'm taller than you now!" I declare with excitement. He gives me a wide grin before pulling me toward him for a kiss.

"I love you, baby," he whispers against my lips. I feel his hand softly rub against my stomach. The last few days I've woken up with Luca whispering to our baby. We haven't told anyone, choosing to live inside this bubble for just a little while. Morning sickness began yesterday, and Luca hovered over me just like he did when he found Arianna and I drunk so long ago.

"You better get back with the team before fans start coming down here," I murmur against him.

"What are you going to do?" he asks as he lifts me and places me back on the ground. I could have jumped down, but something tells me Luca is going to be a helicopter new dad, and hover over everything I do.

"Gonna go find Elsie and see what she'll fess up to about my uncle," I tell him with a devilish grin. Uncle Bennett has been weirdly jovial the last week. Almost too happy. Not only is he getting an opportunity to coach an NHL team at such a young age, but he's finally manned up and admitted his feelings for Elsie.

"I heard him whistling the other day, Pix. Whistling. It's creepy as fuck," Luca whispers, mock horror covering his face.

"It's nice to see him happy."

"It's nice to see him getting laid regularly," Luca replies.

I giggle. "That too."

couple of months later, after Luca and the Wolves went on a tear, winning almost all of their games, we're on our way to Luca's parents' house for dinner. I've never been to his childhood home. I'm interested to see where he grew up. Leo is home for a week before he deploys, and I haven't met him yet. We've FaceTimed him where he's stationed in North Carolina, but I'm looking forward to seeing him in person. Luca mentioned he seems much more reserved than in the past, and he's worried about his older brother.

Alex is home, having some time before he'll report for a deployment as well. I'll also see Gianna, Luca's older sister, and the woman who I replaced as the special events coordinator at the hotel. I'm hoping she'll let me snuggle her newborn son, Carson. Gianna and her husband Travis are very concerned with germs and viruses. Travis is a paramedic, and he is very worried about Carson's immune system. So far, Carson has only been to one family event, a dinner at Dominic's house on Christmas, and no one was allowed to hold him. I understand. I will undoubtedly be a nervous wreck when our child is born.

"There's something I haven't told you about my family, Pixie," Luca announces as he slowly drives down the snow-packed road from our house. Turning to him, I find him oddly nervous.

"Do you think they'll be upset about the baby?" I ask, my hands instinctually covering my baby bump. We're telling the family tonight, and I wasn't nervous about it until right now.

"Oh, no. Not that. They're gonna be thrilled. But we have this weird tradition, and I'm assuming they are expecting me to take part."

"A tradition?"

"It's kind of a test, I guess."

"Testing me?"

"Testing us."

"Luca, you're worrying me."

As we turn into Luca's childhood neighborhood, I see every Santo family member standing outside a large and stately home. "Why are they all outside?"

"Shit. I hoped they wouldn't do this," Luca mutters. He stops the car a house away and turns to me. "Back when Alex was in high school, he got this idea that any Santo kid had to cross the threshold of our parents' house by carrying their partner."

"Okay? That doesn't seem like that big of a deal."

Luca's eyes bare into mine. "No one ever made it, Pix."

"What the hell does that even mean?" I ask, irritation evident in my voice.

"It means that something always happened to the couple. Dropping, tripping, people refusing to participate. It became the way we determined if a relationship would be successful."

"You can't mean everyone, Luca."

"I do. Everyone failed ... until Gia."

"Travis carried her over the threshold?" I whisper.

"No, baby. Gia carried him. That's the tradition. The Santo kid has to carry the partner."

"That's messed up for your sisters, Luca."

"I know."

"Wait! It had to have worked for Alex, right?"

Luca shakes his head. "No. We laughed it off, because they were clearly in love. And then she died, and well, we were all pretty shook. Then Dom's wife wanted a divorce and basically ran out on the kids. Suddenly the tradition took on some merit."

"So you're saying you have to carry me over the threshold, and if something happens, it basically means we are destined to crash and burn?" I ask quietly, tears burning my eyes.

Luca grabs my face with both hands. His eyes are intense, emotion evident across his face, as he shakes his head. "No. Absolutely not. It's a stupid tradition, and I don't care what it says. You're mine, bella. I'm not going anywhere."

I laugh bitterly as tears fall down my cheeks. "You're the most superstitious person I know, Luca. This has more meaning than you're letting on."

"I'm saying that I'm carrying you across that threshold, because I know you're my soulmate, Hannah. I feel it deep in my bones. You'll see. I was just warning you why they were all outside, and how they'll be expecting this."

"I'm scared," I confess, more to myself than him, but Luca hears me.

"No reason to be scared. It's just another day, and I'm confident that we'll be happily sitting down to dinner talking about how dumb this stupid tradition is," he says as he takes his foot off the brake and steers us to Sofia and Nick's house.

I shakily get out the car, my hand cradling my tiny baby bump, and Arianna's eyes zero in on it. She gasps quietly and wraps her arms around me. "He told you about the threshold thing?"

I nod against her, taking in a shaky breath. "What if it doesn't work?"

"It's going to work, Han. You're meant for him. This is just a stupid thing we do."

"Did it ever work for you?" I ask as she steps back. She smiles softly.

"No, but I know it will."

Nick Santo walks toward us, his posture stiff and refined. The most reserved man of the Santo family, I haven't interacted with him much. He appears to sit on the outskirts, studying our interactions. Luca told me he attempted to break up Gianna and Travis before they were married, convinced Travis wasn't the right match for Gia. Once Gia stood up for herself, Nick stepped back and admitted he was wrong.

"Let's get this over with," Nick says. "Sofia made an excellent dinner, and I'm starving."

I let out a pained giggle at his nonchalantness, and he peers at me. "This is just a technicality, Hannah. It's clear to all of us that you're meant to be Luca's."

"I hope so," I murmur, and only Arianna hears. She gives my hand a quick squeeze as Luca motions for me to follow him to the front door.

I get a whiff of food through the open door, and my mouth waters. I'm just at the end of the first trimester, and the nausea has finally begun to wane. I'm craving salt and savory foods constantly.

"Alright. This is super easy. Nothing to worry about," Luca mutters to himself. He might have talked a big game in the car, but I know he's worried. He bends down to scoop me up, and once I'm in his arms, our eyes meet. He gives me a tender smile. "You're the love of my life, Pixie."

"I love you too," I whisper, my hands finding his hair and scratching his scalp with my fingertips.

"I love when you do that," he whispers.

"What?"

"Scratch me."

"Luca, your parents are right there!" I hiss, my eyes widening in horror and embarrassment.

"They know we have sex, Han. Clearly when we tell them you're having my baby, they'll realize it even more," he jokes.

"You're having a baby?" Isabella shrieks.

Luca winces. "Whoops."

"Nice, Luca. We had a whole plan for telling them, and you blurt it out while standing outside your parent's house," I say.

"Technically, I said it inside their house."

I jolt, looking around, and realize we're now well inside the house, standing by a beautiful stone fireplace.

"Told ya we'd be okay," Luca says proudly. I'm still in his arms as he smiles at me.

"You can put me down now," I whisper.

"Not until you give me a kiss."

Luca's eyes sparkle with mischief, love, and adoration, and I've never felt so complete in my life. "I love you so much, baby."

"I love you too, Pixie. Now kiss me."

Laughing, I grab his face in my hands and lay one on him, then listen as his entire family cheers in the background. I finally have a supportive family, and a phenomenal man.

Leaving Georgia, taking a job with a hockey team, and taking a chance on Luca were definitely worth the risk.

Epilogue

Hannah

"What are you staring at, Mommy?" my three-year-old daughter, Melanie asks. I look down at her, my mini-me, and smile broadly. Melanie, the little bean in my tummy when Luca thought about retiring.

"Well," I say, lifting her up to my waist and pointing at one of my favorite pictures, "this picture is from when Daddy won the Stanley Cup at his last game. And you were in my belly."

"Like brudder," Melanie says, patting my heavily pregnant stomach.

"Yes, sweetheart. Just like brother."

If I had to take a guess, I'd say the newest Santo offspring would come out wearing skates, much like his dad and uncles did. As soon as we found out the baby's gender, Luca was over the moon. That's not to say he wasn't thrilled with Melanie's birth. The only other person wrapped as tightly around her little finger is her Nonno, Luca's father. He might seem stoic and standoffish, but Nick Santo lives and breathes for his grandkids. He reserves most smiles for the youngest generation, and I'm fine with that. At least he has a relationship with them, which is more than I can say for my own parents.

Within a few weeks of Caroline being arrested, more information came out highlighting just how involved my parents were in the mess. Caroline folded quickly, explaining how she was the victim. How Woodward promised her he'd leave his wife, but always came up with excuses why he couldn't do it. How she didn't have a great relationship with her own parents, so when her older sister reached out and asked for her help, she jumped at the opportunity. Besides, she claimed, I had been given everything my entire life. I deserved to be taken down a few notches.

Being the consummate professional, Caroline managed to snag a rental on the outskirts of Denver that was fully furnished. She stayed there, far enough away that she wouldn't run into anyone, but close enough she could still meet Woodward. When Jefferson showed up, he stayed with her. She let him into the underground parking lot to slash my tires, and she told him where I worked. Woodward supplied her with my detailed schedule so Jefferson could 'deal with me.' The longer I conveniently evaded Jefferson, the more unhinged both Caroline and Woodward got.

Luca told me about a woman outside the building the day we met, and we learned Caroline was responsible for that too. Evidently, Caroline had propositioned Luca a time or two, and when he kept turning her down, she was pissed. She was the one to start the rumor about Luca sleeping with Woodward's wife. While Woodward was definitely more aggressive with his strategies to get Luca kicked out of the NHL, or at least traded from the team in a haze of disgrace, Caroline was really the puppeteer pulling the strings.

She didn't take too kindly to finding out Luca was involved with me.

That's when she convinced Jefferson to arrive at Claire's apartment and drag me back to Georgia. Since Caroline was also sleeping with Jefferson, and he truly believed she would continue seeing him, he dutifully followed her directions.

She really must give an amazing blow job to have these two successful men willing to commit heinous crimes for her.

She attempted to claim innocence, but the terrible terrors, Jessica and Lindsay, came in clutch. They recorded Caroline in Woodward's office multiple times in the weeks after I quit, ranting and raving about me. She despised me. She was incredibly jealous of me, it seems. Why a successful woman over a decade older would take it this far is beyond me. But here we are.

The case against Woodward was pretty cut and dried. He admitted his guilt, believe it or not, and due to it being his only offense, he received minor jail time and extensive probation. Even with the multiple women within the Wolves organization claiming sexual harassment, it was a case of he said versus she said. I chalked it up to a win that Woodward was banned from coaching any hockey team at any level in the U.S., and hopefully would go off into obscurity. He was handed divorce papers while awaiting his trial, not to anyone's surprise. I held on to the video I recorded of the woman propositioning Luca at his hotel in Boston. Should Woodward ever surface again and try to start anything, I like having a possible insurance net to shut him up.

Jefferson had a worse time. The state of Georgia actually had a warrant out for his arrest, due to him abusing another woman he dated after I left him. He had to go through two cases. Colorado chose not to prosecute, and instead extradited him to Georgia. Multiple woman came out of the woodwork to claim abuse. He received a hefty prison term.

Caroline claimed innocence so strongly that a psychiatric team was brought in to determine if she was even lucid enough to stand trial. She was found incompetent to stand trial, and was forced into a mental treatment facility to help her regain her cognitive and emotional functioning. The trial has been delayed multiple times as Caroline still hasn't been found competent. Each time, as soon as she sees me in the courtroom, she belligerently shouts at me and claims I'm the villain.

Unfortunately, my family did not support me in any of this. My mother went so far as to say Jefferson was a nice man who got himself into a 'lick of trouble,' and I should forgive him. Needless to say, I blocked both of my parents. They've yet to meet Melanie, and I don't care if it ever happens. I don't need that toxicity in my life. Besides, I have Luca's family now.

Nick and Sofia are the most attentive grandparents I've ever experienced. They dote on Melanie the same way they dote on their other grandchildren. It's a beautiful site to witness. Luca and I have date nights often because Sofia will show up and kidnap Melanie, promising movie nights, manicures, and anything else a three-year-old girl is interested in. At this point, Mel sleeps more at their house than she does at our own home. Sofia asked that Melanie call her Nonna, which confused the crap out of poor Mel. Ever the fixer, she now calls Sofia New Nonna and Luca's grandmother Old Nonna. Old Nonna wasn't too thrilled with the moniker, but now accepts it with a shrug of indifference.

Luca's dad walked me down the aisle only a few weeks before Melanie was born, and he proudly announced that he wasn't 'giving away' anything. Instead, he was escorting me into the family. Luca gave me a hard kiss as soon as Nick put my hand into Luca's, which offended the poor officiant, who was already rattled from the chaos the entire Santo family brings anywhere.

It probably didn't help that Luca's grandmother pinched the officiant's ass as he greeted her at the front of the church, then joked she brought her own wine in case there wasn't enough to go around during mass.

We didn't have a Catholic ceremony.

Luca's family isn't Catholic.

The officiant hightailed it out of there as soon as he had signed the marriage license. I wasn't surprised.

"*Bella?*" Luca's voice shouts as the garage door slams closed.

"By the stairs!"

As Luca rounds the corner and gives me a breathtaking grin, I feel the never-ending butterflies take flight in my stomach. Not a day goes by that I'm not captivated by this man. Now almost thirty-four, he has a few gray hairs in his scruff giving him a distinguished look. His arms come around both of us as he gives a quick kiss to Melanie's temple before giving me a thorough kiss on the mouth. I can't even hold in the whimper that melts into his mouth. I've become even more insatiable this pregnancy than I was with Melanie. Luca can barely keep up.

"How was practice?" I ask breathlessly once we finally break apart.

"Good. We've got some great kids this year," Luca tells me as his hand finds my ass and squeezes.

Luca lasted about six months without a job before he finally admitted to being incredibly bored and without purpose. There were only so many odd jobs at the hotel he could take on, and his crabby restless attitude made everyone on edge. By a stroke of sheer luck, the high school hockey coach reached out to him and asked if he'd be interested in a part-time coaching position. He jumped at the chance. He told me all about coaching his cousin's step-daughter whenever he had time in Colorado Springs, and he really enjoyed the challenge.

Luca completely flourished as a coach. So much so, in fact, that when the head coach retired at the end of the school year, the school board and athletic director quickly offered the position to Luca. He made sure I was on board before accepting the job. I thought I had seen Luca happy the times I witnessed him on the ice with the Wolves, but nothing compares to how he is now. He couldn't be prouder of the kids he coaches, and he's really found his purpose. I don't mind the away games being much closer to home as well.

"How's little man doing?" Luca murmurs as he caresses my stomach. Luca has always been the most affectionate man I know, but my pregnancies make him incredibly touchy. If he's near me, he's touching me in some way, whether that be a hand on my knee, fingers twirling my hair, or him pulling me into his lap so he can be all around me. After years of being starved for physical contact due to my uptight family and their 'southern values,' I'm not complaining at all about Luca's attention. In fact, I crave it when we're apart. He's become my missing piece. The part that keeps me sane and nourished. My soul needs his to survive.

"Really pushing on my spine today," I admit. I'm hesitant to tell Luca that I might be in labor. Little man is positioned quite differently from my pregnancy with Melanie, so I'm not completely confident that what I'm experiencing is indeed back labor. All I can say is, I'm in pain, and it doesn't seem to be getting any better. But the nursery isn't fully ready, and I'm determined to push through so I can get some more things done tonight.

Luca studies my face for a moment. "You're in labor, Pixie."

"No!" I sputter. "Not necessarily!"

"Baby, you're nine months pregnant, and you're obviously in pain. Let's drop Mel off at my parents and go get you checked out. If you're not, we can go hit that Thai place you love for a late dinner."

I salivate thinking about it. I've craved a specific Thai dish called Chicken Satay. Luca has dutifully gone into Denver to a hole-in-the-wall Thai place to get it almost weekly for at least half of this pregnancy. It's unlike any Chicken Satay dishes I've ever eaten, and I've begged the owners to give me the recipe. I wouldn't be surprised if little man comes out and wants the amazing chicken and rice dish.

Ninety minutes later, after huffing about how wrong Luca was about me being in labor, I'm admitted to the hospital. Because of course he was right. I'm in labor.

Caleb Nicholas Santo was born just before midnight. I pushed twice and he came roaring into the world. I can already see the resemblance to Luca. Caleb squawked and hollered until he was tightly wrapped in a blanket and placed in Luca's arms. As soon as Luca spoke quietly, so quietly even I couldn't hear him, Caleb grew silent. He stared up at his father, enamored with him.

That connection never went away.

By the time Caleb was three, he was already in skates, tiptoeing around the local rink in Eternity Springs. His favorite thing to do is watch the Wolves, and he recently attended his first game with Luca.

Mel has absolutely no interest in hockey, and we've never pressured her to. She's perfectly happy helping out at the hotel. Next gen Everlasting Inn and Spa could potentially keep this amazing establishment in business for years to come.

We've talked about having more babies, but honestly, I'm happy with two. I've joked with Luca that two kids allows us to play man-to-man defense, but adding a third would mean we'd move into zone defense. I don't want to be outnumbered. Our little foursome is perfect.

But I'd do anything to keep my husband happy, and if Luca says he wants another kid, I'll give him one. Besides, practicing is half the fun, right?

I'd do every aspect of my life again if I was promised to end up here. I'd go on every bad first date, deal with ex-boyfriends, get berated by my mother. All of it. Because Luca, and our family, are worth it.

The End

Sneak Peek

Worth the Trouble, coming April 2024

Arianna

It's official.

I've hit rock bottom.

Sobbing in the middle of the gala I've spent months planning, because my jackass of a now ex-boyfriend decided to announce his engagement. Twenty minutes ago, I still had a boyfriend. Unbeknownst to me, he had a fiancé. Turns out, I was the side chick.

"Ari, what can I do?" My brother's girlfriend, Hannah, softly pats my back as she attempts to keep me calm. Easier said than done, obviously. I'm two seconds away from my sobs echoing across this grand ballroom in downtown Denver. "Should I get Bradley?"

"No!" I sob. "Didn't you hear what he did? Why would I want him near me?"

"What? No, I was with Luca. We stepped out for a moment," she murmurs. Of course she did. I open one eye a sliver and notice her swollen lips and hair that is distinctly frizzier than it was only thirty minutes ago. I don't know why I'm surprised that Luca would grab a quickie at this event. And speak of the devil ...

"Where is that motherfucker?" Luca snarls.

"Baby, why are you shaking?" Hannah asks, grabbing on to Luca's tuxedo jacket. He's taut with animosity, his eyes dangerously dark with venom.

"He's fucking engaged to someone else," he seethes. Hannah gasps, her eyes whipping to mine, as a fresh wave of tears pour down my cheeks. Humiliation. Utter and complete humiliation. Shit. Now I see my mother approaching, my older brother Dominic stalking behind her, and I realize my rock bottom of moments ago just got worse.

I'm the youngest of seven kids. Yep, you read that right. Seven. Two older sisters and four brothers. Four guys who have attempted to reel me in, scare any man I've dated, and tell me I'm not allowed to have sex until I'm forty. Sorry, bros, that ship sailed quite a while ago. And generally I take their thoughts and advice on my love life pretty seriously. But watching Luca fall for Hannah made me horribly jealous, and I met Bradley right after that. Dom hated him immediately. Luca was hesitant, his own lovesick heart making him second-guess his gut decision, I think. He wanted to trust me, and my ability to pick out my own men. My remaining brothers, Alex and Leo, are both overseas on military assignments, and hadn't met Bradley yet.

I'm sure I'll hear about how they felt, regardless of that fact.

"*Paperotta*," my mother soothes as she reaches me, "go. You don't need to be here for the remainder of the event. I'll handle everything."

"It's my event, Momma. I'm not leaving because of that asshole," I pout. I try to catch my breath as a sob threatens to break through. Hannah is in charge of special events, but this gala, the Children's Hospital gala, is so incredibly important to me. My sister, Gianna, finally let me take over planning this event last year, and Hannah only helped a little for this year. When you're in and out of the hospital as a kid, you want to give back as an adult.

"You don't need to prove anything, Arianna. This is the best event we've ever hosted. Everyone is talking about it. You can leave with your head held high," my dad says quietly. He's the voice of reason. The observant one who notices everything, but only speaks when it's truly important.

"I'll be fine," I murmur, my voice stuttering as I try to rein in my emotions.

"Go splash some water on your face. Take five or ten minutes. We're not sad to see him go, *cara*. None of us liked him," Dad says with a flip of his wrist, as if he's casting Bradley away for good. It'll be hard to do, considering he works at the hotel I work at. My family's hotel.

"Okay, I'll be back," I whisper, turning on my heel and quickly walking out of the ballroom and into the closest bathroom. Two stalls are occupied by giggling women, and I scurry into the third stall to hide out until they leave. It gives me a few minutes to control my breathing and focus on calming thoughts.

I met Bradley at work. While I manage the hotel spa and hot springs, he is one of the chefs. He pursued me for months, flirting at every opportunity. I welcomed the attention, but evaded his advances. I worried about mixing business with pleasure. Bradley assured me it wouldn't be an issue. That should have been a major red flag. But I was going through a pretty long dry spell, and I let my hormones make the decision. Now I have no idea how I'm going to deal with seeing him every day at work.

I knew from an early age that I'd work for my family's hotel, Everlasting Hotel and Spa. It's an institution in Eternity Springs, having been part of our family for three generations. First my grandfather, then my father, and now my brother Dominic. We all work here in some capacity, even our mom. But my heart was always pulled toward the spa.

People who don't know me, or those who assume things about me, would think it's because I'm a typical woman and enjoy anything that is labeled as self-care. But in reality, it's how the spa helps others feel. There's nothing better than seeing a frazzled mom come in, stressed about life, and watch as she relaxes and unwinds.

When she's done with her treatments, she vows to make it a priority to take time for herself. Or teaching a teenage girl who suffers from cystic acne how to care for her skin, and watch as she grows confident when the acne begins to fade away. I won't take for granted the times I've gotten to witness a toddler experience the hot springs for the first time. Don't get me started on how amazing it is to help a bride and her bridal party get ready for her wedding. The happiness and excitement are contagious.

I love my job, and I was born to have this role.

Don't get me wrong, it's an exhausting job. The spa is open long hours, and seasonal employees only help so much. It's left to me to cover any open times, and I couldn't even begin to guesstimate how many times I've fallen asleep in my car in the parking lot because it was too much to drive back to my apartment.

This year especially, I regretted my decision to live in western Denver. I wanted to be closer to my friends, and the nightlife of Denver, and didn't take into account how tired I'd be most nights after work. I guess part of the reason Bradley wore me down was because I was too busy to actively look into dating. Obviously, that's a decision I regret more than the location of my apartment.

Once the coast is clear, I sneak out to the sinks and address my makeup. All in all, it's not looking too bad. My eyes are red-rimmed, but the crying jag left my cheeks with a natural blush that matches my sequined baby pink dress. The gown I chose for the gala has thousands of crystals and sequins, a small train that just grazes the ground as I walk, and a plunging neckline that showcases my boobs amazingly. My dad was not thrilled with the dress, but he didn't see it until I arrived at the gala, and he couldn't force me to go home and change. I'll probably get hell from him tomorrow about it.

As I step out of the bathroom, I look down as my favorite pair of Christian Louboutin ribbon ankle-wrap stiletto sandals catch on the hem of my dress, making me stumble forward. I close my eyes tightly as I fall, blindly reaching out to brace my fall, until arms wrap around me, and pull me into a hard body. I gasp as the scent of leather and cedarwood sweeps over me, and I lean into it reflexively. I know this scent. It's the same cologne he's been wearing since I was a teenager.

Stone Dixon.

My brother's best friend, and the one man who has never given me the benefit of the doubt. Why? I don't know. I honestly don't. He's been belligerent and standoffish toward me for well over a decade. My earliest memory of him revolves around one of Luca's hockey games, and me asking Stone if he liked the dress I was wearing that day. I don't remember exactly what he responded, just that he was horribly rude, and he made me cry. That's when he began calling me Princess, and he's never stopped.

I never again asked him what he thought. It's clear he doesn't think highly of me, and I'd rather not learn the specifics as to why.

"Princess," he says grittily. I instinctively shiver as if his voice is speaking directly against my skin. Stone's voice is deep, so deep, but it has a vibration that makes me feel the words. I can only imagine what he sounds like when he's talking a woman through an orgasm. Demanding her compliance as he gets them both there. I take a moment to rake my eyes quickly down his body, admiring how well his tux fits him. Around the time I turned thirteen, I realized how attractive I found Stone. Just over six feet with unruly brown locks that always look perfectly tousled, slate blue eyes that appear to see into my soul, and lips that I'd beg to experience just once against mine. "Powdering your nose for your perfect boyfriend?"

And then he speaks, and I'm reminded of what an ass he can be.

I mean, his fills out his trousers exceptionally well, but still. Stone Dixon isn't a nice guy, and I don't know why my entire family loves him.

I can't even say that lie. He's an amazing guy. Just not to me. Everyone loves him, except for me. Well, and my dad. Dad doesn't like anyone really, though, so his opinion can't be trusted.

"Shows what you know," I retort. "I don't have a boyfriend."

Stone's smug expression falls as his eyes sharpen on me. "What happened? What did that motherfucker do?"

"Why do you care, Stone? Go ask him. I'm sure he'll enjoy the two of you making fun of me all night. He started calling me princess because of you, you know."

"I didn't —" Stone stutters before clearing his throat, "I didn't know he was calling you that."

"Yeah, well, there's a lot of things you don't know about me, old man. Let go of me," I say clearly as I push away from him. He looks down, as if confused to find he's still holding on to my waist. When he lets go, I'm acutely aware of the warmth from his hands being replaced with stark coldness.

"Worried I'll contaminate this perfect dress, Princess?" he taunts. "How much did this set you back? Or rather, how much did Daddy pay for it?"

"Why are you so concerned with my clothes?" I ask. He doesn't need to know that my beautiful dress is a rental. I don't buy dresses for these events. It's a waste of money. The only money I spend on fashion is my shoes.

"I'm not concerned with your clothes."

"But you obviously are. You comment on them almost every time we interact. How much did it cost, where did I get it, did my dad buy it. It's insulting, Stone," I tell him. "I don't comment on your clothes."

"I wear the same six things, Arianna. Pretty sure your mom got most of them for me," he says exasperatedly.

"So? Who cares? I don't. Why should you?"

"I doubt your mom spent as much on the sweater she got me for Christmas as you clearly spent on your fancy shoes," he mutters.

I roll my eyes. Knowing my mom, the sweater might have cost more than my Louboutins. My love of fashion is a genetic trait passed down from her. And while we're both pretty stingy in everyday life, my mom enjoys spoiling her kids. Stone has always been considered an adopted son of hers. Which is why no one, not even my mother, knows that I've had a crush on him for as long as I can remember.

"Excuse me, I need to go back in the ballroom," I say snootily, holding my head up and flouncing past Stone.

I hate that he still affects me.

I hate that I want to impress him.

I hate how I still want him, even though he despises me.

But mostly, I hate myself because I compare every guy I date to him. The man I can't have. The one I don't even know what it would be like to have.

As I walk back into the ballroom, I'm ambushed by Bradley.

"Princess," he sneers.

"Don't call me that. That was never okay," I respond. A tiny blonde approaches him, sliding her left arm into the crook of his elbow, her massive engagement ring proudly on display.

"Darling, who is this?" she whines. There's no other way to explain her voice. It's a whiny voice, that after only four words, already grates on my nerves.

"Sweetheart, this is Arianna," Bradley coos.

"Oh, the easy lay," she says nonchalantly. My mouth drops open in shock, making her break out in a fit of high-pitched giggles. I'm reminded of Janice from Friends. "Did you think I didn't know about you? Oh my God. That's just too adorable. Bradley told me all about you."

"You were okay with him dating someone else? While you're engaged?" I ask incredulously. She hyena laughs again.

"That's not dating, Adrienne. He fucked you. That's it," she snarls. I don't miss her mistaking my name. Now she's just being hurtful. Game fucking on.

"Ahh. Just sex. Got it. You should know, then, that he told me how he's never had it as good as he had it with me, and I rocked his world," I tell her. Her eyes narrow.

"Of course he would say that. We're waiting until our wedding night. That's the only reason why I was okay with this asinine situation," she retorts. "I told him to find some stupid whore and get his kicks before we get married. He found you, and the rest is history."

Before I can respond, my arm is grabbed, and I'm whirled around. I see Stone's eyes only a second before his lips are on mine.

I gasp into his mouth, and Stone takes the opportunity to slide his tongue against mine. I shudder as his arms tighten around me, and find I've slid my arms snugly around his trim waist. I feel his groan as my body connects with his. I'd always wondered what his lips would feel and taste like, and this is so much better than my imagination. This is perfection.

As he breaks the kiss off, his hand cups my cheek reverently. I'm about to ask what the hell is going on, but he discreetly taps my lips before turning me back to face a stunned Bradley and his fiancée. "Hello. I'm Arianna's man. And you are?"

"Her man?" the fiancée asks, turning to Bradley, whose face is getting quite red.

"Your man? You two-timing bitch," he seethes.

"Considering you just announced to the crowd that you were engaged, and half the people in attendance knew you were dating Arianna, I don't think you have any room to judge," Stone points out.

"Always knew you had a thing for her, Rock," Bradley spits out. Stone chuckles.

"You know my fucking name, asshat. Take your trailer trash and get the hell out of here. Oh, and I'd start looking for a new job if I were you."

"I'm very happy where I am, thank you very much," Bradley responds.

"You won't be," Stone says lightly.

"Is that a threat?"

"It's a promise, man. You know much about her other brothers?" Stone asks.

"The ones that don't live here? No," Bradley says warily. His fiancée, who I still don't know by name, watches with interest.

"They're both in the military, man. One is special ops. And,"

Stone says, as he whips out his phone and begins to furiously type, "when they hear about this bullshit you pulled tonight, I can assure you they're going to have all kinds of thoughts."

"Well, they're not here, so ..." Bradley trails off.

"Baby Girl," Stone says, turning to me, and damn it all to hell if my heart doesn't skip a beat at the pet name, "what's that lake that Lex used to take us fishing at? The one he talked about being the deepest in the state."

"I don't remember," I murmur with a smile, captivated by this new side of Stone I've never seen.

"Damn. I can't remember either. I just know he said it would be really easy to drop a body there," he says pointedly, staring at Bradley. "Have I made myself clear?"

"Crystal," Bradley mutters, before taking his fiancée's hand and making a quick dash to the exit.

I turn to Stone, expecting some kind of explanation, but he just shrugs.

"What?"

"What the hell was that?" I shriek.

"You're welcome, Princess."

"I didn't thank you."

"You should. You obviously needed help."

"I was handling that just fine," I growl.

Stone smirks. "Go ahead and keep thinking that."

As he pats me on the ass — THE ASS — and walks away, I stare at his retreating form in complete shock.

I repeat: what the hell was that?

Acknowledgments

This book about did me in. I mean that with all sincerity. I've never had a manuscript tick me off so much that I debated on scrapping the entire thing more than once.

I really enjoy sports. All the sports. Well, except maybe golf. Is that even a sport? In any case, I'll be honest with you: my knowledge of hockey is minimal. I was incredibly worried about writing a book with hockey, knowing it could really upset some hockey romance enthusiasts. My editor had to talk me off the ledge … again … by explaining that she's edited hockey romance manuscripts with even less hockey in them than mine!

But I wanted to tell this story. I had the idea for the Santo family way back a few books ago, and actually began writing this manuscript in October 2022. I had a vision of this "bad boy of hockey" who hated the persona he'd been forced into having, and desperately wanted to change his life. Enter our southern belle, Hannah. She felt trapped in Georgia. Smothered by family expectations and an increasingly uncomfortable boyfriend. Finally getting out from under her family's thumb was eye opening for her. Experiencing all that is Luca Santo was worth it.

Originally, Luca was going to introduce a group of guys who all had a bad boy exterior with a heart of gold, but while writing Matt and Victoria's book (Forever Us), I had a moment of clarity. I envisioned a loud and cantankerous family running a hotel in small-town Colorado, and I was so excited to tie in Luca's story. I have so many plans for all of Luca's siblings. Grab Gianna's novella by signing up for my newsletter!

This book only came to be with the help of my Quill & Cup BFF's, Mandy and Tamara, my PA Morgan, my beta readers Daisy, Anna, and Amarilys, and my editor Brenda. They each had a role in keeping me sane, helping me tell the story, and giving me constructive feedback. I'm so incredibly thankful to each one of you.

Lastly, I'd like to thank my family. To my two sons, who now understand when I'm screwing around on my computer, I'm actually working, but they can't believe I write such long books, and my husband, who is patiently waiting for the moment I'm rolling in the dough and can buy him his dream poker table. And to my eighty-one-year-old father, who proudly tells people that I'm a writer, and had me show him exactly how to find me on Amazon, so he can tell his friends how to purchase my books.

We're in for a wild ride with these Santo siblings. If any of you could please tell the one who will be book six that he needs to shut the hell up, I'd sure appreciate it. He's just yapping away, telling me all about what he thinks he wants. Wait your turn, buddy.

It's been almost two years since you passed away, Mom. I miss you so much it hurts. I hope you're proud of me, and tickled to see me growing in a career you'd have admired. Well, except for the sexy parts. That I know you'd be horrified about.

About the Author

Jennifer was born and raised in Ohio, but currently calls Colorado home. A lifelong lover of romance books, Jen felt pulled to write stories with older characters, because "old farts" deserve love too. Jen prides herself on delivering realistic characters that struggle with normal problems. She spends most of her free time within her zoo: two kids, two dogs, and two cats...all of which are male! When not containing the chaos, Jen can be found lounging on her covered porch devouring books on her Kindle.

Also By

FOREVER SERIES

Forever Sunshine

Forever Yours

Forever Ours

Forever Mine

Forever Us

Forever Together

ETERNITY SERIES

Worth the Risk

Worth the Trouble April 2024

Printed in Great Britain
by Amazon